JODHPURS AND JEANS

'Good girl, Calliphigenia,' I said, walking around behind her to inspect her sweat-slick bottom and back. 'So, no whipping. A treat instead, but I've no sugar lumps. Bend down.'

She reacted immediately, bending to steady herself against the rope and leaving her bottom stuck out and wide, so that I could see where the shaft of the tail disappeared into her anus.

'Legs open,' I ordered.

By the same author:

THE INDIGNITIES OF ISABELLE
(writing as Cruella)
PENNY IN HARNESS
A TASTE OF AMBER
BAD PENNY
BRAT
IN FOR A PENNY
PLAYTHING
TIGHT WHITE COTTON
TIE AND TEASE
PENNY PIECES
TEMPER TANTRUMS
REGIME
DIRTY LAUNDRY
UNIFORM DOLL
NURSE'S ORDERS

JODHPURS AND JEANS

Penny Birch

Nexus

This book is a work of fiction.
In real life, make sure you practise safe sex.

First published in 2003 by
Nexus
Thames Wharf Studios
Rainville Road
London W6 9HA

Copyright © Penny Birch 2003

The right of Penny Birch to be identified as the Author of this Work has been asserted by her in accordance with the Copyright, Designs and Patents Act 1988.

www.nexus-books.co.uk

Typeset by TW Typesetting, Plymouth, Devon

Printed and bound by
Clays Ltd, St Ives PLC

ISBN 0 352 33778 8

All characters in this publication are fictitious and any resemblance to real persons, living or dead, is purely coincidental.

This book is sold subject to the condition that it shall not, by way of trade or otherwise, be lent, resold, hired out or otherwise circulated without the publisher's prior written consent in any form of binding or cover other than that in which it is published and without a similar condition including this condition being imposed on the subsequent purchaser.

Dedicated to Jenny, James, Jim, Jan
and all those who have provided
encouragement and support on
www.pennybirch.com

Prologue

'It's been too long, Amber.'

'Far too long.'

Carrie's response was a kiss, a single, tentative peck on my lips as she closed with me, to straddle my lap. She kissed me again as I hugged her into my body, and this time her mouth stayed on mine, open. Her breasts pressed to mine, small and firm through the wool of our jumpers as our tongues met, and we were kissing.

It had been a long, long time since we last had sex, but the years seemed to melt with our inhibitions. Her arms came around me, holding my head and back. I began to stroke her hair, the same cascade of rich red curls she had worn at school, falling to the small of her back as I tugged the constraining net loose. Her hard hat fell off, ignored as I twisted my hand into her glorious locks and tugged. Her body tightened, her mouth pulling free of mine. She sighed, her eyes closed in bliss as I pulled harder on her hair, until her back was in a tight arch, with her little breasts poking up in two neat mounds beneath the cream-coloured wool of her jumper. I pulled her closer, tugging on her hair again even as my other hand slipped into the rear of her jodhpurs, to find smooth, resilient girl flesh, then the taut elastic of her knickers.

With passion and urgency, she tugged at my jumper and pressed her mouth fiercely to mine. I met her kiss, pulling her head tight in, my hand pushing into the rear pouch of her panties as she obligingly lifted her bottom. My jumper came high, my blouse with it, lifted to my chin in a tangle of material. Her hands went to my breasts, stroking and squeezing with desperate urgency. Her jodhpurs were sticking on her hips, but she reached back suddenly, to push them down and leave her bottom a tight, panty-clad ball beneath her coat tails. My hand slid deeper into her panties as she returned to fondling my breasts, to feel the firm ball of one little cheek, with the roughened line of the welt I'd given her with my riding crop. It was that cut which had reaffirmed what we'd once had, and her kissing became more passionate still as I explored her hurt flesh.

I'd caught her perfectly, full across her seat as she bent in her saddle, her neatly rounded bottom stuck well out, with the harp-shaped outline of her sex showing in sweat through her jodhpurs, a target too good to resist. Her reaction had been a pained squeal and an instant of shock, then she'd smiled. Ten minutes later we'd been in the privacy of the little marble folly, the horses tethered outside, and in each other's arms.

She was beginning to push her bottom out in her urgency, and I decided it was time, burrowing into the soft crease between her tight bottom cheeks. I touched the sweat slick dimple of her anus, tickling, my coat cuff taut against her half-lowered panties. She caught my bra, flipping it up to spill my breasts out. Her panties gave and my fingers were on her sex, slipping into the wet, welcoming hole, finding her clitoris.

As I began to masturbate her she cuddled into me, moaning and gasping, kissing my mouth and my neck, squirming her bottom and sex on to my hand. I got my thumb to her bottom hole. The little sweaty ring gave and I was holding her between the two entrances as I rubbed her. Her grip tightened, her body shivering against mine, the wool of her jumper tickling on my nipples. I pulled hard at her hair, and she was coming, her bumhole and fanny tightening at the same instant. Her breath was coming in pants, then great, ragged gasps as her climax went through her, her body locked tight in my arms, my fingers busy under her out-thrust bottom.

Only when her spasms had subsided and her breathing slowed did I stop rubbing at her underside. Even then I kept hold of her, holding her by her sex. She made no effort to escape, purring like a contented kitten as she cuddled into me. I held her tight, letting her come down in her own time and enjoying the open, sticky feel of her fanny and bottom hole.

When at last she pulled back, it was to rub the tip of her nose against mine, then kiss me once more, gently, but full on my lips. Nothing needed to be said. She knew what I wanted, exactly. I let go of her hair. My fingers slipped from her body. Her mouth came open as she slid down and I fed her my slippery fingers, letting her suck up her own juices before she went lower to kneel on the hard marble floor.

She made no effort to cover herself, leaving her jodhpurs and panties down at the back, but I could see the slight trepidation in her eyes as she looked up to me. I smiled as I turned, and knelt down on the bench, my bottom pushed out. She came close, to flip up the tails of my riding coat. I put one hand on the wall, the other to my breasts, steadying myself as I teased my nipples. Carrie's hands found the waistband of my jodhpurs and tugged. They slid down, slowly, my knickers with them, to bare my bottom right in her face.

My eyes were shut, but I could picture it in my mind: her pretty, freckled face, with her huge, green eyes set in uncertainty as she stared at the full, bare spread of my bottom from just inches away. I knew she'd do it though, and sure enough, a moment later I felt her face press to my flesh. She kissed one cheek, the other, and between, in my crease. I pulled in my back, spreading myself for her. She took hold of my hips. Again her lips found the crease of my bottom, then her tongue, and she was doing it, licking my bottom hole.

I moaned aloud as my fingers slipped down to my sex. I was wet, my clitty aching to be touched. I began to masturbate, focused on the delicious feeling of her tongue lapping at my bottom hole, and thoughts of how she would feel. She was on her knees, her jodhpurs and panties pushed down at the back, bare in the cold air. The welt on her bottom would be stinging, reminding her of her place as she licked the anus of the woman who had done it, the woman who had beaten her and made her lick a bottom, my bottom . . .

I started to come, crying out as it hit me. Carrie's tongue pushed deep up my bottom hole, at exactly the right moment. I felt my ring tighten, right on her tongue tip, and I was there, my sex going into spasm in her face, my clitty burning under my finger, my anus gaping to the attentions of her pretty, sweet mouth, which would be full of my taste as she gave me what she knew I needed.

Even when my gasps had died to contented sighs she carried on licking, stopping only when I reached back to gently pull her away. I sat, the marble cold on my warm bottom, and she came up, into my arms, to kiss me. Her tongue probed at my lips, and I let my mouth come open, tasting myself and allowing her to restore her battered pride by sharing it. Our kiss over, she snuggled into me, sighing as her head settled on to my chest.

'I've wanted that since the moment you arrived,' she breathed.

'So have I. I didn't know if you would.'

'Of course, why ever not?'

'Well, it's been a long time, and you're married . . .'

'Clive is sweet, and he does like to spank me, but he's not like you. He's sort of jolly about it, not really dominant at all. Your girlfriend's lucky. What's her name – Penny?'

'Yes, although she's not in my good books at the moment. Do you remember Morris Rathwell?'

'How could I forget him.'

'Well, Penny managed to get me involved in a spanking party he was running for . . . well, for a bunch of dirty old men, basically. It's a long story, but I ended up having to take a bare bottom spanking from the most horrible man. Protheroe he was called . . .'

She burst into giggles.

'It was not funny, Carrie.'

'Sorry, Amber.'

'He was awful, bald and flabby, and he was really dirty about it. That wasn't the worst of it though. Afterwards I found out it was a paying party!'

'Paying?'

'Yes, paying, and you know what that makes me. I have never been so humiliated.'

'And Penny took you there?'

'Yes . . . not that she knew, or at least she swears she didn't. She tried to make up for it, but only made it worse. She shaved Melody Rathwell's head, and had her served stuffed and trussed at a dinner, like a sucking pig.'

'What, not . . .'

'No, not actually roasted, stupid, just stark naked and covered in sauce with a fried pig's testicle in each hole. Morris was away, but was he furious when he found out, and Penny had told Melody it was my idea in the first place. I've been trying to avoid him ever since.'

'Why not whip Penny or something?'

'Oh I did, thirty-six strokes of the cane. She took it, and she howled the house down, but . . . I don't know. She's never there. She doesn't need me, not the way I want to be needed.'

'At least you can play when she is there. I haven't even dared try Clive with pony-girl fantasy. I know he'd just laugh. Still, I suppose I should be grateful he spanks me. Oh dear, I'm going to have to explain that crop mark, aren't I? That was hard, Amber!'

'Sorry, I couldn't resist it. You make such a pretty target.'

'I'm glad you didn't. I think I'll tell him you did it, as it goes, but as a forfeit, because I lost a bet, a riding bet. He's always doing that sort of thing with his friends, you know, racing round the grounds and the last one back has to drink a pint of port or whatever it might be. It might even turn him on.'

'You with a whip stripe across your bottom? I'd be amazed if it didn't!'

'We shall see. Talking of bums, mine's getting cold.'

She pulled away, to stand and adjust her knickers and jodhpurs, giving me a brief and teasing flash of her bare bottom, as neat and firm in the flesh as it had looked covered. The welt I had given her made a thick red line, running from cheek to cheek. She made a face of mock resentment, and pulled her panties up.

I followed her example, covering myself not only because of the cold but because there had to be at least a faint risk of one of her estate guests stumbling on to us. Theoretically, the little wood in which our folly stood was off limits, but there was nothing to actually stop anyone. It still seemed a shame not to be bare any more, but it was all too easy to imagine the scandal if we were caught together. Lesbianism may be all the rage in London, but in deepest Norfolk it was simply not done for the lady of the house to be caught *in flagrante*, even with an old school friend. Not that I cared much, but Carrie had her business reputation to think of.

'So are you making ends meet?' I asked.

'Well enough,' she answered. 'The estate made a loss last year, but Clive's income covers it. And you?'

'Not too bad.'

'Are you still making pony-girl gear?'

'Yes. Not that it brings in much money, but it's such fun. We manage to play quite a bit too, sometimes with customers, the cute ones, usually with Vicky, the very tall girl, you remember?'

'Sure. Does your godfather still let you use his place?'

'Henry, yes, he loves it. We've got a great chance coming up this summer, as it goes. Some old railway land is being auctioned off, a long strip beside the tracks and two areas that used to be sidings. If we get them, I can join my land to Henry's, which would be great for racing. All we need to do is thicken up a few hedges and do some cutting and we ought to be able to have the girls nude in total privacy.'

'Great. Do I get invited? I'd love to be a pony-girl again.'

'Of course.'

'I shall hold you to that, and just to be sure you remember, you can make me one of those cute tails that go up the girl's bum. I'll write you a cheque when we get in. Speaking of which, we'd better get back. The shooting party'll be back by now, and Cook will want the dinner orders.'

'Right.'

We left the folly, sharing a conspiratorial glance as we walked back to the horses. The wood was as quiet as before, with the sun striking down the long aisle of trees which gave the folly its view, and down which we'd been cantering when the view of Carrie's bottom had proved too much for me. We mounted, and turned for the house, passing a man no more than a hundred yards down the track. He had a shotgun under his arm, but was in combat gear and not tweeds. I saw his face as we drew level, handsome but harsh, sinister even. He turned us a glance I was sure held both guilt and lust, then looked quickly away. Carrie gave him a cheerful 'good-afternoon'.

'Who was that?' I asked, the moment we were out of earshot.

'Gavin Bulmer,' she answered. 'He's with the shooting party. He must have got lost on the way in, I suppose.'

'You don't think . . . he might have been spying on us?'

'God, I hope not! He's a creep . . . No, he couldn't have seen anything. Yuck, I don't even want to imagine it!'

One

It was hard not to be optimistic on the day of the railway property auction. The lots I wanted were small, oddly shaped, had poor access and were hedged around with restrictions on planning permission. One was simply rough ground, a long, five-sided piece of land which had not been a siding since the 50s. It touched the end of my paddock for around twenty yards, and led to the other. That was less good, and I'd hoped they would make two lots of it, with the long strip of land leading to Henry's and the siding separate. Instead it was one, and the siding area did have road access of a sort. Still, even if it went beyond my means, there seemed every chance of the new owner being willing to part with the long thin piece I actually needed. Both had areas of oil contamination, which was a pain, but made them unsuitable for farming.

The auction was not local, not in Hertfordshire at all, but in central London, and it was huge. Nor was it just land, with an immense amount of railway memorabilia and even some old rolling stock on sale. Most of the land lots were far bigger than mine, and scattered across the whole of south-east England, making me more hopeful still. The only fly in the ointment was that it was just the sort of event Morris Rathwell was likely to be at, after land for trading estates and housing developments.

Sure enough, he was there, his great, vulgar gold Rolls-Royce an immediate eyesore in the car park of the small exhibition hall hired for the auction. I parked well away from it, sure that so long as I avoided his attention he would be too busy with business matters to worry about me. Afterwards, with both lots secured, I could tell him.

I collected my auction card at the reception desk and went into the hall, to discover that it would be at least two hours before my lots came up. They were doing the memorabilia first, with young men in anoraks and old men in suits paying extraordinary sums for objects such as original station signs and the great brass dome from a long dismantled steam engine. I watched in fascination for a while, then left, intent on lunch and a little Dutch courage at the bar.

The foyer was nearly as big as the hall, and crowded. Most were men in smartly cut suits, presumably in property. I knew they would include Rathwell, and kept a careful lookout, only to find myself three places behind him in the queue for the buffet. Between us were two big men, and I might have got away with it if they'd only stayed still. They didn't.

'Well, if it isn't little Amber Oakley!' Morris boomed, extending his hand as he stepped around the two men. 'So what brings you here? Don't tell me you're one of the train spotters!'

'Er ... no,' I managed, completely taken aback.

The last time he had spoken to me had been six months ago. I remembered his finally words before I put the phone down – 'demented little bitch'.

'It'll be Lots 417 and 419 then,' he went on. 'Two pieces of land of no practical use to anyone, except perhaps a girl who wants to do some discreet pony-girl racing?'

My heart sank. It was pointless denying it, so all I could do was be nice and pray he wasn't still angry about Melody's hair. I forced myself to smile as he continued.

'I reckon no more than three grand for 417. No access, contaminated soil, and you'd be hard put to get anything but agricultural or recreational use. Two grand maybe, if you're lucky. 419, tricky. It could make a nice little garden centre. Popular out your way, garden centres. Or a builder's yard, something along those lines. I reckon eight to ten grand. Look, sit next to me. If the bidding gets too hot for you, I'll step in. We can sort out repayment later, at minimal interest.'

I knew exactly what form his 'minimal interest' would take, something involving his cock and my body. I opened my mouth to give him the answer he deserved, but shut it again. Annoying him was not something I could afford to do, not now.

'I have ample funds, thanks,' I answered. 'Henry's backing me.'

'The old goat still up for it, is he? Must be pushing seventy. I'm amazed he's alive, big fat bugger like that. Fair enough then. I'll keep an eye on you anyway.'

We had reached the head of the line, and he turned his attention to the buffet. I did the same, all the while worrying about why he was being so friendly, so that it was only when I reached the till that I realised I'd poured custard over my chicken breast and salad.

Rathwell fell into a conversation with another developer, and I was left to try and eat the disgusting mixture, too embarrassed to change it. He could not simply have forgiven and forgotten. It would have been completely out of character. So he was up to something, and it was almost certain to involve buying the two lots I wanted. After all, he'd made the effort to find out about them. I could not outbid him, and I knew only too well that he was capable of spending several thousand pounds just for a chance to humiliate me. Besides which, knowing him, he would probably manage to sell the land at a profit. With his contacts he might even get planning permission and do something really awful, like put up a block of flats overlooking my property.

Unfortunately it was very hard to see what I could do. What he wanted was my sexual submission, degrading dominant women being his favourite kick. He wanted revenge as well, so it would be that much worse. In normal circumstances I would even have offered to suck his cock in return for holding off. Undoubtedly he'd have been really disgusting about it, like making me do it kneeling in the gents' toilets, and he'd definitely have come in my face. It would have been worth it, and normally I'd have trusted his word. But now, not after the incident with Melody's hair. He was more likely to make me do it, then buy the land anyway.

I realised I was grinding my teeth, and stopped, trying to look at least faintly ladylike, and to think calmly and logically. If Rathwell wanted the lots badly enough, he would buy them. Being Rathwell, he would be prepared to bargain, as he always was. Being Rathwell, my side of the bargain was likely to be both painful and degrading. On the other hand I wanted the land badly, and worse, there was no telling what he might do with it. He had trapped me, something he was infuriatingly adept at doing.

As I ate I pushed the problem back and forth in my head, barely tasting the food, which was probably just as well. In the end I found I simply could not bear to back down. That meant bargaining.

He was with a group of other men at a table on the far side of the eating area, and my heart was in my mouth as I walked across. Some of them looked up as I approached, but Morris was facing the other way and I had to put my hand on his shoulder to get his attention. He turned, dabbing at his mouth with a napkin as he looked round.

'Amber, hi.'

'May I have a word, Morris?'

'Sure, fire away.'

'In private.'

My words drew a round of guffaws and one or two lewd remarks from his companions. He laughed as he pushed his chair back to rise, smiling as he lifted his hand.

'It's not like that, boys, more's the pity. This is Amber, old Charlie Oakley's girl.'

One or two obviously knew my father as their expressions quickly changed. I felt a touch of gratitude at Rathwell's words, but bit it down, knowing it was a ploy to make me more vulnerable, more suggestible. I bit down another, entirely different emotion as his hand settled on my bottom to steer me across the room, but managed to contain myself until we had reached a quiet space by the doors.

'Changed your mind?' he asked.

'There's no need to play games, Morris. I know what you are trying to do, and I'm willing to make a bargain.'

'I don't know what you mean, Amber.'

'You know full well what I mean. You're planning to buy the land, aren't you, and then use it to apply some sort of leverage . . .'

'Nonsense!'

He sounded genuinely hurt. I didn't believe it.

'So what bargain did you have in mind, exactly?' he asked innocently.

The blood came rushing to my face as I struggled to get the words out, but I managed, my opening bid.

'I'll . . . I'll suck you, if you don't bid for my lots.'

His face broke into the familiar dirty leer. He glanced at his watch.

'Sounds good to me, girl. The back of my car will do, but we'd better hurry.'

'Not now, after the auction. You're not catching me that way.'

'As if I would! I'm good for my word, Amber, you know that.'

'Afterwards.'

'If you don't trust me, how am I supposed to trust you?'

'I'll keep my word, you know I will.'

He nodded thoughtfully. He knew I was telling the truth. So did I.

'All right, you're on.'

'You promise not to bid? Not at all, even to push up the price?'

'I'll do better than that. One of the guys wants to talk something over privately, very privately. I'll sort it so he and I come out to the foyer while your lots are up. That way I won't even be in the room. Fair enough?'

I nodded. My stomach was fluttering, but I was amazed I'd got off so lightly. I'd expected him to laugh at my proposal, and come back with something truly awful, like being taken back to his house to be beaten and sodomised in front of his wife. At the least I'd expected to end up nude with a sore behind.

He made the agreement with his colleague and almost immediately went into the auction room. I came to watch from the door. They were already at Lot 350, and on to the land, of which my own two pieces were among the last. Rathwell began to bid at Lot 360, an area of sidings in the East End, which attracted some pretty fierce competition. By the time they reached Lot 400 he had spent more money than I am likely to see in my lifetime. The big lots were gone and he stopped bidding. Then, as Lot 414 went, he slipped out, nodding to me as he went. He'd kept his word, and I found myself blowing out my breath with the sudden release of tension, only to catch it again at the prospect of keeping my own.

There was a hard knot in my stomach, and it was as much from the tension of the auction as the prospect of sucking Morris Rathwell's penis. Bidding had become desultory, but there were an awful lot of people still in the hall, and most of them looked pretty wealthy. Lots 415 and 416 were similar parcels to the south of the village, and I was pleased to see both go for under five thousand.

I'm quite used to auctions, and there's always a jolt when a lot you want comes up. This time I was prepared to spend a lot more than ever before, and the jolt when the auctioneer announced Lot 417 was enough to leave my stomach feeling weak. I'd exaggerated when I told Rathwell that Henry was backing me. He was, but only to a maximum of five thousand. Anything above that came out of my own pocket.

It was a breeze. The bidding opened at two thousand and nobody showed the slightest interest. A woman in one of the front rows put her card up at one thousand and I was forced to bid. A man near me topped my bid, one of the railway fanatic types, which surprised me. I bid again and again he topped me, bringing the bid back up to two thousand. He turned his head to see who was bidding against him, and smiled. I smiled back and raised my card.

There seemed to be something familiar about him, but I put it down to nerves. He hesitated and for a moment I thought I'd got it, only for him to raise the card once more. I topped him, raising my card in what I hoped was a casual manner as he once more glanced back. This time he failed to respond, and when the auctioneer glanced at him he shook his head. There was a last moment of tension as the auctioneer looked around, the hammer came down, and it was mine.

Lot 418 was a tiny piece of land on the far side of the railway, and so of no use to me. I expected my rival to bid, thinking he must be a local, because I was certain his face was familiar. He didn't, and it went to the woman near the front for just eight hundred pounds.

My tension rose again as 419 was announced, and grew worse as I saw my rival give a determined nod. The bidding opened at three thousand and he put his card up immediately. Several others joined in, quickly pushing the bid up above the five thousand mark, only to slow abruptly. He had the bid, and I topped him at six thousand. Instantly he raised his card. I countered, but there was a sinking feeling in my stomach as he countered in turn.

The bid stood at seven thousand. I'd promised myself not to go over ten in total. My promise melted as I raised my card. Immediately he raised his. In grim determination I raised mine again, only to be topped immediately. That meant eight thousand five hundred pounds and an unpleasant meeting with my bank manager . . . unless I sold off the larger piece of land and kept the narrow strip I actually needed. I raised my card.

He raised his, without the slightest hesitation. My teeth were gritted as I raised mine once more. I was countered, and the bid stood at ten thousand pounds. It would now go up in thousands, and he showed no signs of flagging. Maybe it was better to let him win and try to negotiate the purchase of the narrow bit. Unless he was working for Rathwell. I found my arm coming up to raise the bid once more. He topped me immediately, the auctioneer met my eyes and I just shrugged. I had lost, and spent nearly three thousand pounds on a piece of contaminated wasteland.

The sale had to be fixed. The man had to be an agent of Rathwell's. My anger was soaring even as the hammer came down, and I left the hall absolutely steaming and fit to kill. Rathwell was in the foyer, still talking business. I didn't care.

'You are a bastard, Morris Rathwell!' I spat as I came up to them.

He looked angry as he turned, but it made no difference. The other man looked up in surprise and began to get up.

'Just a little problem here, Gerald,' Rathwell said quickly. 'Do excuse us.'

Gerald made a hasty exit, leaving Rathwell and me in a glaring match.

'Look,' he began, the instant Gerald was out of earshot, 'do not, ever –'

'No, you look,' I cut in. 'Who the hell do you think you are, doing that! I mean –'

'Doing what?' he demanded.

'You know damn well, what! Getting your crony to buy the piece of land I wanted –'

'What? Look, Amber, just calm down. Now –'

'I will not calm down. You –'

'Have done nothing. Don't get your knickers in a twist, girl, or I might just have to take them down and spank that pretty bottom for you . . .'

His anger was dying down. Mine wasn't.

'Just try it, you cheating old bastard!'

'Look, just calm down, will you? I don't even know what you're talking about. Somebody bought the land you were after and you think it was for me?'

'Yes, as you know very well. I know you. You've arranged it all neatly in advance. I wasn't born yesterday, Morris.'

'I don't know the first thing about this, Amber, I swear it. If you don't believe me, just ask whoever the bloke is.'

'Sure, Morris.'

'No, seriously. Come on. Where is he?'

I looked round, just in time to find the man coming out of the hall, with his face set in an expression of smug satisfaction.

'Over there,' I said, 'in the black T-shirt, as you know very well.'

'I don't know the guy. I swear it. Let's ask him, yeah?'

He was already up and walking across the room, and I had no choice but to follow. The man looked around as we came close. I got in quickly before Rathwell could say anything.

'It's all right, he's told me. You can have your laugh now.'

'What?'

'You can have your laugh over buying Lot 419, both of you.'

'Um ...'

'This gentleman and I have never met before,' Rathwell cut in.

'No,' the man answered, 'but ...'

'We're terribly sorry to have bothered you,' Rathwell went on. 'Do excuse us. Come on, Amber.'

He had taken my arm, and pulled me away before the man could say anything more. I could feel my face going red as it sank in that the man really didn't know Rathwell, but I was still refusing to accept the truth.

'So now do you believe me?' Rathwell demanded.

'Maybe you could still have set it up.'

'Oh, crap! You're just trying to squeeze out of your blow-job. So much for keeping your word!'

'No ...'

'When did I fix it then? When did I get a chance to speak to the guy?'

'You'd guessed I'd be here, you could have worked it out in advance.'

'Yeah, and I knew you were going to offer a blow-job for keeping my nose out of it? Sure, Amber. Look, if I'd been after that property I'd have had it. Getting you down on me isn't worth that much, girl ...'

'Sh! Morris!'

People were staring, and I was sure they'd heard what he had said. I could feel the blood rushing to my face faster still as I glanced around me. One expensively dressed woman was giving me a very odd look indeed. An enormously fat man with a red, sweaty face glanced quickly away as I met his eye. The man who had outbid me was watching too. Morris went on. 'Look, if you don't believe me, let's go and see who the sale is registered to.'

'Will they tell us?'

'Sure, unless they've been instructed not to.'

He made for the registration desk. I followed him, trying to bite down my anger and disappointment. Rathwell spoke briefly to the girl behind the desk, who made no objections at all, pushing a file across to us with one red painted fingernail pointing to a line: '419 – Bidder 201 – Razorback Paintball'.

'Razorback Paintball?'

'Does that sound like one of my outfits?'

'No, but . . .'

'Look, girl, if you want to back out, just say . . .'

I shook my head. He took my arm, leading me towards the door. I went, feeling numb, unable to back down, unable to believe that I didn't have my land and was going to have to suck his dirty little penis anyway. Several people were watching us as we left, including those who'd been near us. My feelings of humiliation were rising steeply at the thought of them knowing what I was going to do, of thinking of me sucking on his cock, of how they'd look at me when we came back. Morris seemed oblivious, keeping a firm hold on my elbow as he steered me across the car park to where he'd parked the Rolls in the shade of a tree. He got in and I followed, for once grateful for his bad taste in that the windows were tinted.

'Tits out,' he stated casually as he unzipped his fly.

I shook my head.

'Come on, love, for embarrassing me in front of one of my business associates, a titty show is the least I could ask.'

He had pulled his cock out as he spoke, and slid down the seat, making it ready for my mouth. I swallowed, my fingers shaking, my emotions a mess. Again I shook my head.

'Come on, Amber, your nipples are like fucking corks.'

I glanced down. He was right. They were hard, making two large and embarrassingly obvious bumps in my blouse. Rathwell was grinning at me.

'Oh God, OK!'

I was biting my lip with shame and resentment as I began to undo my blouse, button by button, with his eyes fixed on my chest and his hand on his cock. It had begun to get hard, and as I tugged my blouse wide he reached in to pull out his balls. I was shaking harder than ever as I took hold of the cups of my bra, to tug them up, spilling out my breasts. Rathwell's Adam's apple bobbed in his throat.

'Fucking gorgeous. I swear you're bigger than ever, Amber, bigger than Mel, and just look at those fucking nipples, like little hard cocks. I want to feel them while you suck, OK? And stick that big bum well out. Come on, get down on me.'

'OK, you can touch, but just one thing. Don't do it in my face, please don't do it in my face.'

'Why not? I love that stuff.'

'Because it's messy, Morris! I've got make-up on, damn you! Men, honestly! Do you have any idea of the mess it will make? Yes, I suppose you do . . .'

He had started laughing. This was Morris Rathwell, a man who would happily spend an hour twiddling his thumbs while a woman got her make-up perfect just so that he could ruin it by coming all over her face. Arguing would only excite him more.

'Do what you bloody please!' I snapped and went down on his cock.

He was hard, his stiff little erection poking into my throat as he pushed my head down on to it. I began to suck, my senses filling with the taste of cock, my humiliation at what I was doing burning in my head. There I was, me, who so many people knew as dominant, and lesbian as well, down on a sixty-year-old man's cock in the back of his car, my boobs hanging loose and bare, my bottom pushed out behind. He began to fondle my breasts, and reached down to take one in each hand, so that he was holding my upper body as I sucked him.

'I love a pair of fat tits,' he groaned. 'Fat tits, skinny waist and a big arse, that's what makes a woman, and you've got it all, Amber. Yeah, like that . . . Oh you are one good little cock-sucker. Slower . . . slower, or I'll spunk . . .'

He broke off with a little choking cry as I pushed my throat suddenly down on the head of his cock, hoping it would make him come. It was getting to me, having a cock in my mouth, being bare-chested, having my nipples stroked. If he didn't come soon I was going to have my knickers down too, masturbating.

'Do that once more and I swear I will spunk down your throat,' he groaned. 'Come on, doll, take your time, nice and slow. You've got the happy stick in your mouth, yeah? Enjoy it.'

I ignored him and put my hand to his balls, stroking them as I sucked faster and faster, pursing my mouth to get as much friction as possible. Once more I pushed hard down, to jam his cock head well into my throat. He gasped, and suddenly my mouth was full of thick, salty come. I swallowed frantically, trying not to gag as his cock was forced yet deeper into my gullet. His hands squeezed hard on my breasts as a second lot of sperm was shot down my throat, and a third. He held me tight by my hair, so that I could feel the blood pumping in his cock head as he emptied his full load into my body, until at last he was done and I was allowed to pull back, gasping for breath. He wiped the last of his sperm off on the tip of my nose and gave a contented sigh.

'Nice.'

I sat up. My hands were shaking hard, too hard to do my blouse up. I felt utterly humiliated. I wanted to masturbate, and my humiliation was making it worse.

'If you want to rub your cunt, don't let me stop you,' Rathwell said casually as he pushed his cock back into his trousers.

I shook my head, delving into my bag for a tissue to wipe the come off my nose, and for my compact. Rathwell went on as I inspected my face.

'No? Suit yourself. So, what made you so sure I was after your land? I mean, yeah, we'd like to come and play on it maybe, but I'm not out to give you a hard time.'

'No? What about Melody? I thought, after Penny shaved her head . . .'

'Oh that? I made a deal with Penny. We got her for six spanking parties.'

'She didn't tell me anything!'

'Well, she wouldn't, would she? She's like you, gets funny about being paid for what she'd do anyway. D'you know, if I live to be a hundred I'll never understand you posh birds.'

I didn't answer. I was grinding my teeth again and cursing Penny under my breath. I'd just sucked Morris Rathwell's cock for nothing, just because she hadn't had the common sense to tell me she'd sorted things out with him. If she'd been there I'd have spanked her stupid bottom for her in the car park, and to hell with the consequences. As it was I had to content myself with fantasising over what I would do to her as I adjusted my clothes and repaired my lipstick.

Unfortunately, I knew that I could never really hurt her, or rather, never push her beyond her own boundaries, as there was no way to pretend that two dozen strokes of the cane wasn't going to hurt, however much she enjoyed it. I'd beat her and sit on her face, and we'd end up cuddled together in bed, but I'd have still sucked Morris Rathwell's cock.

I still needed to finalise my purchase, as did Rathwell. I also needed something to take the taste of his come out of my mouth. So we started back for the exhibition hall, only to find the man who had outbid me lounging against a car just fifty yards down the line from Rathwell's Rolls. He now had a combat jacket slung across his shoulder, and finally I put a name to the face – Gavin Bulmer.

The car was a jeep, painted in camouflage colours with 'Razorback Paintball' on the side in brilliant scarlet and orange letters with yellow highlighting. There was a picture too, of a huge razorbacked boar pig, standing on his hind legs, his body criss-crossed with ammunition belts and a gun in his hands, or rather, his trotters. He was also wearing shades.

From the instant I recognised him I was worried. To have met him at Carrie's and then for him to be bidding against me at the auction was pushing coincidence. I'd told her about the land. I'd told her a lot of other things as well, very personal things. I'd had sex with her.

Morris was talking, trying to persuade me to be one of the girls at his next spanking party.

'. . . they really loved you, especially old Protheroe, and mostly because you did get into such a state. They love to make a girl cry, just love it. You can handle it though, always could. I don't see . . .'

'Excuse me, Morris,' I interrupted. 'I need to speak to this man.'

'Sure. See you then, and, you know, think about it, yeah?'

He walked on, completely casual, as if having me suck him off was no more than a pleasant encounter, something that might happen at any time, or not. I bit my feelings down once more and tried to look as pleasant as possible as I approached Gavin Bulmer.

There had to be at least a chance that it was simple coincidence. I wasn't even sure if he'd recognised me before and, after all, it had never occurred to me, but the piece of land was ideal for the sort of macho war games he seemed to be into. Possibly he was genuine. Possibly the narrow section beside the tracks was of no use to him. He looked round as I approached.

'I like your pig,' I remarked to break the ice.

He glanced at the pig as if seeing it for the first time. 'Yeah, cool.'

I went on. 'I do apologise for my outburst earlier, Mr Bulmer. Very silly of me, I know ...'

'No problem,' he answered. 'Amber, isn't it, Amber Oakley? You were at the Butterworths' for the shooting, weren't you?'

'Yes, although not really for the shooting. Caroline and I were at school together.'

'I see.'

He went quiet, his face setting into a dirty little smirk, his eyes firmly on my chest. My mind went back to the cold January day Carrie and I had made love in the folly, and I found my face growing warm at the thought of him listening, watching even. I'd shown everything. I'd put my fingers in Carrie's fanny. I'd put my thumb up her bottom. I'd made her lick mine while I masturbated in her face ...

'I understand you run a paintballing club?' I said, as casually as I could manage.

'Yeah,' he answered. 'Razorback. That's me.'

'Is that what you'll be using the land for?'

'Yeah, mainly. I need to get some of the money back first. I get what I want, as you found out, but twelve grand ... sheesh!'

'I may be able to help you with that ...'

'Yeah, you may,' he interrupted.

I was starting to really despise him, just talking, but I went on sweetly.

'My interest was really in the northern section of the land, the piece running up beside the railway track, which joins on to 416, which you made a bid for. I don't pretend to know quite how paintball works, but I imagine it would be too narrow for you.'

'A bit, maybe. But it's not too narrow for you, is it?'

'I'm sorry?'

'You play straight with me, I'll play straight with you. You be nice to me, I'll be nice to you. I heard you with Caroline Butterworth. I know what you did. I know what you're about. I want some of the same.'

It was blatant blackmail, nothing less, and it left me speechless. He went on. 'You don't have to pretend with me. I know what you posh girls are like. Pony-girls, eh? Swish and all. I've been looking on the net, I have, so I know all about it. Now I want my share. Fuck me, but Caroline Butterworth looked cute with that whip mark across her arse ...'

'Look, Mr Bulmer –'

'Gavin, Gavin, please. Look, don't get all high-and-mighty with me. Just be nice, and we can cut a deal here. What, say ... six grand for your piece of land, I get to come and play with the girls, and a blow-job settles the deal.'

I was left speechless again, my mouth wide in sheer indignation. He gave me another dirty smirk.

'Hey, you just gave the old boy one, why not me?'

'I did not!'

'Why's there spunk in your hair then?'

I'd put my hand to my hair before I could stop myself. He laughed and shook his head.

'I knew it! I fucking knew it! You are one dirty little bitch, aren't you? So, do we have a deal?'

Rathwell was one thing. He may be a dirty old man, a pervert and an absolute bastard, but he understands. He's one of us. He's also very male, very dominant. I'd felt badly put-upon sucking his cock, abused even, but in a sexual way, in a submissive way, and however I felt, it had left me turned on. Gavin Bulmer just gave me the creeps.

I just turned on my heel, my anger boiling inside me as I walked away to the sound of his mocking laughter.

I was turned on, I might have needed sex, but not with Gavin Bulmer, and certainly not when he was trying to blackmail me. Before I'd gone a dozen steps he called after me.

'I want in, you pretty little fuck-toy, you, and I mean to get in. When you change your mind, we're in the book. It's Razorback Paintball. 'Bye.'

I made for the hall to arrange payment for my purchase. Even after I'd done it I was shaking so hard, and so angry that I didn't dare drive, while the double brandy I bought to calm my nerves only made it worse. The sheer arrogance of the man was hard to take in, to demand sex in return for being allowed to buy the land, and not just with me, but with my friends.

Rathwell had been at the desk, filling in the forms for the various properties he'd acquired. My emotion must have showed in my face, because as soon as he'd finished he came over and sat down opposite me.

'Hey, come on, doll, it wasn't that bad.'

'I'm not worried about that,' I answered, waving him away.

He took no notice.

'So what's eating you?'

Normally he was the last person I'd have confided in, but he was there, and I knew he'd understand at least in part. So I told him everything, leaving out only the juicy details of what had happened between Carrie and me. He listened, nodding thoughtfully from time to time, but silent until I'd finished.

'That's the world, doll. You should have let me help you out.'

'Maybe I should.'

'You see, Amber, sometimes you've got to give it over, let your friends help you out. Not you, you're always on your high horse, playing Miss Dominant, and look where it's got you.'

I just shrugged, not wanting to admit he was right.

'Look. I'll tell you what I'm going to do. I'll call this Bulmer guy and offer him fifteen and the option on a little bit of land I've got down in the Lee Valley, with much better access for this paintball crap he's into. That or eight for the bit you want. He has to go for it. You and old Henry can pay me back in your own time, only when Henry gets to spank the arse off you for fucking up, I get to watch!'

He laughed as he finished, re-igniting my anger. I didn't rise to it, and even managed to sound moderately grateful as I thanked him, despite the vision of the long sequence of punishments and humiliations he was likely to put me through before he was done. He got to his feet, leant in and pinched my cheek between forefinger and thumb before I could stop him.

'Cheer up, girlie! Morris will see you right, just you wait.'

I watched his back as he walked away, trying to tell myself I hated him, but without all that much success. I did, in a sense, but he had always exerted a sort of horrid fascination. Deep down I knew the problem. He liked to be in control. So did I, and that made him want to control me more than if I'd been a willing submissive. Unfortunately it aroused me, and more unfortunately still, he knew it. I found myself mouthing the word 'bastard' as the door closed behind him, then swallowed the rest of my brandy.

One thing I was not going to do was add a drink driving charge to what had been a disastrous day. So rather than try to get out of London before the rush-hour, I decided to wait until after it. I meant to go shopping, but on reaching the car I decided to relax for a while. I was drained, emotionally and physically, and I was asleep before I really knew it.

I came awake with pins and needles in one foot and a foul taste in my mouth. Fortunately I had a bottle of water with me, and a quick walk around the now empty car park restored my circulation. It was gone five o'clock, but I knew the traffic would still be heavy and went back to sit in the car for a while. Immediately my thoughts began to drift back to the events of the afternoon: first Bulmer, which made me angry again, so I focused on what I'd done with Rathwell instead.

It had felt so dirty, so humiliating, with my breasts out and a cock in my mouth in a public car park. Worse still, it was only because he had come so quickly that I'd held back from really disgracing myself, masturbating in front of him, even climbing on to his lap to take his skinny little cock up my fanny as I did it . . .

I shook myself, trying to push the rude thoughts out of my head. I'd held back. I hadn't come, but I wanted to. It was so tempting, so easy. All I needed to do was ruck my skirt up a little. I had stockings on, and loose silk knickers, just right for slipping a hand in under the gusset to stroke and flick at myself as I let my naughty thoughts run riot. It wasn't even risky. I'd parked in the shade of a high concrete wall to stop the interior of the car getting hot, which meant I could see the whole car park, including the attendant's box, which was empty. I could see people in the distance, but that just added to the sense of being naughty. Nobody could see what I was doing, and if anyone did chance to approach I could cover myself in seconds and just drive away.

The temptation was simply too great. Telling myself I was every bit as much a slut as Rathwell made out, I lifted my bottom to ease up my skirt, just far enough to get into my knickers. I was very wet, and I closed my eyes in bliss as I began to stroke at my fanny, with all the tension in me just draining slowly away to the delicious feeling of masturbation. It wasn't going to take long at all.

It wasn't going to be over what Morris Rathwell had done. The dirty, eager part of my mind was telling me to work up what had really happened into a full-scale fantasy. I could imagine him putting me across his knee for a bare bottom spanking, long, humiliating and painful, then fucking me across the back seat, even sodomising me. It would make me come, but I'd feel bad afterwards. What I really needed was a dominant fantasy, to restore my injured pride.

The easiest thing was to imagine what I could do to Penny once I caught up with her. She'd admit her crime, she always did. She would accept whatever punishment I chose to give her. She'd be in jeans. She nearly always was, tight on her lovely round bottom, hugging her beautiful cheeks . . .

I'd make her take the jeans down in front of me, panties too, and stand with her hands on her head as I lectured her. She would try to look sorry, but it wouldn't be real, at least not until I got her down across my knee, spanked and squealing with her bottom all rosy and bare. Even if she was sorry I wouldn't stop. I would cane her, two, even three, dozen strokes across her bare bottom as she knelt across my dining-room table so that she could see her bottom in the twin mirrors as she was beaten. It would put her in such a state, probably in tears, almost certainly in tears, blubbering out her emotions into my arms as I stroked her hair, soothing her, caressing away her hurt as I eased her gently down to the floor.

She'd go down, her eyes still full of tears as I put her on the floor. Her legs would come up, her thighs spreading wide, to masturbate, naked and caned on my floor, touching her welts, slipping a finger up her bottom, even as I settled on to her face, to pull aside the crotch of my knickers and her tongue slipped into mine . . .

It was glorious, just to imagine it, with her naked underneath me, her tongue well up my bottom, licking me in abject, grovelling apology. I shut my eyes to allow myself to concentrate properly, knowing that my orgasm was close. Once more I imagined Penny, with two dozen cane strokes decorating her beautiful bottom, maybe three dozen, on the floor with her tongue up my bottom hole, pleasuring me in such a dirty, intimate way, just as Carrie had done, only without some creep watching us ...

My fantasy broke, Gavin Bulmer intruding himself when I was right on the edge of orgasm. I opened my eyes, cursing under my breath in frustration. The car park was still empty, my safety absolute. Not that I'd have stopped anyway, not unless somebody was coming right towards me. I was too close, my clitty aching for those last few touches, the muscles of my sex and bottom already squeezing.

I tried to concentrate again, but the thought of him had spoiled it for me, and I knew that trying to come over having my bottom licked would just bring me back to thoughts of him watching Carrie and me, every time. I cursed again, this time aloud, wishing him to hell for his dirty, prying behaviour. Again I tried to focus on Penny as I caned her, on the little sobs and whimpering noises she makes, only to stop. My real orgasm had to coincide with my imaginary one, and I knew what she would do after her caning, what she most wanted to, and what I needed.

My fanny was getting sore with my fingers still working between my lips, keeping me there just short of orgasm. I gave in, my eyes closing even as I remembered how it had felt to be told to unbutton my blouse, to show my breasts as I sucked on Rathwell's cock. He was always so crude, so vulgar, using the words that brought me the deepest humiliation not because he knew, but by instinct. 'Tits out', he'd said, telling me to expose myself as if it was normal, inevitable, just something girls had to do, like sucking men's cocks. I'd done it too, unbuttoning my blouse, pulling up my bra, letting him touch me up as I paid court to his dirty little cock, fondling me, molesting me. It was just as well he'd come when he had too, or I'd soon have been out of my knickers, nude even, masturbating, as I was now, in a lewd, dirty display. He'd have taken advantage of me too, bending me across the seat, sticking his cock into my body, up my fanny, up my bottom, only to pull it out at the last moment and stick his dirty penis in my mouth as I came under my own fingers . . .

I did, my back in a tight hard arch as the orgasm hit me. My muscles went tight, my fanny and bottom hole went into frantic, rhythmic contraction, my eyes shut, and I came, to a single, blinding peak, even as the great wave of shame I'd expected engulfed me.

Two

I had expected Gavin Bulmer to have his paintball operation up and running by the following weekend. From the piece of land I had managed to get, which I had long before come to think of as the Old Siding, I could look over his. It was a maze of derelict and near-derelict buildings, sheds large and small, housing for electrical apparatus, even a squat pylon the purpose of which I was unsure of. I thought it looked ideal for the sort of boy's own army games he liked, but apparently it wasn't. Nothing at all happened at the weekend, adding to my frustration at Penny blithely accepting that she ought to be punished, laughing over me leading myself into sucking Morris Rathwell's cock, and then saying she couldn't come to see me until the following weekend.

My own piece of land was better than his, for pony-girl play anyway. Whatever buildings had once stood there were long gone, as were the old railway tracks. All that remained were two long mounds of overgrown rubble, lying parallel to each other to leave a trench between. I had no intention of trying to get rid of them. Each one obviously contained many tons of brick and concrete, while the buddleia and rosebay willow herb which had grown up along them were not only quite pretty, but provided excellent concealment. All I needed to do was clear the central track and I would have a perfect pony-cart run, or I would have done had there been anywhere for the pony-girls to run to. As it was, the property ended in a large muddy pool and a rusty fence of iron mesh, with the narrow strip of land I had wanted so badly beyond.

I was fairly optimistic that Bulmer would accept Rathwell's offer. After all, I'd made it pretty clear that he wasn't going to get what he wanted, and while he might try to hold out for a while, it was hard to see him refusing. So I waited, only to have Rathwell call me on the Monday to say he had been refused. Bulmer, apparently, was a money broker in the city, on some ridiculous salary, with the paintball games simply a hobby. If there's one thing Rathwell really hates, it's finding himself unable to impose his will on someone else, particularly a younger man. He was not happy about the call, describing Bulmer as a 'spoiled mummy's boy' and a 'vindictive little shit', which I could only agree with. The next morning a firm of contractors arrived and began to demolish the buildings on Bulmer's land.

I stood and watched for a while, feeling thoroughly fed up, until the workmen began to make comments. So I went back indoors and tried to put the whole thing out of my mind, but failed miserably. I really needed to talk to someone, someone who would understand and with whom I could be completely open. Henry was the obvious choice.

He was always in, and always prepared to listen. I couldn't face opening the saddlery anyway. So I drove round. He knew, of course, but I gave him the whole story again, in detail, including what had happened between Carrie and me, and the consequences, which I had conveniently omitted before. Anyone else might have been annoyed. After all, he had nearly as much interest in the land as I did, and it was, ultimately, my indiscretion which had cost us. Henry simply shrugged his shoulders and tousled my hair as he went to pour us both a glass of malt whisky.

'So there it is,' I said as I accepted the glass. 'What can I do?'

'Do you mean immediately, or in the long term?'

'Both.'

'In the long term, it is rather hard to say. This Bulmer fellow sounds spiteful, and is doubtless smarting over your refusal to be drawn into his nasty little scheme. You can do nothing, unless you wish to give in, which I know you won't. So stand aloof.'

'I see your point, Henry, and you're probably right. I just don't want to admit it. And in the short term?'

'In the short term, what you need is a good spanking.'

I laughed. 'No, Henry, what you want me to have is a good spanking. What I need is that piece of land, and preferably to see Gavin Bulmer dipped head first into one of the barrels of waste oil on it.'

He just chuckled, but I could see the disappointment in his eyes. I immediately felt bad. It was a long time since I'd let him put me across his knee, and he never pushed the issue. As my preferences for taking the dominant role and for other women had grown, so it had seemed less appropriate, despite all he had done for me.

I understood what he meant as well. I can see the appeal of submission. Sometimes it is nice to just let somebody else take charge. A spanking would do me good, if only because with some of my own arrogance smacked out of me I would feel less angry about my loss. It was still difficult to do it.

'Oh, all right,' I managed, and I could hear the pique in my own voice as I stood up.

Henry just smiled and took a sip of his whisky. I was feeling humiliated and put-upon despite myself, and for a moment I wondered if I should leave myself covered, and let him spank me on the seat of my jeans. He likes me in jeans, and they were tight enough to make a good show of my bottom, so I was sure he wouldn't complain. On the other hand, when I spank girls I very, very rarely let them keep even their panties up. Not to go bare felt hypocritical.

I held back a sigh as I began to undo my jeans. Henry just watched, very casually, as I popped the button and peeled down my zip. My thumbs went to my waistband, and I was doing it, lowering my jeans for him, for a man to spank me. I had to wiggle a bit to get them over my hips, which made me feel girlish and vulnerable, with my panty-clad bottom wobbling behind me as I squeezed the jeans down over it.

Henry's smile grew broader as I pushed the jeans to my knees. I stood again, very aware that the front of my panties was showing, and wishing I'd chosen something a bit more elegant than I had – white cotton with a pattern of little yellow ducks. Unfortunately, when I'd put them on I hadn't imagined myself having to show them to anyone. Henry just chuckled, his eyes lingering on the bulge of my pubic mound.

'Shall I . . . shall I take them down, or do you want to do it?' I managed.

His hand went to his chin.

'Hmm . . . you do.'

I swallowed, rather wishing I hadn't asked. Once I'd been over his knee I wouldn't have had much say in it anyway, which would have been easier. Now I had to take them down myself. My fingers were trembling as I took hold of my waistband. I shut my eyes, pushed, and they were coming down, rolling off my hips and bum, down over my fanny, to leave me with my hair showing. I was blushing, and cross with myself for being so wet about it, but for all my dominance I'm a baby when it comes to taking it, and always have been.

Determined to behave with a bit more self-confidence, I turned to make a deliberate show of my bottom. Again

I pushed. The back pouch of my knickers came free of my bottom and I was showing behind, bare cheeks, then the rear view of my pussy as I bent to push the panties down into my lowered jeans. I was shaking all over as I stood, bare front and back, and very, very aware of it. I turned back to Henry, awaiting my order. He simply patted his lap.

I went down, draping myself across his lap, closing my eyes as I steadied myself on the floor. My breathing was deep and a bit ragged, my trembling hard. I was lying across an old man's knee with my jeans and knickers well down, my bottom bare to the world, so that I could be spanked, smacked, like a naughty girl, and for my own good.

At least it was Henry. Whatever he does, his affection is genuine, and he will always think of me as an equal. That didn't help all that much, and when his hand settled on my bottom I felt an immediate jolt of anger, which I forced myself not to show. He was feeling my bottom, stroking my cheeks, leisurely and intimate. I took it, staring angrily at the carpet, my lower lip caught hard between my teeth, praying he wouldn't pull my cheeks apart to show off my bumhole, or finger my fanny.

He didn't, but he did begin to spank, or rather pat. With that I began to melt. I'd expected a punishment spanking, hard and fast, to make me wriggle and kick, my resentment simply ignored until it had been smacked out of me and I was ready to give in. The little pats he gave instead caught me completely by surprise, and they were too nice to resent. It was not punishment, or at least no more than a gentle admonition for my arrogance, just to be bare behind and have it attended to.

I let my mouth come open and shut my eyes, my embarrassment and self-consciousness at the position I was in slowly fading as his big hand worked over my bottom, pat ... pat ... pat ... It was getting harder, my cheeks quivering to the little slaps, until at last they had begun to sting, drawing the first gentle sigh from my lips. Immediately he changed his technique, using just the tips of his fingers, but hard, to sting my skin and send the most delicious tremors through my flesh, and straight to my sex.

It was really getting to me. Already I was beginning to want to let my legs open, to show myself off, fanny and all, to let him see me, to let him touch me. I couldn't. My sense of dignity was eroded but not broken, the idea of making a deliberate display of the back of my fanny too strong. Then my legs came apart as I hung my head lower still, my arousal finally conquering my shame.

'Good girl,' Henry said.

I just moaned. My toes were just touching the ground, my legs were well spread, my fanny on show, wet and ready, probably enough for a finger. My cheeks had come a little open too. I was wondering if I was showing my bumhole, and if I was, if he would take any real liberties, tickling my ring, even putting a finger in. He did nothing, just continued to spank me, bringing my whole bottom up to that wonderful, warm, rosy glow that comes no other way, yet is so hard to accept.

Again he changed technique, cupping his hand to catch most of my cheek with each swat and set the sound of my spanking ringing out around the room. It was harder too, enough to make me gasp. I usually cry when I'm punished, when it really starts to hurt. This time it wasn't going to happen. He had handled me too well, warmed me enough to keep my arousal above my pain, and as the swats grew firmer still I was pushing my bottom up for more, and not just showing my fanny, but flaunting it.

He took the hint, and I just sighed as his fingers found my sex, at exactly the moment I needed it. One big, callused thumb slid up into my body, a knuckle found my clitty and I was being masturbated, having my fanny rubbed, bare and spanked, spread rude and wanton. He could have got me there, easily, but he stopped, and went back to spanking me. It was harder than before, a full-bloodied, vigorous spanking, the way to punish a girl, to make her sorry, to hurt her. In my case, to help me to what I knew was going to be the most glorious orgasm.

I cocked up my bottom, opening myself fully, so that my bumhole showed. I wanted him to touch me there, in that rudest, dirtiest, most intimate of places. Not that I could have asked if I'd dared, with each smack making me gasp and jerk over his lap. I didn't need to ask. He kicked up my middle with his knee, spreading me more blatantly still. His hand went back to my sex, cupping my fanny, the thumb that had been up me on my bumhole, smearing my own juice over the little lewd dimple. I cried out as my ring popped and the top joint of his thumb was up my bottom, holding me as he once more began to masturbate me.

My orgasm was an instant away when he stopped, to leave me moaning in disappointment, only to gasp in shock and pain as the spanking began again, harder than ever. With that I lost control, bucking up and down on his legs, begging to be brought off, squirming my bottom about in the most lewd, uninhibited, frankly dirty show imaginable. He took me around my waist, hard, holding me down. He began to alternate, spanking and rubbing, rubbing and spanking, as hard as he could, full heavy-handed swats to make my bottom bounce and set me squealing, then screaming.

I'd started to come, and as I did he let go of me, rubbing at my sex and bumhole as his other hand belaboured my bottom with every ounce of his strength. His thumb went up my bumhole and I screamed louder still, my ring tightening on the digit, my thighs locking tight on his hand, and I was there, at climax, my shoes drumming on the floor, my eyes screwed up, my fists clenched, my whole body tight, until at last it burst and every bit of tension, of anger, of disappointment began to fade away.

When it was over I still lay slumped across his lap, letting him enjoy my bottom. Everything he had done had been focused on me, but I could guess just how aroused he would be. Short of sodomising me, anything he wanted was his, and as he began to ease me very gently into a sitting position I realised what it would be. I was going to be sat in his lap and fucked.

I made no resistance at all, but waited, with my bottom lifted as he freed his cock, took it in hand and guided it to my sex. Henry is big, and he was already rock hard. I moaned as my fanny stretched, taking his head, then the long, thick shaft, until I was well and truly filled, with my bottom settled against his belly and his big balls pushed up against my sex lips.

He took hold of my hips and began to fuck me, pushing up into my body with short, hard jerks. I sat up straight, very prim, except for being bare from my tummy to my knees and having a great big cock inside me. He was puffing a bit, and I was worried he might not have the energy to finish off in me, so I took over, bouncing on his cock. His immediate moan of pleasure told me it was the right thing to do. It was doing wonderful things to me too, smacking my fanny on his balls and making my boobs jump, until I had once more begun to gasp in pleasure.

His hands came around me, to tug up my blouse and flop my boobs into his hands. I let him do it, enjoying me as he pleased, and all the time wriggling and bouncing my bottom on his erection. He began to grunt, and to squeeze at my breasts as he held them, also to jam himself into me from beneath.

Sure he was coming, I pulled off, to go down on to his cock, tasting my own sex as my mouth filled with his huge, solid penis. He grabbed it, jerking at the shaft, frantic, to tug it loose at the last second, by accident I hoped, as he came. My squeal of protest was cut off as my mouth filled with sperm. A second spurt shot high, to land in my hair and down over my nose, then his cock was stuffed rudely back into my mouth, to make me suck up and swallow the rest of his sperm.

I was still sucking as I began to masturbate again. Henry let me have his cock to play with as I reached back to touch myself, exploring my spanked bottom. I was so hot, my flesh burning, my skin roughened, and it felt wonderful. I let a finger sneak down between my cheeks to tickle my bumhole, finding myself moist and open. Up went the finger and I got down to business, back and front, rubbing and teasing myself as I nuzzled my sperm-soiled face into Henry's crotch, licking and kissing at his cock and balls. I was smearing sperm everywhere, but I didn't care, intent only on the feelings of my body as my second climax rose, rose higher still, and burst.

My cry of ecstasy rang out, a second, and a third, before I was finally done. Slowly I pulled away, to rock back on my haunches as I pulled my finger free of my bumhole with a sticky sound. I was smiling, dizzy with pleasure and utterly content, all my woes forgotten in a welter of dirty, submissive sex.

'Better?' Henry enquired.

'Much better, thank you,' I answered. 'You were right, I needed a spanking.'

'Girls frequently do,' he remarked. 'It's just a shame they so seldom realise it.'

I just smiled at his blatant piece of sexism. After all, it was true in my case, and many others. In any case, he'd certainly made me feel better. I didn't bother to pull up my jeans and knickers, but took them off. It felt nice with my bum bare and my fanny showing at the front, in total contrast to the way I'd felt just a short while before. That was before I'd been spanked. Now it seemed no more than proper, to leave the evidence of my punishment on show as I cleaned up the mess I'd made of my face and sorted out coffee and chocolate biscuits for us. I left my blouse open too, and my bra up, a fine dishevelled mess I didn't bother to do anything about until lunchtime, when Henry's housekeeper was due to come in.

When I finally came to leave, after a leisurely lunch and a bottle of Chablis, I was feeling a great deal less emotional and a great deal more rational. That was despite being slightly tipsy.

Henry sent me on my way with a smack to my bottom, walking, as the distance straight down the railway was shorter by far than the road and I wanted to think. I also wanted to look at the land, and while I was technically trespassing, it seemed highly unlikely that I'd run into Bulmer on a Tuesday afternoon. There was still a frisson of naughtiness as I climbed the fence which separated the most southerly of Henry's fields from what I'd started to think of as the Strip.

It was heavily overgrown, completely untended, and obviously had been for years. There were oaks that must have been there before the railway was built, and other old trees, even elm trunks, some still alive, others rotting in the ground. The understorey was mainly hawthorn, along with several other thorn trees, while there was no shortage of bramble, gorse and nettle. I barely got ten yards before I'd scratched my face twice and decided that it was better to walk along the edge of the fields instead. They were owned by one of the big agricultural combines, another plus factor in making the Strip ideal for pony-carting. The state of the undergrowth made it yet more so, although I could see that clearing a path was going to be a major undertaking. Once done though, it would provide us with a perfectly concealed track nearly two miles long, in summer at any rate. Or rather, it would provide Gavin Bulmer with a perfectly concealed track nearly two miles long, assuming he chose to do anything with it at all.

As I walked I tried to decide what to do. Whatever Henry might have advised, I was not prepared to simply stay away. It might have piqued Gavin Bulmer, but knowing that I had mildly irritated him was hardly something to look forward to. Nor was I prepared to give in to what he wanted. Henry was one thing, Rathwell another, but Bulmer absolutely out of the question. From what he'd said it was pretty obvious that he wanted to be in the dominant role, if he even understood the concept. So I couldn't even take the pleasure of setting him up to be whipped by Melody Rathwell or maybe Vicky Belstone. It was a satisfying thought in any case, and one I let my mind dwell on as I walked slowly along the edge of the huge, empty field.

I couldn't let him loose on any of my friends any more than on myself. It was just not a reasonable thing to do. That left me out of options, so I tried to turn the problem on its head, thinking of what he'd want rather than what I was prepared to give. Money was obviously not going to work, or at least not any sensible sum. He had money. What he didn't have was sex, presumably because no woman in her right mind would be with him, for all his looks. Sex I wasn't prepared to provide, but I might be able to deflect his lust, perhaps by suggesting how he might go about finding some willing playmates.

It was a thought, although not a brilliant one. For one thing, if I felt it immoral to inflict him on my friends, what right did I have to inflict him on anyone else? Then again, they could choose, and would probably turn him down. What mattered was that he felt I was being helpful, and so might be prepared to sell. That still left the problem of how to deflect his interest away from me.

There seemed little point in telling him that I was a lesbian. He knew I'd sucked Morris Rathwell's cock, and somehow I couldn't see him accepting the excuse anyway. He struck me as the sort to regard lesbianism as either something girls did to entertain men, or because they couldn't find men. I'd heard it before. It was an option, but not a good one.

Trying to explain the implications of my being dominant was better, so long as I could lead him to believe that forgoing the pleasure of me as a plaything meant he would get more in the long run. I had no reason to think he was obsessed with me personally, after all, just with girls in general. It was far from perfect. Even if I succeeded, it meant ending up with him as a neighbour, but that had already happened. I realised I could try combining the two options, and by the time I'd reached the edge of my own property I had decided to try.

It could not be done on the telephone, but I still had to make a call. Swallowing my pride to an extent I could never have done had I not been so recently spanked, I made the call, arranging to meet him in the local pub that weekend – 'neutral territory' as he called it. Only as I put the phone down did I remember that Penny was coming up.

Penny arrived at mid-morning on the Saturday. I'd meant to have a serious talk, pointing out that she was being a bit too casual about our relationship. She was so loving, and so full of enthusiasm, that it was impossible. As soon as she was through the door she had hugged herself to me, cuddling with her head between my breasts before looking up for a kiss. I responded, postponing my lecture as our tongues met.

I know exactly how she likes to be greeted, so the moment we'd finished kissing I took her by the ear, to drag her into the kitchen. She came, protesting playfully, but squealing for real, as I was twisting quite hard. Sitting on a high-backed chair, I dragged her down across my knee, twisted her arm tight into her back, and set to work with a kitchen spoon.

She'd expected the spanking, but by hand, so she really squealed. I held her tight down anyway, ignoring her protests as I slapped away at the denim-clad cheeks of her fleshy little bottom, thoroughly enjoying myself. Only when her cries of pain had taken on that familiar, aroused tone did I go further, undoing her jeans and tugging them down off her bum, white cotton panties and all, to leave her bare and trembling. She was already showing signs of bruising, and I only realised then how severe I'd been. It didn't stop me, because what I was doing had become a genuine punishment. My satisfaction grew as I laid into her again, her self-control slipping as she began to howl and kick, wriggling her bottom in a frantic and futile effort to escape the smacks. I held on tight, really taking my feelings out on her, until at last she burst into tears and I realised I was being unfair.

An instant later she was in my arms, cuddled tight to my chest, her whole body shaking, the tears streaming down her cheeks. I held on to her, feeling a bit of a bitch, but with my arousal growing steadily stronger. Holding a trembling, beaten girl in my arms is very, very powerful for me, maybe even more than giving the actual punishment. When she began to nuzzle my breasts through my jumper, I just gave in.

She was making little purring noises as she started to pull at my clothes. My jumper came up and she was nuzzling my boobs through my bra, even as her fingers found the button of my jeans. It came open, and my zip was pulled down. My nipples had gone hard, and she had taken one between her lips. As her hands dug into the top of my jeans I found myself lifting my bottom, and a moment later they were down, panties and all, around my ankles as she buried her face in my fanny.

I shut my eyes in pleasure as she began to lick. She is so good, not just experienced, but utterly uninhibited, and dirty too. As soon as I'd slid forward on the chair her tongue was up my bottom hole, well in, licking me clean before turning her attention back to my clitty. I pulled up my bra and took my boobs in my hands, giving in completely to the pleasure she was bringing me.

Her tongue went back up my bottom, deeper still, until I could feel my anus opening to her mouth. She was masturbating too, and I could hear the wet, squashy sounds as she rubbed at her own fanny. I knew she'd want her tongue up my bottom when she came, but I also knew she'd make me come first. Sure enough, she changed technique once more, her tongue moving over my flesh with little, quick dabs, to my fanny lips to my vagina, to my bumhole, never to my clitty.

I still had my eyes shut, and I didn't need to open them. I could picture her, kneeling between my thighs, her face in my sex, her top high over her little breasts, her smacked bottom stuck well out, one hand busy with her fanny, the other with her bumhole. She is so rude, so filthy, always wanting to be bare, always wanting to be shown off, punished, humiliated, penetrated, usually in the dirty brown ring between her chubby little bottom cheeks.

Her tongue went back to my clitty just as I was about to lose patience and grab her by the hair. I started to climax immediately, my mouth coming wide and my back tightening into an arch as it all came together in my head. She was spanked, her bottom a mass of bruises. She was licking me, kneeling between my thighs in abject submission, with the taste of my fanny and my bottom strong in her mouth. She was crawling on the floor with her own spanked bottom stuck out behind, punished and grovelling, beaten and humiliated ...

She was also masturbating, utterly delighted by what I'd done to her, with her fingers in her body, bringing herself off in a crescendo of rude, sloppy noises as her tongue slipped down to my bottom hole again.

I was there, but I hadn't finished. I grabbed her by the hair, twisting my hand hard in it, to draw a pain squeak from her even as she went back to licking at my clitty. My orgasm had broken, but it took no time at all to come back, and I held her face to my sex, forcing her to lick me properly, to keep me on a long, beautiful plateau of ecstasy. I let her go only when I could bear no more. Her mouth went straight back to my bottom hole, her tongue burrowing up as the wet noises of her masturbation became louder again. I gave her what she wanted, making no effort to stop her as she fed on me in the throes of her orgasm, on and on.

She pulled back in the end, by which time I had spittle and juice running down between my bum cheeks. Her face was covered in it too, wet and messy all around her mouth, which was set in a happy, satisfied smile. Pulling herself up, she kissed me, mouth to mouth, giving me the taste of my own body as we cuddled together.

When she finally broke away it was to tell me she loved me, then to jump up, giggling as she craned back over her shoulder to inspect her bottom, and to show me. At the moment I'd picked up the spoon, I'd genuinely intended to punish her. It was hopeless. Her bottom was one huge bruise, all red and purples blotches. Any normal woman would have been in floods of tears, or furious. Not Penny. She was proud of herself, sighing before she spoke.

'That was gorgeous, and exactly what I needed. Thank you, Amber.'

I shrugged and smiled, then slapped her bottom to push her in the direction of the bathroom. We showered together and I let her wash me, but no more. When I'd finished dressing she was still inspecting herself in the mirror with a big, cheeky smile on her face. Telling her that what I'd just done was supposed to have been a real punishment was plainly pointless.

The beating and sex had in no way diluted her enthusiasm. Downstairs, she immediately went out to her car to fetch some boots she'd had made up for her for pony-play. They were hoof boots, like platforms only with the front part of the sole modelled into the shape of a horse's hoof, and simply superb. Made in black patent leather, they were calf length, and tight, with lacing at the outsides. Unlike most I'd seen, there were no heels, so that she would be forced to walk on her toes, keeping her legs and bottom constantly tight. They were also shod with small iron shoes, which must have been cast to fit.

I had to get the shop open, and lunchtime was going to be taken up by Gavin Bulmer. What I wanted to do was play, but it was hardly practical. So I gave her the keys to the old forge building in which everything to do with erotica is kept locked away and told her to get ready. That way I could at least see how she looked in the boots, and play with her in between customers. I needed to think too, and eventually to have a serious conversation with her.

My feelings had changed in the half hour since she'd arrived, and were muddled. She took such an eager, uncomplicated delight in me that it was impossible not to respond, while pushing her away would have been like kicking a puppy. She had said she loved me, and I believed her. On the other hand, I hadn't seen her in weeks. I like to think of a girlfriend as a partner in life, and for all her love, she was simply too casual. There was also the matter of getting me into difficulties, which she just seemed to find funny.

There was the usual rush of Saturday morning customers, buying everything from second-hand riding clothes to jumps. It was an hour before I managed to get a break long enough to see what she was doing. My yard is closed, completely invisible except from my own windows, and secure as long as the gate is locked. It was, which was just as well.

Penny was standing in the yard, stark naked but for her pony-girl harness. She was in full gear, bridle and body harness, the black leather straps and brass fittings accentuating her nudity. She had even put wrist cuffs on and hitched her reins to a post, so that by fastening a single strap I would be able to render her helpless. The boots looked glorious, not just cute, but adding to her vulnerability, with her effectively on tip-toe. Her waist belt was tight, enhancing her hips and bust, to make her seem more sexual still. The only thing she hadn't put on was her tail, which she was holding out to me, butt-plug up, along with a large tube of anal lubricant.

I shook my head in mock despair at her behaviour and took the tail. Immediately she turned, giggling as she pushed out her bottom. Reaching back, she spread her cheeks, stretching out the dun-brown star of her bumhole. I held up the lubricant as she looked back, her eyes full of mischief and excitement as I squeezed out a thick worm on to the plug. Her tongue flicked out to moisten her lips and she bent lower still, with her fingers digging into the soft flesh of her bottom to stretch her anus wider still, in open invitation. She pushed out her bit with her tongue.

'Please, Amber, fill me. Finger my bottom for me.'

'I intend to, slut, and who said you could talk?'

She was still watching as I lubricated my finger, but her eyes closed as I reached down, and she sighed as I found her bottom hole. The skin of her anus felt hot beneath the cool lubricant and as I wiggled my finger to open her up, but not so hot as inside her. She was moaning as I fingered her, and squeezing her bumhole on my finger, utterly wanton in her enjoyment of having her rectum explored. She was loose too, and when I pulled out her hole stayed a little open for a moment, a tiny dark cavity that shut only slowly, to squeeze out a piece of lubricant.

I reached to pull her bit free once more. My finger went to her mouth, to be sucked clean. I stroked her throat to make her swallow and take down the lubricant. It must have tasted revolting, because her face was a picture as it went down, screwed up in humiliation and disgust. Not that it stopped her sucking on my finger until I pulled free.

She was trembling again, and still holding her bottom wide. I paused for a moment, just to admire her and let what she was doing sink in. Her bottom hole was winking, with lubricant oozing out to run slowly down to the wet, ready hole of her vagina, making me think of strap-ons, and what could so easily be done to her. The tail was a start, but no more.

I put the tip of the plug to her hole, and watched it go in. She moaned as her anus filled, and again as I pulled back to watch her hole close. Again I pushed, easing the plug slowly in, to let her hole open naturally, and enjoy the sight of the little pinkish-brown ring stretching to take its load. She was working her muscle as I did it, tightening and relaxing, to make it squeeze on the plug, open and squeeze again, until she was mushy enough to take it. The thick part popped in and her anus closed on the stem.

'That's lovely. I can feel it inside me.'

'No talking!'

I slapped her bottom, drawing a squeak as my fingers caught the bruised flesh. Her anus tightened again, squeezing on the stem. I slapped her thigh, making her squeak once more and let go of her cheeks. She stood, clenching to hold the stem of the tail in place until I could tie it into the laces of her waist belt. Done, I stood back, to leave the long black hank of hair bobbing behind her, as if rising from her spine, just as a real horse's would. She wriggled her bottom.

'So,' I said, 'what shall we do with you? A little dressage perhaps? Maybe practise walking with your nice new hooves? Or should I put you on the cart?'

She nodded eagerly at the last suggestion, which I immediately discounted. What with one thing and another I wanted to be cruel, to take her to her limits. The idea came to me just as the shop bell went, and I was forced to go back inside, leaving her hitched to the post with her hands fastened behind her back.

It only took a moment to serve, and on the way back I took a crop from the rack, one with a deer horn handle and silver fittings. It look painful, long, with a leather sting at the tip, just right for coaxing her to more effort. The handle also had potential, the grip a length of ridged horn, rough, but not too rough, with a four-inch prong of polished horn at the tip. I also took a rope.

Penny was as before, waiting patiently in the sun. She was fully in role now, and gave no more than a gentle tug and a muted snicker as I unhitched her and led her into the paddock. I'd been clearing the hedge which had shut off the view from the Old Siding, and the ground was littered with pieces of Leyland cypress, some of which had been twenty feet tall. She stood patiently as I fixed the rope to her waist belt in a long loop and knotted it off on the biggest of the trunks.

'Haul,' I ordered, stepping close, and as the rope took the strain I laid a cut across her legs.

She jerked and gasped through her gag, giving me that delicious thrill of pure sadism which simply never fades. Again she strained, and the tree began to move slowly, dragging across the damp ground, into which her hooves were sinking. I gave her another cut, making her stumble and almost fall, and was about to put a third across her shoulders when the shop bell went.

'Pull it across the paddock, Calliphigenia,' I ordered, using her pony name. 'If you're not at the far side by the bonfire before I'm back, it's six strokes across your legs.'

She stamped once and again took the strain. I hurried for the shop, to find one of my neighbours, a Mrs Millet, looking at the display of riding boots.

Twenty minutes later she had decided that she didn't like any of the styles I had available in her size. I went back, to find that Penny had managed to cross the paddock, and was standing in the corner opposite her starting point, by the ashes of the bonfire site. She was wet with sweat, so much so that her fringe was plastered to her forehead. One leg was shaking slightly too. Her eyes followed me as I approached, doubtless wondering if I would find an excuse to whip her thighs anyway. I considered it, but decided to let her tension build a little more.

'Good girl, Calliphigenia,' I said, walking around behind her to inspect her sweat-slick bottom and back. 'So, no whipping. A treat instead, but I've no sugar lumps. Bend down.'

She reacted immediately, bending to steady herself against the rope and leaving her bottom stuck out and wide, so that I could see where the shaft of the tail disappeared into her anus. I could also see her fanny, which was puffy and wet with juice, the inner lips glistening with fluid where they projected from between the outer, her clitoris standing proud beneath the milky flesh of the hood.

'Legs open,' I ordered.

Again she obeyed immediately, spreading her fanny to me. I turned the whip in my hand, reaching out to poke the heel into her hole. It went easily, and I began to tease her, rubbing first the smooth, then the rough horn on her sex, until she had begun to whimper and her muscles were tightening in her excitement. Stepping closer, I slid the prong fully into her vagina and pulled gently up, making her gasp and keeping her helpless as I began to stroke the bruised flesh of her bottom.

'Right,' I said, 'as I can't attend to you properly at present, I think I shall keep you working. After all, you may as well do something useful. So . . .'

She stamped for the right to speak.

'Yes?'

'More work? Aren't you going to have me? I need it, Amber, my bum's really glowing, and –'

'Later. For now, I have to see to the shop, and I'm meeting somebody in the pub for lunch. Once you've been like this for an entire afternoon, I imagine you'll be all the more ready.'

'The whole afternoon!? Oh, Amber, please! At least rub me off with the crop handle, or . . .'

The shop bell went. I gave her a smile, took her reins and twisted them off on the top of the jump. She gave me a pleading look, to which I responded with a pat of her bottom.

This time there was a girl behind the counter who did not look like one of my typical customers. She was shorter even than Penny, but with a very different figure. A brilliant pink skinny top held in breasts bigger than my own, which seemed all the more enormous for her tiny waist, which was bare, her little round tummy showing, with a green stone in a belly-button piercing. She had cut the waistband off her jeans, leaving them so low on her hips that it was impossible not to wonder if the top of her bottom crease showed at the back. I gave her a big smile, hoping she had come for SM equipment, but cautious, as I do my very best to keep my sideline secret except for those who appreciate it.

'Hi,' she greeted me. 'Are you Amber Oakley?'

'Yes.'

'Hi, I'm Jade. A friend, Heather, recommended you.'

'Heather?'

'Heather. Heather Ryan I think it is, or O'Ryan. She's Irish anyway, a care nurse, about five foot six, dark-haired, very pretty . . .'

'Heather, yes, I know who you mean. She recommended me? Good.'

'Yes. You . . . er . . . you made something special for her, so . . . so that . . . oh, shit, so that she could be a . . . a pig, a sort of pig-girl. That is what you do, isn't it?'

She was looking so earnest, and so embarrassed, that it was almost tempting to deny it. It would also have been very unfair.

'That's me,' I answered, smiling, 'but only to those in the know. So you want to be a piggy-girl?'

She nodded, her face still pink, but smiling.

'Yes.'

'You want a snout and tail, then?'

'Sure, a harness too, just like Heather's, to cover my mouth and nose. I suppose you do a standard design?'

'A truffle harness, we call them, and they're custom-made to measure. Is it for you?'

It was the crucial question. I was praying that the answer would be yes and that she wasn't going to turn out to be a wife pushed into dominance by a kinky but possessive husband. It is a type who make up a depressing proportion of my SM gear customers. Jade was not one of them.

'Yes, for me,' she said happily, and just opened up. 'We played with Heather as a pig ... a piggy-girl, my uncle Rupert and I. It was great, and I've been dying to try it ever since. Do you think I'd be good?'

'Perfect,' I answered truthfully, thinking of her great heavy breasts swinging beneath her and her fat bottom wobbling behind.

It was true, she was the perfect pig. Plump in all the right places, her face both pretty and cheeky, with a little snub nose not far off being a snout in its own right.

'She, um ... Heather,' she went on, suddenly shy again. 'She says you are a lesbian?'

It's not always an easy question to answer. To a girl who liked to play at pigs with other girls it was very easy.

'Yes, and you?'

'Yeah ...'

She had trailed off, and there was just a touch of doubt in her voice.

'Bisexual?' I asked. 'Don't worry. I am.'

'No . . . yes . . .' she said. 'I don't know. Maybe . . . not really, no.'

I gave her a sympathetic shrug, not wanting to go into the details of my own lack of purity. She went on. 'What I was going to say is that I hadn't seen you at any clubs. Not your thing?'

'Not really, no. I prefer to play with my friends. There's a yard and a paddock at the back. The paddock's grown round with a thick-set hedge . . .'

I stopped. I wasn't normally so open, but she was disarmingly frank. For an instant a horrible thought crossed my mind, that Bulmer might have sent her in to sound me out. I dismissed it. She knew Heather, and anyway, piggy-girls were one of the things I hadn't mentioned to Carrie, and it wasn't something he was likely to think of off the top of his head. She went on cheerfully.

'Cool! So you can play without the nosy neighbours finding out. Uncle Rupert has a garden a bit like that, only some of it is overlooked. That's where we played at piggy-girls with Heather. We made this big mud puddle for her, and she went in, and she was rubbing her tits in the mud and everything, and we gave her a good switching, and Rupert fucked her and everything.'

It had come out in one long sentence, and my last doubts dissolved. She was genuine. I didn't want to push her, but I badly wanted to hint that if she wanted to be a piggy-girl I would be more than happy to help with more than just making the accessories. I was still wondering how to express myself subtly when she solved the problem for me.

'You've got gorgeous big tits.'

It took me aback. She was so casual, as if complimenting a girl she'd met five minutes before on her breasts was the most natural thing in the world. Maybe in the company she mixed in it was. I managed a smile and returned the compliment.

'Thank you, and so have you.'

Her response was to glance at the door, snatch the hem of her top, and jerk it up. For one glorious moment I was staring at two absolutely huge pink breasts, each snuggled into the confines of an enormous bra, with a cleavage I'd have had to hold mine together to achieve, and maybe not then. She covered herself, giggled and threw another glance at the door.

'Thanks,' I managed, 'but careful, please. I have some very straight-laced neighbours. So, the snout and tail? The tail's easy, but the snout has to fit to the contours of your face, which is tricky. Once that's done it normally takes me about a week. You can try it on when it's ready if you like?'

'Yeah, love to. So, Heather says you invented the piggy thing?'

'Yes, in a way. I mean, it's not entirely original, but yes, I worked it out from scratch, for my girlfriend. She's here, as it goes. Would you like to meet her?'

Jade nodded. It had been more than I could resist. She was so outgoing, yet perhaps just a little bit smug, with her piercing and her club-going and casually flashing her boobs. I showed her out to the back, she chatting casually as we went.

Penny was standing where I'd left her, at the edge of the bonfire patch, still attached to the cut tree. A look of alarm grew on her face as we approached, far stronger than I'd have expected when she knew full well I'd only bring out people who could be trusted. As I drew closer I realised why. She was standing in a puddle of pee, the dark stain blatantly obvious among the pale ashes. It had run down the insides of her legs too, filling her beautiful new boots to the brim. I glanced at Jade, wondering if she'd be shocked. She wasn't. She was giggling, her fingertips pressed to her mouth in a gesture both amused and pleased.

'You might have squatted down,' I told Penny, who returned an accusing look.

55

Jade had come close, and her expression turned from amusement to something more serious as she saw the state of Penny's bottom.

'Oh, you've smacked her. Beautiful.'

She had ducked down, to inspect Penny's spanked bottom. Her mouth was a little open, her eyes full of excitement as they ran over the bruises.

'Hairbrush?' she asked.

'Spoon, and a riding crop.'

'Lucky thing!'

Penny gave me a quizzical look.

'She wants to be a piggy-girl,' I explained. 'She's called Jade.'

Penny's own eyes had brightened up at the mention of piggy-girls. I had a delicious vision of the two of them together in a pool of mud.

Jade had completed her circuit of Penny and stood up.

'That is beautiful leatherwork, Amber. She's beautiful too, aren't you, girl?'

Penny gave a little snicker, pushing her face out towards Jade. Jade giggled.

'May I touch?'

'Of course.'

Jade reached out, to stroke Penny's cheek with a single finger. Penny nuzzled in response.

'She is so cute! And she's the original piggy?'

'Yes.'

'But a pony now. That is so beautiful.'

Jade was rapt in her attention, one finger tracing a slow line down Penny's body, to her neck, to her chest, tickling one hard nipple, and lower, over the gentle curve of chest and tummy.

'Can I finger her, Amber?'

'She's a bit wet.'

'I don't care.'

'Ask her. She'll stamp for yes.'

Penny promptly stamped. It was getting good, and all I needed to do was take control of the situation, something I was fairly sure would meet with no resistance whatsoever. I glanced at my watch, wondering what I could fit in before my lunchtime appointment, only to discover that I was already five minutes late.

'Hell! Look, you two, I have to meet someone in the pub, now. Penny, look after Jade. Show her your snout and tail.'

Penny nodded. I went, biting my lip in frustration. I was feeling very aroused, enough to need to check that there wasn't a damp patch at the crotch of my jeans, which was the last thing I wanted when I was going to meet Gavin Bulmer. There wasn't, but my nipples were hard and, as always, blatantly obvious even through a bra and jumper.

I tried to think neutral thoughts as I walked to the pub. I also forced myself not to hurry. The last thing I wanted was to appear flustered, while there was no harm in being a little late. I even stopped for a few minutes before crossing the green, pretending to look at the parish notice board, although the only new thing it held was a garish poster advertising some sort of carnival.

The Coach was crowded, as ever on a Saturday. Bulmer was already there, in the beer garden, looking as smug and creepy as ever. He was in full combat gear, including a flack jacket with the pig logo on the chest. Feeling badly in need of a drink, I ordered myself a double gin and tonic and took it out to his table. He'd been reading a book, something to do with guns, and waited until I was seated before putting it down to talk to me.

'Changed your mind?' he said. 'I knew you would. So –'

'Not really, no,' I interrupted. 'Look, I might be able to help you, but I need to explain something to you first.'

'Fire away.'

'OK. So you spied on Carrie and me –'

I broke off. I'd expected a look of guilt, the reaction, surely, of a Peeping Tom accused face to face with the woman he has been spying on. At the least I'd expected embarrassment. Gavin Bulmer was grinning, thoroughly pleased with himself. I pushed on.

'You spied on Caroline Butterworth and me. You know we had sex –'

'And what sex! You dirty bitch, Amber.'

There was immense satisfaction in his voice, and not the slightest trace of shame. It was almost conspiratorial, as if the fact that he had spied on such an intimate moment created some sort of intimacy between us. It was not an easy attitude to take in, much less understand, but I went on, determined to make my point.

'Lesbian sex, Gavin, and as lesbian sex goes, not so very unusual.'

'Bollocks! She reamed out your asshole, Amber, and the pony-girl stuff, and the swish. Bizarre!'

He lifted his pint to his mouth. I could feel the blood rising in my cheeks as he spoke. He was so crude. He managed to make it seem so seedy as well, just by the tone of voice, so different from the air of playful naughtiness Penny and I like, or Jade's open sensuality. It was turning my stomach, but I held myself in. I could see where he'd picked up his vocabulary. It was pointedly vulgar, heavily Americanised and littered with violent and misogynistic images. That almost certainly meant the Internet, which he'd mentioned before. I'd spent enough time surfing for the rare worthwhile pony-play content to recognise the style. It seemed likely that many of his other attitudes to sex came from the same source, which was not something I knew a great deal about. It did give me a fresh detail for my argument.

'What I'm trying to say,' I replied, frantically concocting a new story, 'is that you've misinterpreted the situation. Caroline and I were lovers at school –'

'Fucking shit! That is so horny! How old were you? Go on, I want to hear it all.'

'Mr Bulmer! Could you listen for a moment, please?'

I took a deep breath, forcing my temper down, and went on.

'Caroline and I had a lesbian affair when we were both in the sixth form. What happened when you spied on us was . . . was like a piece of nostalgia. My girlfriend doesn't even know, and she would be very upset if she did. Yes, I do the things you heard, but it's not as sexual as you think. The images on the net are mainly provided as pornography, made by men, with paid models, and intended for men. They give a false impression. Above all, what we do is between lesbian women, and not appropriate . . .'

'What, getting spanked by dirty old men?'

'No . . .' I began, and stopped.

It was a thought. I knew most of the girls who attended Morris's parties, but taking a spanking from Bulmer couldn't be any worse than from Protheroe. Morris made sure the guests behaved themselves as well. He was talking again, lust dripping from every word.

'I'd love to have seen that. Bare bottom spanking. Did he pull your knicks up your crack then, or right down so everyone saw your cunt?'

He was trying to rile me. He had to be. Nobody is that insensitive.

'That was all a misunderstanding,' I said quickly. 'But the thing is, I could introduce you to Morris Rathwell's spanking club.'

'Nice.'

I was getting somewhere. Not far, but somewhere. I carried on.

'It's not all that expensive. Two hundred a head, I think.'

'I don't pay.'

'Everyone pays, that's the whole –'

'Not me. You see, there's two types of bloke in this world, punters, and men. I'm a man.'

'I'm sure you are, but Morris has a standard charge, for which you get to spank two or three girls, maybe even cane them. It's done bare too, it's always done bare.'

'Yeah, nice, but I don't pay. You can get your mates in, can't you?'

'I don't go. I only went to Morris's house that night as a favour for my girlfriend. We didn't even know there was a party, never mind what sort. Morris just . . .'

'Yeah, sure. Come on, babe, I wasn't born yesterday. Let's cut the crap, yeah? I know women, me. You bullshit that you don't like it, but underneath, you're gagging for it. So you get off on being spanked, and you have to get a dirty old man to do it. Think how much better it would be with a handsome young stud. Look at me, am I a bad-looking bloke?'

'That's not the . . . No, I . . . I don't enjoy . . .'

I stopped, feeling confused and angry. He was getting to me, prying into my most intimate feelings, things I could talk to with only my most intimate friends, like Carrie. I'd lost track of my argument as well, and struggled to get back.

'What I'm trying to say, Mr Bulmer, is that I can help you, not personally, because I am a lesbian, and a dominant at that, but I can, and I will. All I ask in return is that you allow me to purchase the northern section of your land, the strip beside the railway.'

He took another swallow of beer before speaking.

'Maybe, maybe. I'm not an unreasonable bloke, Amber. I just like a fair deal, that's all. So what about this girlfriend of yours? She sounds a dirty bitch. What she did to that girl, fucking marvellous!'

'What girl?'

'The girl whose head she shaved, and stuffed fried pig's bollocks up her cunt and arse. Jesus, a detail like that and you don't even remember. Fuck me but you must have some sex life!'

I'd forgotten just how much I'd told Carrie, and was earnestly wishing I hadn't.

'Yes, but ... but ... that's my private life, Mr Bulmer, part of a very intimate, very complicated friendship, between lesbians ...'

'Not the girl you stuffed the balls up. You said she was that bloke Morris's wife. He's a dirty old bastard and all, ain't he?'

I didn't answer, but blew out my breath in sheer exasperation. Swallowing a good half of my drink in one, I went on.

'The thing is, Mr Bulmer, Gavin, as far as sex is concerned, actual sex, my girlfriend and I are monogamous. Please, I'm not trying to be funny here, believe me. It's just the way things are. I do understand what you need, but I can only help you if you allow me at least a little leeway. Please?'

He frowned, doubtful for once. I pushed on.

'Yes, we do rude things with other women, occasionally, but only with a few old friends, and as I said, they're not really sexual. What I did with Carrie was an exception, and very personal.'

I'd put a lot of resentment into my voice at the end, again trying to shame him. As before, he took no notice whatever, but finished his pint in two swift gulps before speaking.

'Here's the deal. You get me the introductions, and get a few of your dirty bitch friends up the first time. I provide the land to play on. Once I've got that place enclosed, it'll be perfect. Once things have got going, we'll make a deal over the bit of land you want.'

I nodded, trying to think over the implications of what he was saying. He still wanted me to help directly, but he seemed to have accepted that sex with me was not on the cards. I still needed to stress that my sex life was not as interesting as he imagined, but I had at least made some progress.

'So have you seen the posters for my carnival?' he asked.

'Those are yours?' I asked, remembering the gaudy picture I'd seen on the village green.

'Sure. It's a great scam. It's some arty crap, funded by the lottery, so they pay top dollar. Hold it regular, and my money'll be paid back in a couple of years.'

'So it's on your land then?'

'Yeah. Come and see what we're doing. Look, Amber, babe, I know we got off to a bad start, and perhaps I was a bit hasty and that, but only because I fancy the knickers off you. Take it as a compliment. We're the same sort of people, you and I, so how about a fresh start, yeah?'

He put out his hand. I knew he was still trying to manipulate me, but I still felt a bit of a bitch as I accepted the gesture. It didn't stop me continuing my efforts as we walked from the beer garden.

'To tell the truth, what I said to Carrie was a bit exaggerated. I wanted to show off, I suppose. I do have the contacts though.'

I continued to talk as we walked back through the village, past the station and up the track that led to the land. I'd been up the track before, but never inside, it having been firmly shut off ever since I'd moved there, and not even fully visible from the train.

Nobody was there, but the contractors had been busy, as I knew from the constant noise over the previous week. Many of the structures had been flattened, leaving only the brick sheds and the pylon. There was rubble everywhere, and they still hadn't got rid of the five great iron drums of waste oil I'd seen before, but only moved them into a corner. They had been planting Leyland cypress too, but even then it was going to take a while to screen it off properly.

'... I'm into it, yeah,' Bulmer was saying, referring to paintball, 'but it's the perfect cover for girlie stuff. The big hut will be HQ, and there's existing plumbing, so we can have bogs, and proper changing rooms, all for Razorback, but just as good when we get down and dirty. I'm keeping the spotlight pylon, might even get it working again, for night games. It'll make a great frame for bondage and whipping, like the Jap stuff.'

I nodded, not really wanting to agree, but immediately picturing Penny strung up by her hands from the lower members of the pylon. He went on.

'What I reckon will be cool, yeah, is to combine our skills, right. To have games, but sexy. Like we can do stuff with teams of girls, and the losers get a good whacking. Or the girls get hunted, with paintball guns, and ... I don't know, maybe six hits earns a good fucking. Believe me, babe, I am full of ideas.'

He was, and I could see the appeal. On the other hand, if he thought I was being hunted down, shot with paintballs and fucked by a complete stranger he had another thought coming. I kept my peace, letting him talk as we walked up the length of the siding, until we reached the point where it joined my own purchase. Bulmer was still talking as he jumped up on to a pile of broken concrete slabs.

'... and here, we can join the two bits of land, for when we need more space. I reckon ... fuck me!'

His mouth had come open, and he was staring at something on my land. It didn't take a genius to work out what it would be, and I was immediately scrambling up on to the concrete.

Sure enough, Penny and Jade had taken it into their heads to use the big mud puddle at the end of the Old Siding to play piggy-girls. Both were there, brown and filthy, plastered from head to toe, snouts in place of noses, little rubber tails waving above muddy bottoms. Nor was that all.

They were kneeling, head to tail, bums up, and playing with each other's fannies. Jade had her back to us, her big, round bottom stuck high, her thighs wide, her huge boobs dangling in the mud. She was filthy, brown all over, except for the pink opening of her vagina, her visibly aroused vagina. Penny was masturbating her, fully intent on the fat, filthy bottom in front of her face, one finger tickling Jade's anus, others working on the muddy fanny. Jade was doing much the same, alternately rubbing between Penny's thighs and slapping at her bottom, to spray mud out around them with every impact.

I suppose it took about a second before Jade realised that somebody was watching. Unfortunately she knew nothing about the situation with Gavin Bulmer. All she knew was that I was bisexual, and had gone to meet someone in the pub. She giggled, gave Penny a harder slap and sat up, to cup her great, fat, muddy boobs in her hands and bounce them for us. Penny looked around, realised immediately, and whispered something into Jade's ear.

Both stood, and ran off towards my house, bare, muddy bottoms wobbling behind them, their tails bouncing above. It was a gloriously rude sight, and one I could not have resisted. Nor could Gavin Bulmer.

'Your girlfriend?' he demanded. 'With the big knockers?'

'No,' I sighed, 'the other girl.'

'Cute. They're both cute, and I love the pig stuff. Now that is my kind of shit!'

Three

It was partly my fault, but only partly. Mostly it was Penny's who really should have guessed Bulmer might come out to inspect his land. Her argument was that she thought I'd been having lunch at the pub, not just a single drink.

One way or the other, I was right in it. Before, Bulmer had only heard. Now he knew for certain. He also knew I had been lying, or at least bending the truth, which was worse. He was also privy to my piggy-girl fantasy, one of the dirtiest and most intimate.

I couldn't be hostile, there was too much to lose. So I had made a joke of it, and more or less agreed to his terms. I even let him kiss me when we parted, just on the cheek, but it still stung my pride. The slap on my bottom as I turned away took more swallowing, but I did it.

So I was left feeling wounded, sulky and not on the best of terms with Penny, which was how it stayed for the next week. On the Sunday she rang and apologised, offering me the chance to punish her in any way she wanted. I'd mellowed enough to accept, only to discover that she was leading a university field trip to Ireland and wouldn't be back until the weekend of the carnival. Jade came to collect her order, but we didn't play, which I was sure we would have done had it not been for the incident with Bulmer.

Work continued on Bulmer's land, which I went to inspect each day, watching it slowly being cleared. By the day before the carnival it was empty but for the shells of those buildings Bulmer intended to renovate, and the oil barrels. That evening a truck-load of portable toilets and a marquee arrived, followed by Bulmer himself. I was standing by the fence, and could hardly pretend not to have seen him, so accepted the bundle of free tickets he pressed into my hand with as much good grace as I could muster.

It seemed petty not to go anyway. Also, it would give me an afternoon with Penny that didn't involve sex, which I felt I needed. I also invited Anderson and Vicky, in the hope that meeting a man so obviously more attractive in every way and a woman several inches taller than him might intimidate Gavin Bulmer.

They came up together on the day, in fine spirits, and we walked over to Bulmer's land together, in brilliant sunshine. The carnival turned out to be all to do with performance art, fire-eaters, jugglers, mime-artists and so forth, which really didn't do a great deal for me. There were stalls too, selling such things as occult jewellery, crystals and dried herbs. Prices were extortionate, which was justified by all proceeds going to some charity I'd never heard of. I could see it was just the sort of thing that would get lottery funding, but it didn't really appeal, at least until Penny laughed out loud and tugged on my arm.

'Amber, look, pony-girls!'

She was right, after a fashion. One of the acts was a sort of pony-cart, which was giving customers rides around the edge of the plot. The cart was really more like a rickshaw, with two girls between the shafts, in tandem formation. They weren't even harnessed, and their costumes were showy but not overtly erotic. That was hardly surprising considering they were offering rides to all-comers, children included, so it was impossible not to wonder if they were really into being pony-girls.

Both were certainly attractive – if in rather a conventional way – tall, elegant girls so similar they might have been sisters, and the more so for brilliant emerald hair and make-up, accented with black and silver, as were their costumes. The cart was in the same colours, and the stall, behind which the third member of the troupe was taking the money.

If the two pony-girls were attractive, then she was absolutely gorgeous, and far more to my taste. She was tiny, maybe no more than five foot, and very slim, with small apple-like breasts and a cheeky, spankable bottom, accentuated by her tiny waist. Her tight, low-slung jeans fitted beautifully, tucked well under, to make her bottom seem more spankable still. She was also very pretty, with a delicate oval face, a tiny nose and a mop of tawny blonde hair half covering her large blue eyes. I could only stare, until I felt a sharp tweak to my bottom and turned, expecting to find Anderson or Vicky. It was neither, but Gavin Bulmer, who took my involuntary look of annoyance with as little reaction as ever.

'I thought that would get you going,' he said. 'Cute, ain't they?'

'Gorgeous,' Penny cut in before I could answer. 'Are they . . . for real?'

'You mean up for it? Nah.'

'You're sure?' Penny asked.

'Yeah. I tried, didn't I. Would've got my face slapped if I hadn't stepped back smartish.'

'By who?'

'Her on the left, as you look at them, Lisa. Her sister's Shelley.'

'They're really sisters?'

'Yeah. Frigid bitches and all.'

I nodded to myself, wondering if their response had been to what he'd said or the way he'd said it. What I could be sure of was that they weren't likely to slap my face, let alone Penny's, but to find out we'd have to get rid of Bulmer. The sensible solution was to take a ride on the cart, which was a two-seater.

Unfortunately, it was not so easy. He stayed with us as we queued, as we paid and even as we went round. It was fun, but a very pale reflection of real pony-carting. It was nice watching the gentle, rhythmic movement of Lisa and Shelley's bottoms as they walked, and they did have a certain natural elegance. What they didn't have were bare cheeks, tails or reins, while I had no whip and urging them on with a well-placed toe was obviously not acceptable. So I made the best of the view and tried to ignore Bulmer, hoping he'd go away.

He didn't, and other people took our places in the cart as soon as we'd relinquished our seats. Only when one of the stewards came up to consult him about some problem to do with parking did I manage to get rid of him. By then I'd lost Penny too, as she had gone to look at a stall that sold little glass shells and sea animals. So I went to get a drink, which took a good ten minutes, by which time she'd moved on.

The stall was one of the closest to the line of portable loos. All four had queues, short for the men, long for the women. Penny wasn't among them, but the girl from the pony-cart stall was, and she looked far from happy, her face set in grim determination, her fingers locked together in one continuous fidget. She wasn't the only one, and there were a good ten people ahead of her, and it was impossible not to wonder if she would make it.

I hoped she would, but I was not going to deny myself the pleasure of watching her squirm. It's one of Penny's favourites, to be tied helpless until she wets herself, and it is nice to watch. She gets in such a state, wriggling her toes and squeezing her thighs together, even crying, until she lets go and does it in her jeans. Even voluntary, it is immensely powerful, and this was not voluntary.

Promising myself that I would invite her over to my house if she really looked like she was going to have an accident, I sat down on a trailer for one of the stalls. There were nine women ahead of her, some chatting together, some admiring the view, a couple looking worried, but not as worried as the little blonde. I began to sip at the cold beer I'd bought, feigning indifference as I watched from the corner of my eye.

The queue was moving painfully slowly, but it was at least moving, down to nine, then eight, then seven, with my blonde getting gradually more desperate all the time. I knew all the symptoms, and was seriously wondering if she would be able to hold on. Her toes showed in her open sandals, and she was wiggling them, as well as fidgeting. She was crossing her legs as well, and would occasionally give her fanny a surreptitious little squeeze when she thought nobody was looking. Her jeans were tight anyway, but all her wriggling and pressing had pulled up her crotch, until her sex lips were showing clearly, with the denim seam caught tight in the groove. She kept turning around as well, to provide me with an even better view of her little fat bottom cheeks squeezing as she struggled to hold herself.

It was when she began to shake her head that I knew she really wasn't going to make it. There were still seven people ahead of her, with an elderly woman in the loo. I got up, only to see her bend into herself, both hands now pressed to her crotch as an expression of pain and frustration came on to her face. I stopped, feeling an absolute bitch, and promising to wait just a moment more. She had straightened up and taken her hands away from between her legs, but her jaw was set tight, and her shame showed in her eyes, along with the strain of holding on to her bladder. It was too late anyway, with a tiny wet patch showing in the tight crevice of her sex. She had begun to wet herself, and at any moment she was going to let go completely.

It was impossible not to watch. The stain spread, slowly at first, just in the narrow valley of denim where her jeans had caught up in between her fanny lips. As it grew bigger, so the expression of agonised humiliation on her face grew more intense. Suddenly her eyes shut tight, and her expression changed, to despair, then utter, complete disgust. She clutched frantically at her crotch, but it did no good. Piddle burst from between her fingers, to spray out on to the ground, soaking into the denim of her jeans as well, the stain spreading quickly as it soaked in. I watched, the wet patch growing, around her crotch and down the insides of her thighs as the urine trickled down her legs.

Either the whole thing was too emotional for her to cope with, or she had just given in, because she stayed where she was, wetting herself in full view of all four lavatory queues and a good many others. Her only vague attempt at modesty was to turn her back to the main crowd. That left her gloriously rounded bottom stuck out, side on to me, with a star-shaped pee stain growing slowly up the cleft of her bottom, in either tuck beneath her cheeks, and in the valley between her still tightly clenched legs. The piddle had begun to run out of the bottoms of her jeans too, into her sandals and on to the hard packed ground, until she was standing in a little yellow puddle of her own making. A trickle began to run down towards the loo, other women in the queue stepping quickly to one side. Most ignored her. Some were too worried by their own condition to notice. Two exchanged looks of disgust and disapproval.

I just stared, feeling very, very sorry for her, but also very, very aroused. I wanted to go and comfort her, with my arm around her shoulder. I also wanted to tell her off for being so dirty, to pull her across my knee, spank her lovely, cheeky bottom, hard on her wet seat. More, I wanted to pull her jeans down, and off, to spank her bare and let everyone watch, to stuff her pissy panties in her mouth as I punished her . . .

It really was too much. Besides, it was hardly fair to leave her in such an awful state, when it probably meant going home on the train in her wet jeans. Telling myself that I was being kind, and responsible, and not at all trying to take advantage of her plight, I stepped forward. She looked round sharply as I laid a gentle hand on her shoulder, and I saw that her eyes were full of tears.

'Are you all right? No, you're not, are you. Look, you can't stay like that. I live just a little way down the road, so come and clean up.'

'I'm all right, really . . .'

'No, you're not.

'Really, I am. I just have to find my friends.'

'Well, if . . .'

'No, actually. I'm not all right. That would be great if you could help me.'

Taking her by the arm, I led her gently away from the queues. She made no effort to pull away, and after a moment her hand tightened on my wrist as she spoke again.

'Oh God, this is so embarrassing! How could I! Oh, how could I!'

'Don't worry, it could have happened to anyone. It's ridiculous having only four loos for this number of people.'

'I know. You'd at least have thought they'd have the sense to have more for the women than the men!'

'Not Bulmer. The man's an idiot,' I answered, desperately trying to get off the subject of her wetting herself.

'Bulmer?'

'The guy who owns the land. I thought he'd spoken to you?'

'Oh, him. I thought he was the caretaker or something. He pinched Lisa's . . . my friend's bum.'

'That sounds about par for the course. What's your name?'

'Kay.'

'I'm Amber. I like your act. Where did you get the idea?'

'Oh . . . it . . . it just came to me.'

She was embarrassed. That almost certainly meant there was some connection with a sexual image. I was wishing I could be as open as Jade, and just ask straight out. I couldn't, at least not with her in pee-soaked jeans and panties, and my own not all that much drier. I'd seldom felt so aroused, but I kept telling myself that it was not the time, and just carried on talking, asking neutral questions about her act until we reached my house.

I showed her to the bathroom and left her to it, not at all sure I could resist if I helped her, or even saw her naked. I wanted her, badly, but the only constructive thing I could think of doing was to offer to put her soiled things in my washing machine and let her pick them up later. She accepted gratefully, bringing them out tightly bundled up, and with just a towel wrapped around her, as her top had got wet where the piddle had soaked up the back and front of her jeans.

There were various things of Penny's around, which fitted her far better than anything of mine would have done. I said she could borrow some, and brought them to the bathroom door, to find it open, and her bent, drying one leg, with her bare bottom towards me. She was well down, her lovely fleshy cheeks stuck out and slightly parted, to hint at a dark anus, but make a full, rude show of the rear of her fanny. I found myself swallowing hard, my eyes locked to the little fat sex lips peeping out so sweetly from between her thighs and the lush, fleshy hemispheres of her bottom.

What I wanted to do was grab her, force her down across my knee, spank her until she was howling and her bottom was crimson, then sit on her exquisite face and make her lick my fanny and bumhole until I came.

What I did was drop the fresh clothes on to a chair and tell her I'd wait until the wash was finished and peg hers out so that they'd be dry for her to collect later.

She thanked me, and picked up Penny's knickers, a white pair, plain, which make her look so, so spankable. They were no less cute on Kay, and I had to turn my head as she tugged them up, the cotton pulling tight to her chubby cheeks and settling into a gentle valley between them. She didn't have a bra at all, and as she turned I caught a glimpse of her breasts, two fist-sized balls of girl flesh topped by upturned nipples. As she reached for the blouse I'd put out she gave me a big smile, which was almost too much. I turned away, making an excuse about checking the washing machine cycle.

Five minutes later she came downstairs, thanked me again, and left, hurrying back to the carnival. I was alone. I just had to come over the memory of Kay wetting herself. I didn't feel particularly good about it, because it had been a genuine accident, but I had to anyway. My fingers were shaking, there was a dry, hot feeling at my neck and my nipples were so hard they hurt.

So I went upstairs, hurrying, with my mind full of guilty excitement as I played the scene over in my head. She had been so desperate, her emotions there for all to see, her discomfort, her shame, her distress at what was about to happen to her. Then she'd done it, peeing in her panties, in her jeans, peeing herself ... pissing her panties, in public ...

I lay down on my bed, grappling with my jeans. The button popped and they were down, to my ankles, my knickers too, allowing me to spread my bare, urgent sex to the warm air. My blouse came up, and my bra, letting my boobs free into my hands. I began to massage myself, teasing my nipples, my eyes shut, thinking once more of Kay.

She had looked so forlorn, just standing there in her own puddle, with the dirty, tell-tale stain on her jeans making it quite obvious what she'd done. I'd felt her embarrassment, the hideous, agonising shame that had shown in her face, her, a grown woman, wetting herself in public. I knew I could have stopped it, by speaking to her at first. I had rescued her, and that was the only thing which made it bearable, which pushed back my guilt and justified my ecstasy. In any case, she might not have made it to my house, and done it in the street, even indoors.

That really was too much. My hand went to my fanny and I was masturbating properly, holding my lips wide as I dabbed at my clitty, with the image of Kay's bottom in her tight jeans fixed firmly in my head. She would have come through my front door and run for the stairs, utterly desperate, her thighs pressed tight. It would have been a mistake. On the way, she'd have been walking in little, waddling steps, and talking to me to keep her mind off her bladder. As soon as she dashed for the stairs she would lose control, perhaps tripping on the bottom step, to go down, on her knees.

Her bottom would be right up, stuck out at me, her fanny a sweet, plump bulge between her thighs, the seam of her jeans caught deep in her groove. It would happen, her pee bursting out, soaking into the pale blue material as she gasped in shock. She'd just do it, whimpering with shame as her piddle sprayed out, coming through her jeans in a little yellow fountain, just like Penny's did when I made her do it on purpose. It would soon be everywhere, soaking in, up her bottom and in the creases to either side, but mostly down her legs. Soon it would be running down my stairs, a cascade of warm yellow pee, running down behind her as she sobbed out her misery on her knees . . .

I came, sighing as my body tightened, a long, slow climax, with the image of Kay's pee-soaked bottom burning in my mind. I held it as long as I could, and I was smiling as I finally sank down on the bed, still aroused, but with that first, desperate urgency gone.

As I tidied up I began to feel a little guilty again, knowing that in reality she almost certainly would have made it. It had been good though, and the thought of Penny's reaction when I told her soon had me smiling again. She was almost certain to want to be made to do it herself, or more.

When I finally got back to the carnival I found Penny beyond the stalls and acts, talking with Anderson and Vicky, also Jade and Bulmer. Anderson was wearing his best look of aristocratic contempt, but as ever, Bulmer seemed immune, talking rapidly with all his normal crude enthusiasm.

'Hi, Amber, I've been telling your mates what we're going to do,' he announced as I approached.

'Nothing until you've screened the land properly,' I pointed out.

'Details, details,' he answered. 'Anyway, I reckon we can put a track up the long skinny bit you want and do some great stuff, pony-girl racing, breakthrough –'

'Breakthrough?'

'It's a paintball game, where one team has to break through another's line, only we do it with bare-arsed girls, forfeits for losers, the works.'

'It does sound quite fun,' Vicky put in.

I gave her a glare, but she just shrugged. 'Come on, Amber, it's a great game, and after all, we can talk the rules through.'

It was hard to deny what she was saying. I didn't share Bulmer's obsession with all things military, or pseudo-military, but it was easy to imagine the hunted girls' fear and excitement, and my own in response. It also meant Bulmer would clear a track through the Strip, which I needed anyway.

'The way I see it,' he said, 'is to have a territory for each guy, with his own colour. It's going to be easy to hit, but only shots on the arse count, so –'

'Hang on,' I broke in. 'One thing. It's not just men in the dominant role, just women as the submissives –'

'Marks.'

'As you please. That's fine by me, but I'm not playing if . . .'

I stopped, realising how sulky and childish what I'd just said sounded.

'Yeah, whatever,' Bulmer said, 'just as long as there's plenty of bare ass babes. So what d'you reckon? Up for it, babe?'

'Sure,' Vicky answered, 'sounds good.'

Penny gave me a quizzical look, but I could see in her eyes she wanted to. Jade bit her lip.

'Maybe a girls only event.'

'Come on, girls, all you get is a bruised arse, and don't tell me you're not used to that!'

'Not from men,' I pointed out, Jade nodding vigorous agreement.

'What's it matter? I mean, they ain't even going to touch, and if you get horny and fancy a bit of lessie action after, that's OK. I'll just watch!'

He finished with a laugh, and nudged Anderson with his elbow.

'Seriously, babe,' he went on, 'we can work out the rules any way you want, only there's got to be some sort of challenge, like a prize for the guy who gets the most hits –'

'And for the girl with the least,' Vicky cut in.

'We'll work it out, babe, we'll work it out, but I don't want any bollocks. It's got to be down and dirty, you know, a blow-job for the winner or something.'

I drew my breath in. It was not easy. Vicky was always game for anything sporty, while she was highly unlikely to lose. The idea obviously turned Penny on, but then humiliation is her favourite thing. I'd made her suck men's cocks before, but this was Gavin Bulmer, if he won . . .

'You can do it if you like, Penny,' I offered.

'Thanks, Amber,' she answered immediately.

'Two girls then,' Bulmer stated.

'OK, I'll do it,' Jade said suddenly.

'Three, ace. We need, maybe ... ten or twelve to make it good. You sure you're not up for a bit, Amber?'

'No. As I said. I'll take a dominant role ...'

'A sniper.'

'Exactly.'

'How about if you get to buy the land for a quid if you make a clean run?'

There was a dirty smirk on his face. I didn't trust him.

'One pound, if I get through without being hit? And this will be drawn up as a legally binding agreement?'

'Sure. The only condition is, I still get to use it for games.'

It was my turn to bite my lip. He might still want to use it for games, but things change. It would be mine. In time he might grow bored. It would only be on odd weekends anyway ...

'OK,' I said, although there was already a knot of fear and humiliation tightening in my stomach. 'Depending on the rules.'

'No problem.'

He was grinning like a schoolboy, a particularly dirty-minded, nasty little schoolboy. I could only turn away, fighting down my hurt pride.

I was still feeling extremely vulnerable and not a little angry by the time the carnival began to wind up. Other than a break for lunch, we'd stayed all day. It had been impossible to go, with Bulmer sticking to us like glue, in the hope of exploiting the sexual tension building up between Penny and Jade. Having persuaded us to play his game, he was clearly hoping to be invited to join in whatever happened later, and from the state the two girls were in, it was obvious that something would, or at least, could.

Penny could sense my anger, and wanted it taken out on her, both for my sake and her own. Jade also seemed to understand how the dynamic worked, either from experience or because Penny had managed to tell her. Vicky seemed amused and also aroused, as I knew Anderson would be, despite his outward calm.

Our chance came when Bulmer had to deal with the problems of dispersing the carnival vehicles. He didn't actually know my address, but it wasn't going to be too hard to work it out, and I was sure he was capable of coming round. So we hurried back, locking the front door behind us, and went into the kitchen. Penny and Jade were already touching, and their tension was palpable. Jade was uncertain, glancing at Anderson, but I knew she could make allowances, and was in no mood for argument, or subtlety. I wanted to be in charge as well.

Pulling out two of the kitchen chairs, I sat down, nodding to Vicky. She smiled and sat down opposite me, pulling her chair in until our legs were locked together. Crooking my finger, I beckoned to Penny. She nodded, her eyes downcast as she came towards us. Anderson settled against the work surface, his arms folded across his chest. Jade stayed standing, looking nervous, with her big nipples standing to attention beneath her top. I patted my knee and Penny came down, draping herself across us, with her hands and feet on the floor to steady herself, and to push up her bottom for our attention.

Vicky smiled at me as her hand settled on the tight seat of Penny's jeans, and we began, stroking her bottom and squeezing her cheeks until she had started to sigh and push herself up against our hands. I slid one between her thighs, to find the crotch of her jeans warm and moist, immediately making me think of Kay wet with pee. Vicky moved too, to tug up Penny's top, to cover her head and leave her little breasts hanging down. I took one, Vicky the other, to tease her nipples to erection as I masturbated her. Her fanny felt hot, even through her jeans, and swollen too, making me wonder if she would come with enough friction, and just why she was so turned on.

'Why so wet, little slut?' I demanded.

'Just things,' she said quietly.

'What things?'

'Things. Aren't you going to spank me?'

'Yes. The question is, how hard. Have you been thinking about Bulmer's dirty little games?'

'No!'

'Are you sure?'

'I promise!'

'I'm not convinced. Let's see just how wet you are. Vicky, help me get her knickers down.'

I took a leg, Vicky the other. Penny squealed as she was lifted, and again as I pinched the flesh of her tummy trying to get at her jeans button. On the second attempt it came open, and I peeled down her zip. Vicky already had the back of Penny's jeans, and was tugging them down. Her bum came out, soft and pink and as spankable as ever, with her big white knickers left in a tangle around her lower cheeks as the jeans came down.

Vicky took the jeans to Penny's ankles as I dealt with the knickers, peeling them right down. Bare from her neck to her ankles, Penny lay back across our laps, completely surrendered, her head hung in mute submission, her bottom lifted and ready, her cheeks a little wide, hinting at the hair that concealed her anus.

'Let's see then.'

Penny cocked her knees apart and lifted her bottom, into a position both awkward and revealing, her fanny coming on full show. She was soaking, her flesh moist, her hole a little open, while a glance down showed the crotch of her knickers soiled with creamy fluid. I pushed a finger into her vagina, sliding it up without the slightest resistance. A second went in, and a third. She gasped.

'Yes, fist me, please.'

'Shut up, slut.'

Jade giggled. I continued to explore Penny's hole, opening her until I could fit a fourth finger, and sliding my thumb in with the others, to grant her wish, with my hand in her sex, almost to the knuckles. She was gasping and moaning, a reaction which grew stronger as Vicky began to massage her bottom, squeezing her cheeks and spreading them, to show off her tight brown bottom hole in its nest of fur. I nodded to Anderson, indicating the row of wooden spoons hanging above my work surface. He grinned and reached out to take one down, and another, the two largest.

'Well?' I demanded as I took a spoon, laying it on the table.

'Not Bulmer's game ... no ... it was Jade,' she blustered. 'She was ... she was teasing me, saying I ought to be a pig at the carnival, and ... and greased, like they used to do at country fairs, so whoever caught me could use me as they pleased.'

'Hmm, not a bad idea for a game. Is this true, Jade?'

'No,' Jade answered casually. 'She was getting horny over the paintball thing.'

'No! You liar!'

'You were too!'

'No, I ...'

'Shut up, both of you! I think we've heard enough. Vicky?'

Vicky took her cue, and brought her spoon down hard across Penny's bottom even as my fist slipped from the sopping hole. My fingers were slimy with juice, and as Vicky laid in to the sound of Penny's squeals and gasps, I was reaching down. Penny gave a still shriller squeal as I twisted a handful of T-shirt and hair into my grip, forcing her head around, then went abruptly silent as I stuffed my fanny-soiled hand into her mouth. Her eyes came wide as she sucked up her juice, with her body still jumping to Vicky's smacks.

With my hand clean, I let go of Penny's head and picked my spoon up, to lay in to one bottom cheek as Vicky did the other. She was a little uneven, and I was forced to do it fast and hard to catch up, smacking my cheek to the same even red glow Vicky had already achieved before I could slow to a more even pace. Penny was making a fuss, as always, kicking and squealing and writhing about on our laps, until we were forced to take hold of her waist to keep her bottom still. That didn't stop her wiggling, but it made it a great deal easier to punish her properly, and we were soon beating out a steady rhythm on her buttocks, with even her squeals in time.

'She'd make a good greased pig,' Vicky remarked. 'We must try that.'

'Yes, we'll do it in the paddock, tomorrow if you can stay over.'

'Sure. We've brought our things, and I'm sure you can get good pig-grease at B&Q.'

'Do you think so?'

'Well, something. I imagine any heavy duty grease would do.'

'I think a garage one would be better.'

'Maybe.'

'I'm being spanked here!' Penny suddenly wailed from beneath us. 'Will you two please pay attention?'

'Oh, shut up,' we chorused.

'Not like ... Ow!' she yelled as we laid in harder, quickly reducing her to an incoherent whimpering as she struggling to break free from the merciless torrent of blows to her bare bottom.

She was beginning to bruise quite badly, and I didn't want her spoiled for the weekend, so stopped. Vicky gave her one last smack, full across both cheeks, and also stopped, letting go of Penny's waist. I did the same and she stood up, her top falling down to reveal her head, with her normally neatly bobbed black hair in wild disarray around her face, her mouth open and her cheeks flushed. She immediately began to rub her bottom, blowing out her breath as she touched her roughened cheeks.

'Corner time for you, Miss Birch,' I instructed. 'Right, let's see about your little friend.'

Penny scampered into the corner, to stand with her red bottom showing to the room. We hadn't beaten her as hard as I had the last time I'd used a kitchen spoon, but she was very red, and showing a few darker marks where bruises would come up. Jade was biting her finger as she looked at what we'd done.

I lifted my finger, crooking it at Jade. She licked her lips, a sudden, nervous gesture, but she came, stepping forward to lay herself across our laps. I was grinning as she went down, to lift her bottom in meek acceptance of the spanking she knew she was going to get. She'd been playful, and rude, from the start, but I hadn't been sure. Now I was.

With her bent over our laps and ready, her bottom looked delightfully fat, really bulging out of the seat of her jeans. They were the same ones as before, or identical, with the waistband cut off to leave a frayed edge well down on her hips. Only the zip kept them up at all, and with the size of her bottom in comparison to her hips, I was surprised it held.

It didn't for long, popping open as I took hold of the seat of her jeans and pulled hard. They came down, exposing the deep, meaty cleft of the bottom and her glorious cheeks, along with a pair of lemon yellow panties, too tight by far.

'Panties down, naturally,' Vicky said, suiting her action to her words as she jerked Jade's knickers low. 'And boobs out too, I think, my girl.'

I nodded in agreement and tugged up Jade's shirt as Vicky pulled the lower clothes down properly. Jade's bra was held with a four-clip catch, holding together a strap a good two inches wide. I tugged it open, feeling the weight as her breasts moved, heavy, considerably heavier than my own, which are not small. Intrigued, I reached under her to tug up her cups, one, then the other, to spill out her breasts, like two big udders under her chest. I took one, cupping it to feel the weight, with her big, hard, nipple pushing into the palm of my hand. She was huge, and natural too, and as I let go I was promising myself a little breast torture if we became regular playmates.

Like Penny, being stripped and fondled had her sighing and moaning with pleasure. She was wet too, as we discovered when Vicky hauled her cheeks apart to show off a plump pink fanny, shaved, and a tight, wrinkly bottom hole.

'A slut, like the other,' Vicky remarked. 'Come on then, let's give her what she needs.'

She had put the spoon down, and she laid in by hand, which was only fair as we had no idea of how much Jade could take. I did the same, catching Vicky's rhythm, Jade's big cheeks wobbling beautifully with every double smack, and parting too, to flash the lewd details down between. She took it well, better than Penny, panting and kicking a little, but no more. It only encouraged us, our smacks growing harder, until her bottom was flushed a rich all-over red, and still she did no more than grunt and gasp.

'A tough nut, eh?' Vicky said. 'Spoons, Amber?'

'Spoons.'

Penny would have protested. So would I. Jade just sighed and stuck up her bottom, her now sweaty cheeks pulling wide with a sticky sound. I picked up my spoon, and patted it on the crest of the cheek I'd been spanking.

'No. Spank my sweet spot. I come.'

Her words had come out in a sigh, almost a sob. I patted the spoon to the chubby tuck of her bottom, right over her anus. She nodded, the mane of long brown hair which had fallen around her head bobbing to the motion. I patted again, harder. Suddenly Jade's weight increased, and I realised that she had begun to feel her breasts. We began to spank, now across the fat of her bottom, Vicky's spoon landing above mine.

Jade's breathing quickly became deeper as the smacks grew harder and faster. Slowly her legs began to come apart, exposing more, her fat pink fanny, then the dark spot of her anus. She was wet, sopping, with the flesh between her lips glistening with juice. Not many girls come just from spanking, but both her holes had already begun to pulse, and her muscles were flexing to the same, lewd rhythm. I laid in harder still. She began to pant, fast, and faster still, really gasping, then suddenly babbling, pleading with us to beat her harder, to hurt her and to make her come. We obliged, working the spoons hard down on her bottom, until her voice broke to a long cry of bliss. She went into frantic bucking motions, her body sliding forward, nearly off our laps, so that she was forced to steady herself. The orgasm broke as she squeaked in shock, then she was giggling and thanking us.

She made no effort to get up, or to hide herself, keeping her thighs well apart so that her fanny was wide to us. I could smell her, rich and feminine, making me want to get her mouth to my own sex. The juice was running out of her hole too, which was still pulsing, and she had made a fair-sized puddle on my leg. Again I thought of Kay in wet jeans, and wished I had her in line for a spanking.

I had been paying attention only to Jade's bum, but caught a slurping noise, then Vicky's giggle. Penny was no longer in the corner, but on her knees in front of

Anderson. She was masturbating as she sucked on his erect cock, and his eyes were fixed firmly on Jade's open, glossy bottom.

He wasn't the only one to be aroused. I wanted to come, and I was sure Vicky did too. I glanced towards Penny, but she was too busy with Anderson to notice, or care, holding his cock and licking it like a lollipop while she rubbed at herself. Her bottom was well stuck out, the reddened cheeks wide to show off her hairy crease, with her fingers working in the wet flesh of her fanny and her bumhole winking lewdly behind.

She was going to come at any moment, and I could have waited, only Jade was already down on the floor, clearly understanding exactly what a spanked girl is expected to do to say thank you. She had picked up that I was dominant to Vicky too, and was kneeling to me, looking up out of big, brown eyes, waiting. I tried to be cool about it, rising to undo my jeans, and pushing them down, knickers and all, with as much grace as I could manage.

As I sat back down I spread my thighs and slid forward, giving Jade the chance to lick my bottom as well if she wanted to, but not wanting to push her. She went down without hesitation, to feed greedily on my sex, clumsy and eager for a moment, then applying her tongue tip to my clitty as she set to work at making me come. I was urgent, but not so urgent that I couldn't take my time over my first lick from such a lovely girl. She was good too, obviously experienced, and as her bunched fingers began to work my vagina open I realised I was to be fisted as well as licked.

Across from me, Vicky had pulled up her skirt, splaying her long legs, to pull the crotch of her lacy panties aside so that she could play with herself as she waited her turn. As she masturbated she was watching Jade and me, also Anderson and Penny. He was nearly there, with his hand twisted hard in her hair as he fucked her mouth with short, hard thrusts. So was she and, as I watched, she came, her fanny and bumhole squeezing, with her finger working on her clitty in bursts, her red bum cheeks clenching and opening in her ecstasy. Even as she came, so did he, groaning, as sperm burst from one side of her mouth and her eyes flew wide in surprise.

She drew back, gasping for breath, but already crawling towards us as she caught it. I sat back to watch as she went down between Vicky's thighs. She still had sperm running from the side of her mouth, and as she opened up I saw the full, sticky mess Anderson had given her. There were thick strands running between her tongue and the roof of her mouth, and a pool caught behind her teeth. Then she had buried her face in Vicky's crotch, smearing the come over the neat sex lips and into the groove between, then settling down to lick.

I closed my eyes, concentrating on what Jade was doing. Her hand was well inside me, fisting me as she licked, so that I felt wonderfully full. All it needed for perfection was a little attention to my bottom hole, but I was coming anyway, regardless. I felt my vagina tighten on her hand. Her licking became suddenly more intense, and I was there, held on a long, lovely peak under her expert tongue. My cry of ecstasy mingled with Vicky's and I realised she had come too, both of us brought to a climax by the girls we'd spanked, as it should be.

Jade snuggled into me as I came down, and I cradled her head in my lap, still with my eyes closed. When I did open them it was to find Penny cuddled into Vicky in much the same way, with a happy smile on her face. I immediately felt a pang of jealousy, which was ridiculous in the circumstances.

There was more to come, anyway, hopefully a full evening of rude delights, and I promised myself that I'd make sure Vicky's bottom got its share of attention before bedtime. For the moment, I just needed to exert my authority a little.

'Right, you two, into the corner, and you can keep your jeans down.'

They went, without hesitation, into the same corner, which didn't surprise me. Jade's hand went straight to Penny's bottom, to stroke the hot cheeks, a favour returned more or less instantaneously.

'Hands on your heads,' I ordered.

Jade obeyed immediately, Penny turning to give me a sulky pout but following suit. Stood still and unprotected, it was possible to inspect them at leisure. We had certainly spanked them well, both bottoms well coloured, also very female and very appealing, Jade rosy and gloriously plump, Penny neater, but no less rosy, and no less feminine. The way their panties and jeans were tangled around their thighs was also delightful, helping to show off their bottoms and accentuating the fact that they were bare.

I was enjoying the view far too much to let them move, and left them there as we chatted, knowing full well that being made to display their bare red bottoms would be rapidly building up their arousal. It seemed a good idea to have them make dinner, maybe nude except for their pinnies, and to serve us completely nude. I was going to suggest it, when the doorbell went.

'Knickers up, girls, I suspect that'll be Bulmer,' Anderson stated.

'Or Kay, from the pony-cart ... rickshaw thing,' I said. 'Open the windows. It reeks of sex in here.'

There was a brief flurry of activity as we made ourselves decent and threw open the windows, before I went to the door. It was Kay, who gave me a slightly embarrassed look in greeting.

'Come in,' I offered. 'Your stuff is ready. Coffee?'

'Sure, thanks,' she answered, 'but I can't stay long. Lisa and Shelley are just packing our gear into the van.'

'Oh, right. Did you make all that yourself?'

'The costumes, yes, not the rickshaw. We got that at a theatrical auction. It was what kicked the idea off, sort of.'

There was embarrassment in her voice again, and once more I wondered if I dared simply tell her that harnessing girls to carts was more or less part of my job.

She'd spoken to the others, all of whom had taken rides in her rickshaw, but I made a quick round of introductions as we came into the kitchen. The room still smelt of sex, and as I bent to retrieve her clothes from the drier I caught her wrinkling her nose from the corner of my eye. Penny had already started coffee, which was helping, but I was sure she had guessed something had been going on.

Just looking at her was enough to make me want to take the risk. She was standing sideways on, looking out at the yard, with the contours of her svelte figure in perfect profile. Her face was just so pretty, maybe lacking in Penny's vivacity and intelligence, or Jade's pure impudence, but cheeky just the same, and delicate, vulnerable.

It felt odd, when I'd just spanked the other two, and knew I could as easily have spanked Vicky, with sex for afters. After all, I'd only known Jade briefly, yet she had come to me through a mutual playmate, Heather and I having been to bed twice. I was used to that, or the opposite, people who I knew would be horrified even by the suggestion of lesbian sex, let alone pony-play, spanking, or any of the other kinky things I so badly wanted to do to Kay. She fell between the two camps.

None of the others were being any help. Anderson was being charming in a rather neutral way, Vicky was being friendly but no more, Penny and Jade were talking together. I was trying to tell myself that as I was never likely to see her again unless I did something the best bet was to be open, but I was also worried about the possible consequences if she turned out to be a prude. I still hadn't reached a decision when the doorbell went again.

This time it was Bulmer.

Even though I'd been in the room most of the time I could still smell the prevailing scent of hot fanny when I came back, giving me a horrible vision of him demanding a blow by blow account of our little orgy. Fortunately, he didn't seem to notice, which seemed to suggest either total innocence of real sex or a complete lack of a sense of smell. Unfortunately, he didn't need anything to trigger his imagination. As soon as he saw Kay he gave a smug nod.

'You signed up then, babe? Fast work, Amber, fast work.'

'Signed up for what?' Kay asked.

The tone of her voice would have warned anyone less thick skinned. Not Bulmer.

'No, she's . . .' I managed, but it was too late.

'Bare-ass paintball!' he said happily, and slapped her bum as he passed her, to take the coffee Penny had just put down for herself.

I thought Kay was going to slap his face, but she didn't.

'What's this?' she asked, and the question was directed at me.

'A game Mr Bulmer has invented,' I answered quickly while he still had Penny's erstwhile coffee cup to his mouth. 'Essentially the women have to run a sort of gauntlet, along the Strip, the wooded land to the north of where the carnival was held. Men with those paintball guns try to shoot us before we reach the far end.'

'On your bare arses,' Bulmer pointed out. Kay ignored him.

'And you're going to do this?'

'Yes,' Vicky answered for me. 'I mean, I know he's a creep, but it's a good game. You should join in.'

Bulmer gave her an offended look, but didn't say anything. Kay was looking doubtful, then she spoke.

'Not really my thing, I don't think. Look, Lisa and Shelley will be waiting for me. I'd better get going. Thanks for everything, Amber. See you again sometime, maybe?'

'Anytime,' I said quickly as she started for the door.

She gave me a smile, wry, still a touch embarrassed. I followed to open the front door for her, speaking as she stepped through.

'Sorry about Bulmer, he's . . .'

'Don't worry about it. I know his sort.'

She gave me another smile and hurried away, leaving me standing on the doorstep, wishing I'd said more, wishing I'd kissed her, or at least had the courage to ask her a straight question. The idea had seemed to intrigue her, and I wasn't at all sure that it wasn't just Bulmer who had put her off, which was infuriating.

I was feeling really angry as I walked back to the kitchen, with Bulmer, with myself, with the world. Penny passed me a coffee as I came into the kitchen. I took it, sipping the hot liquid, blowing, then sipping again, so that I could hide my feelings. Bulmer was talking.

'. . . twelve has to be about right, but we could go fifteen or more. Then maybe eight or ten snipers, to give each guy a decent chunk of territory and neutral ground between. So how many girlies do you reckon you can get together, Amber?'

I shrugged, too angry to reply sensibly. Vicky took over.

'It depends. For the hell of it, not that many. If you pay, plenty.'

'I don't pay.'

'Then us four and maybe a couple more. Ginny would be up for it. Katie Linslade maybe?'

'What about Caroline Butterworth?' Bulmer demanded.

'Her husband doesn't know,' I pointed out. 'I'm not sure she'd want to anyway.'

'There are others we could ask,' Vicky went on. 'Maybe with a decent prize on offer we could get ten. If you want lots of girls, the guy to know is Morris Rathwell, but most of them will expect to be paid.'

'Morris Rathwell, the guy Amber sucks off? He's the man, is he?'

Vicky and Anderson looked at me. I gave them a despairing shrug.

'Ten's all right, I suppose,' Bulmer went on, 'but give this Rathwell bloke a call. Tell him if he's in, and brings a couple of girls, he can be a sniper.'

'It would be three at least,' Penny said. 'His wife, Melody, her twin sister, Harmony, and Annabelle, Melody's slave. We might get Sophie Cherwell too, but you'd need to let Annabelle's boyfriend, Marcus, be a sniper.'

'Fair enough. So we're talking, maybe, fourteen? Cool.'

'Maybe,' Vicky answered him. 'So what about prizes, and rules?'

'Prizes are simple. Sex. I reckon the winning sniper gets to fuck the losing mark ...'

'I'm not fucking. I'll suck if I have to,' Jade cut in.

'All right, a suck,' Bulmer answered sulkily.

'And for the winning girl?' Vicky demanded.

'Well, we could have the guys put some money into a pot ...'

'Maybe, but I reckon the winning girl gets to give the losing man a dozen of the cane.'

'Fuck that!'

'Look, we have to suck your cocks.'

'Exactly,' Penny agreed, Jade nodding her agreement.

'It seems fair to me,' said Anderson.

'Yeah, but my mates won't go for that stuff,' Bulmer protested.

'Well, I'm not prepared to play with anyone who won't take a risk in return,' Vicky stated firmly, both the other girls immediately chorusing their agreement.

I could see what they were doing, taking the whole thing out of his hands.

'It's completely unreasonable,' I added. 'Look, with you, Anderson, Morris, Marcus, and Ginny and Katie's husbands, that's already six snipers. There's Henry as well. It will be a lot easier if we can end up on his land. That's seven.'

'Bart will play,' Anderson added.

Bulmer looked doubtful. Anderson went on.

'Actually, if that's the sniper team, we can probably get a few more girls. They won't mind if it's men they know, or for whom we can vouch, and we'll put in a good word for you, of course, Gavin.'

Bulmer responded with a grateful smile. I nearly laughed. Unfortunately he wasn't quite that dim.

'What about the land deal? If all the snipers are your mates, they're going to let Amber through.'

'Not at all,' Anderson answered, sounding both hurt and offended.

'Marcus Sowerby certainly wouldn't!' Penny laughed.

'Marcus Sowerby?' Bulmer queried. 'Who used to be floor manager for Komatsu Securities, goes with some blonde bird?'

'You know him, clearly, and Annabelle,' Anderson said. 'As Penny says, he is unlikely to spare Amber.'

Bulmer nodded and stuck his lip out sideways in a peculiar expression that made his face seem rubbery. When he spoke again it was with more confidence.

'Yeah, still, I'll get a couple of the lads from the club to make up numbers, and be sure.'

'So long as they are prepared to risk the cane,' Vicky said firmly.

'They won't be losing,' Bulmer said, now with absolute confidence, 'but yeah, I'll tell them the deal. I'll tell you another thing. Whichever of you loses, it'll be a Razorback cock you end up sucking.'

I wasn't so sure about that. Marcus and Bart Pelham both played at paintball regularly, while Anderson had been more than once. We were going to be easier targets for our friends too, or at least the others would be. I had to get through unscathed. It still sounded tough, with ten men to get past on a strip of land no more than fifty yards wide. On the other hand, hitting me wasn't enough. They had to hit my bottom. All I really had to do was be brave and face my attackers, something Gavin did not seem to have considered. I was not going to tell him, but as the others began to thrash out the details of boundary marking, head protection and so forth, I was wondering how it felt to get hit with a paintball, especially on my breasts.

We'd actually got away with a lot. On a similar deal Morris Rathwell wouldn't have settled for a simple piece of cock sucking. He'd have wanted nothing less than public sodomy for the losing girl, with a few subtle humiliations thrown in for good measure. Bulmer knew what he wanted, but he didn't quite seem able to believe he could actually get it.

He left but only after I'd spent ages pointedly making up beds not just for Anderson and Vicky, but for Jade. Finally he accepted that our tiredness and disinterest in his attempts to bring the conversation round to sex were for real, and I managed to hustle him out. Even then we waited a half hour, sharing the last of the bottle of wine we'd been drinking, until at last it seemed safe to assume that he was not coming back.

There was no question that Jade would be coming to bed with Penny and me, no discussion at all. She just came up, took her turn in the bathroom, and bounced in to where I already had Penny cuddled on to my shoulder. As she dropped her towel she was smiling, and she crawled straight on the bed to join us. Nude, she really was like a little fat pig, all boobs and bum and impudence. It was more than I could have resisted, even if I'd needed to. I didn't.

She climbed on to me, nuzzling my face, and Penny's too. A moment later we were kissing, three mouths open together, tongues entwined. I let my hand stray to Jade's bottom, and it had begun. I had put pyjamas on, but they didn't last long, open at the front and down at the back in no time, with the two of them eager to get me bare. Jade began to suckle me as Penny pulled off my pyjama bottoms.

I shrugged the top off and we came together, nude, in a tangle of legs and arms, breasts and bottoms and hair, kissing, cuddling, exploring each other. At first I tried to impose some order on things, hoping to exert my dominance. It was hopeless. They were both too eager, and with Penny's mouth already busy between my thighs, I allowed Jade to mount me, head to tail, presenting me with her sex.

With her big bottom right above my face and her plump, smooth sex lips over my mouth, it was impossible not to lick, and to touch. I began to stroke her still well-smacked bottom as my tongue found her clitty, and she was moaning in no time. She was the first to come too, full in my face, or so I thought, until I got up to discover that Penny had been masturbating as she licked me. I was ready myself, and wondering if I could get away with sitting on Jade's face, when Penny made my decision for me. She had sat back on her haunches, thighs well apart in careless nudity, Jade beside her between my own well-open legs.

'I'll show you her favourite thing,' Penny said happily. 'Roll over, Amber.'

I rolled, without hesitation, lifting my bottom for her attention. Her face pressed between my cheeks, a wet, eager tongue found my bottom hole, and she was licking me anally, as she said, my favourite thing. To my utter delight, Jade giggled, and spoke a moment later.

'Me, me, me! I like to brown-nose too. Oh, you two are so dirty! Mmm . . .'

She trailed off as she buried her face in my bottom, her little snub nose right in my hole, burrowing in as she licked my fanny.

'Lick her bumhole,' Penny advised, 'leave me her pussy.'

Jade responded with a happy purr, moved just a tiny bit, and she was doing it, her tongue in my already wet bottom hole, and well in too. I could only sigh in pleasure.

Penny pushed in beneath me, and I was truly in heaven, with two eager and experienced tongues working between my legs, fanny and bottom, licking, probing. Jade put a finger in my bottom hole to open me a little more and went back to licking. Penny stopped for one instant and I knew the finger had gone in her mouth. Then I was being licked again, and I knew I was going to come.

Even as they tended to me I was thinking of how they'd look, two pretty faces smeared with my juice, eyes bright and eager, tongues stuck out into my most intimate places. Their mouths would be full of the taste of my fanny, my bottom too, and still they were licking, more eagerly than ever, feasting on my juice, on my bumhole. I was coming, my mouth wide, my fingers locked in the coverlet. As it hit me the dirty, wanton image in my head changed, to include a third face, every bit as pretty, every bit as rude, her tongue well in my bottom hole . . . Kay.

Four

We didn't get to play greased pigs with Penny and Jade the next day. Bulmer had either arrived extremely early or slept in his car, because he turned up at my house before I was even dressed, asking for coffee. He had to supervise the clearing-up after the carnival, but that meant he was likely to turn up at any moment, and that he and others could see into the Old Siding and the top of the paddock. So we took things easy instead, lunching outdoors and talking together until mid-afternoon, when Jade had to go. Unlike so many girls, she had showed not the slightest trace of embarrassment over what we'd done, happily teasing me over my love of bottom-licking in front of both Vicky and Anderson. It was especially impressive as she was still in her early twenties.

I did insist on giving Vicky a spanking before they left, brief, but over my knee with her knickers down. It was only fair, when she prefers to be submissive, but gets so little chance with other women, her six-foot height and sleek, muscular build making her many girls' ideal dominant. Things might have got better, only for Bulmer to turn up yet again, and they left with me feeling annoyed and not a little frustrated. I was anxious, too, about the whole idea of the paintball game, and most of all, about being shot with one. Penny had done it, but on an enormous adrenalin rush, and even then she'd said it had hurt. She could always take more than me anyway.

So the evening was spent feeling insecure, and also regretting Kay. She had seemed open-minded, playful even, despite what must have been the most appalling embarrassment at wetting herself. It seemed entirely possible that with time and a sensitive approach she might have ended up as a playmate. Now it was not going to happen. Bulmer's approach would have been enough to put Vicky off, never mind Kay. I ended up taking an early night, and not even masturbating, despite the events of the weekend.

It took Bulmer a fortnight to prepare the Strip, which was now the official name of the long piece of land. I was there all the time at first, harassing his contractors, as I was determined to make sure he kept it well sheltered. If anything, he was keener on privacy than I was, coming up every evening to check on the work. After a couple of days I decided that I could safely leave him to it. I had to grudgingly admit that the design was good too. He was making not one track, but two, intertwining, and with frequent connections between them. The result was a maze, and ideal for both his game and pony-cart racing.

He also continued work on what he had named the Razorback Ground as well, finishing the toilets and changing facility as well as his 'HQ'. At the weekend he came to supervise the installation of cover for his paintballing games, some fixed, some mobile.

I needed the time, as organising the team was not a simple matter of making a few phone calls. For a start I needed to explain the situation in detail to everyone I wanted to invite. Some were easy, some not. Matthew and Katie Linslade had some big agricultural show on that weekend and couldn't come. Michael Scott was keen, but Ginny doubtful on the grounds that she presented too easy a target, but after nearly an hour on the phone I managed to persuade her. Bart was enthusiastic, and even talked his Finnish girlfriend, Sari, into joining in, which made up for Katie. Henry agreed easily enough, and when I saw Bulmer at the weekend he told me he'd invited three men from his paintball club. That gave us eight men and six girls.

The big problem was Morris Rathwell. I knew he would want to take the whole thing over, but we needed his influence. Penny was close enough to Sophie to invite her, but that meant Rathwell getting to know in a matter of hours, she being a hopeless gossip. Penny and I agreed to make our calls on the same evening, but Rathwell still managed to pre-empt me, full of enthusiasm and ideas, and wanting to discuss it over dinner.

Rathwell had behaved decently enough at the auction, for him anyway. So I went, telling myself that it would be perfectly easy to stick to business and not allow myself to be teased or tricked into sex, especially submissive sex. I knew Melody would be after me, but I was used to her. Harmony was always the easier of the two, generally following her sister's lead, and not nearly as aggressive.

The dinner was the most extraordinary exercise in ego. There was no attempt at all to balance the sexes. Morris was there, and five women: Melody, Harmony, myself, Sophie and Annabelle. Not even Annabelle's boyfriend had been invited, which was probably just as well, as she was not a guest, but a maid.

Melody always wants to flaunt her dominance at me, but this time she had excelled herself. She had Annabelle nude but for a collar and black leather ankle boots, which not only had six-inch heels, but were joined by a short chain, hobbling her, so that she could only walk in tiny, precise steps. Her head had been shaved, doubtless in a piece of vicarious revenge on Penny. Her sex had been shaved too, to show off her tattoo. I hadn't seen it before, and I had to admit it was cute. The legend was 'Slave Annabelle, Property of Melody Rathwell', executed in flowing script, deep red, and decorated with blue and yellow flowers, leaves too, set out ever so neatly across her bare pussy mound.

Seeing her so beautiful and so submissive did give me a pang of envy, but it was high bondage and domination in style, which isn't really my thing. I said as much to Melody, trying to look indifferent as Annabelle offered me a drink from the tray which had been chained to her wrists. Melody just smirked.

Sophie was also a maid, but in Rathwell's most vulgar style. Her dress was pink PVC, a confection of pleats and frills, with a ridiculous amount of lace and froufrou petticoats. Her bare bottom showed beneath, with the skirt and petticoats projecting a good two feet out around her hips. She was topless too, her plump little breasts supported in puffs of nylon lace, while she too had a collar and high-heeled ankle boots joined to stop her walking properly. She had at least been allowed to keep her fine blonde hair, which she had pulled up into a high-set ponytail.

Cute they may have been, and they certainly looked submissive, but they were painfully slow with their hobbles on, so Harmony had to do most of the actual work. I enjoyed the view anyway, as we ate, but remained cautious.

I explained the game over the soup, and had a wonderful moment when I had to tell Melody that she would be a mark and not a sniper, tempered only by having to admit that I would share her fate. Annabelle was actually serving her as I said it, but to my surprise she barely flinched. I had thought she might object, but by then Morris had latched on anyway, and for all Melody's dominance, she very seldom crosses him. As I'd expected, he was full of enthusiasm, and also ideas. All four girls' services were volunteered immediately, although only the twins were actually asked. He had never fired a paintball gun in his life, but had already produced a detailed plan of how it ought to work by the time the maids served out the fish.

I had actually done what I needed to do, but I could hardly wander off in the middle of dinner. Besides, Melody seemed happy as long as she could show off, which she was doing in abundance. Annabelle had clearly been taught to bend at the waist to serve, and told to make sure her back was towards me as often as possible. That meant repeated views of her neat little bottom, which was decorated with a set of six perfectly delivered canes marks in a five-bar-gate pattern. She was also so slim that the pose left the neat pink lips of her shaved fanny on open show, along with her bumhole. Even when she was face on to me I had her little breasts dangling more or less into my plate, that or her tattooed mound inches from my face.

She had been one of those girls who found it difficult to express her true sexuality. Modern society makes it very easy for women to be dominant. In fact, it's almost obligatory, at least to be strong and confident. Ironically, Annabelle was both strong and confident, but not quite enough. She was also very, very submissive, but with her height and looks, had found it far easier to enter London's SM scene as a dominant. She had fooled the men, even Anderson, but not Penny or Melody, and becoming a dominant black girl's regular slave had proved to be her ideal. Hence the tattoo. As a side effect, while trying to come to terms with her true self, she had put Penny through some of the harshest and most humiliating erotic tortures I'd come across. Penny didn't mind, but I was not entirely happy about it. Unfortunately I was in no position to bargain with Melody.

Rathwell, or rather Harmony, had served wild salmon, which was worth paying attention to, and I began to relax. The wines were also good, despite the inevitable pink Dom Perignon as the aperitif. So by the time Annabelle had tiptoed in with a roast sirloin of beef on her tray, I was feeling pleasantly mellow. Strawberries in cream followed the beef, along with a sweet Vouvray, before Morris led us through to another room, for port and cigars, with the sexual services of the maids as an extra.

I'd guessed he'd do something of the sort, and I knew he'd have done it anyway, with or without me being there. To have me play, and show myself off, would be satisfying for him. To get me to go submissive would put the icing on the cake. Not that he seemed bothered, and there was none of the usual banter or remarks about me being too attractive to be dominant all the time. Instead he simply chose the most comfortable armchair, accepted a glass of port and a cigar from Sophie, and ordered her down on his cock.

She had already served me, and I sat back to watch, refusing to show even the slightest reaction as she unzipped his fly and pulled out the little cock I'd had in my own mouth only weeks before. Unlike me, Sophie has no compunction at all about sucking men's cocks, which applies to more or less anyone with the skill to bring out her submissive feelings. She is a natural exhibitionist too, and has no illusion about the appeal of her small, compact body, pert face and natural blonde hair. She certainly looked good with her ponytail bobbing up and down as she sucked, and her bare bottom stuck out behind, with the fleshy cheeks settled on her heels.

The twins were watching too, with Annabelle at Melody's feet, serving as a foot rest. I wasn't at all surprised when Melody lifted her bottom to hoist up the black leather skirt she was wearing. She was in a bodysuit of black silk, and calmly pulled open the poppers to reveal her fanny, her hair shaved into a neat triangle, her full, dark lips swollen and a little open to reveal the pink centre between. As she slid forward in the chair to let her thighs come apart she clicked her fingers.

Annabelle had been well trained, and rose immediately, to bury her face between her Mistress's thighs. That was well worth watching. Sophie might have been more my type, petite and just a little cheeky, but she had Morris's cock in her mouth, a sight which made me feel vulnerable as well as arousing me. Watching Annabelle, slim and elegant, stark naked but for the little boots with their linking chain, with her face buried in Melody's full, black sex, really got me. She still had her tray, making her clumsy, which added to the pleasure. There was a little jealousy, and I would have liked to see the woman who had tortured Penny so severely between my thighs rather than Melody's, but it was still good.

Harmony was directly opposite me, sipping her port. She was trying to catch my eye, and I could imagine exactly what she was thinking – if she gave the same display of casual dominance as her sister, would I go down on my knees for her? We both knew the answer too – yes, but not in front of Morris and Melody, let alone Annabelle. I had my issues, but she didn't. So I met her eye, smiled, and began to hitch up my dress.

Her mouth came a little open, she swallowed, and glanced at Morris. He failed to notice, too intent on watching Sophie's mouth working on his erection. I had lifted my dress, right up to my tummy, exposing my lower body, complete with stockings, suspender belt and French knickers, in matching cream silk. It was a choice made mainly on the grounds that if I was going to end up over Rathwell's lap, then I might as well be dressed properly. Now it looked like being a good one for other reasons.

Rathwell had noticed what I was doing, and this time Harmony managed to catch his eye. He chuckled.

'Oh, Amber's in that mood, is she? Go on then, lick her cunt for her.'

Harmony made a face. I beckoned to her. Looking sulky, she stood up, gave a last envious glance to her sister and came over, to kneel at my feet. I considered pulling my gusset aside, to keep my exposure to a minimum, only to decide that if I was going to show my fanny it was pointless trying to cover anything else. Besides, to finish the evening without my knickers down would have been too much to ask. So down they came, and off, as there are few things less dignified than a woman with her panties around her ankles. Taking Harmony firmly by the hair, I pulled her into my fanny.

She took her time, and I didn't hurry her. Long before I was ready Sophie had her mouth full of come and Rathwell was sitting back smoking his cigar with a look of absolute contentment on his face. Melody came soon after, with a long sigh of bliss as she stroked the bald dome of Annabelle's head. Done, she ordered the maids into a sixty-nine, so that I soon had the gorgeous sight of Sophie's bare bottom in Annabelle's face, and vice versa. That really was too much, and I let myself go, coming under Harmony's tongue, unspanked, and with my mouth full of the taste of fine vintage port instead of Morris Rathwell's sperm as I'd expected. Harmony had been masturbating as she licked me, and when she came, that was that. It looked like I'd got away with it.

My trip to the Rathwells' ensured the success of the paintball game, or Sniper's Alley as Bulmer had so charmingly christened it. Sensitivity was obviously not his thing. Penny had been hard at work too, and managed to sign up her cousin, Susan James, and also Natasha Linnet, both pretty, vivacious girls who had played paintball before. Both apparently saw the game as just an amusing and pleasantly erotic sport.

That made it twelve girls, and a stroke of pure luck brought it up to thirteen. Carrie called, feeling bored and lonely because Clive was in New York for a month, just to talk to me, but when I mentioned what was happening she jumped at the chance. Basically she wanted some excitement, and to judge from the tone of her voice found the idea of ending up obliged to suck off a complete stranger as pleasantly titillating and a little dangerous.

The final addition was even more satisfying, and a complete surprise. I'd been doing my best to push Kay from my mind, and content myself with the memory of her wetting herself and bare in my bathroom. Certainly I was sure Bulmer had put her off anything to do with Sniper's Alley, or any other erotic games. So I was pleasantly surprised when she came into the shop on the Wednesday afternoon. What she said was that she thought she might have lost some keys from her jeans pocket when I'd washed them. I knew she hadn't, and so did she. Evidently she wanted to know more about the game, about what was going on in general, maybe about me personally.

If she was too embarrassed to ask a straight question, I was not going to spoil it by being hasty. So I played it carefully, admitting just so much and no more, and telling her that she'd be very welcome to come and play on the Saturday, or just watch if she preferred. I thought she'd come and watch, but she said she would like to play, with the colour rising into her cheeks as she did, a blush which had my heart hammering once again.

The temptation to take her into my arms and kiss her was almost overpowering, but I resisted. We talked instead, for the rest of the afternoon, until I was seriously wondering if she wanted to be taken to bed. There seemed a real chance, but her mobile went just as I was about to ask her if she'd like dinner, and she left. I'd barely managed to lock the shop after her before I was in the kitchen with my jeans and knickers in a tangle around my knees and my fingers on my fanny.

That made fourteen girls as marks: Kay, myself, Penny, Carrie, Vicky, Jade, Ginny, Melody, Harmony, Sophie, Annabelle, Sari, Susan and Natasha. There were ten men as snipers: Bulmer himself, Anderson, Henry, Michael, Morris, Bart, Marcus and the three from Razorback. It was certainly enough, leaving me with the problem of how to get from the Razorback Ground to Henry's without getting shot.

Most of the details were already worked out. The Strip was to be divided into ten territories, each two hundred yards long, and evenly spaced. Between the territories were areas of neutral ground, to give the girls a chance to rest and reduce the risk of the men shooting each other. We had no idea what order the men would be in, as they were going to draw lots for the positions in secret. What we would have were lists of who had which colour of paintball, just to make certain that they had the satisfaction of us knowing who had got a shot home.

Each man would have paintballs of a distinctive colour, and as multiple shots were likely to be hard to count, the winner was to be the one who had hit the most girls. In the event of a tie, they both got their cocks sucked by the unfortunate loser, who was whichever girl had been hit by the most of them. If two girls drew, the man got to choose, a rule Bulmer had insisted on.

The winning girl was whoever got hit by the fewest men, and won the right to dish out six of the best to whichever man, or men, made the fewest hits. If two or more girls came out equal, they had to share out the cane strokes. That meant that if I got through unscathed I would not only get to buy the Strip for a pound, but if my luck was really in, to cane Gavin Bulmer. It would not be erotic, but it would be immensely satisfying.

Protective headgear was the most essential item of clothing, which Bulmer was able to provide for everyone. Otherwise, the men could wear what they pleased,

We girls also had a choice, so long as it left both buttocks fully exposed. That meant no knickers, and trousers were obviously more sensible than skirts. Our tops had to be short enough to leave our bottoms properly vulnerable. Vicky, Penny, Ginny and I had decided that the best thing to do was cut the seats out of old pairs of jeans, thus exposing the target but nothing more.

They came up on the Friday night, along with Anderson and Michael, and we made the alterations then and there. Seeing the three of them and myself in the mirror, with our jeans tight on our waists, hips and legs but with our bare bottoms bulging out at the back, I found myself wishing fervently that I was one of the snipers. Practical it might be, but there was something intensely humiliating about going around with a bare bottom and everything else covered. The boys thought it looked hilarious, and both Vicky and Ginny had been pulled across their partner's knee for impromptu spankings before we retired.

Humiliating it might be, but with fourteen girls competing I wasn't too worried about having to suck anyone off. After all, while I could hardly compete with Vicky or Carrie, even Annabelle, I was up with the rest. I was certainly faster and fitter than Ginny, who had been big and voluptuous at school, and was now frankly plump. Plump and beautiful, yes, with a sort of Earth Mother look, but that was not going to stop the boys shooting her big, wobbly bottom, just the opposite. I couldn't see Jade being very athletic either for she was also a city girl through and through. So was Sophie, who was likely to run to one of the snipers for comfort if she saw a spider. Sophie was also a slut, and not likely to try very hard. The same was true for Penny, although as the two smallest girls they would not make easy targets. Susan looked fit. So did Natasha, but she was altogether too vain to be much good at country sports.

Melody and Harmony were very much in my own class. Sari I had never met, and for all I knew she had one leg.

She and Bart were two of the first to arrive on the Saturday morning, and she turned out to be tall and slim, with strikingly pale hair. They breakfasted with us, the others drifting in throughout the morning, until by eleven everybody had arrived.

Even before Bulmer turned up the atmosphere had become charged. We had separated into two groups, men and women very much separate, with a lot of whispering and discussion of tactics in both camps. Even our own male friends were behaving like overgrown schoolboys, comparing their equipment and combat clothing. Rathwell was as bad as any of them. The only exceptions were Anderson and Henry, both dressed in country tweeds, and their conversation more appropriate to the hunting field or a pheasant shoot. Anderson had even brought a shooting stick.

I was feeling very self-conscious with my bottom bare. I'd chosen a pair of jeans I'd been using to paint in, along with an old but thick jumper, cut short to leave me unprotected behind. Trainers had been an obvious choice, also a sports bra to stop my boobs bouncing as much as possible, and to provide extra protection.

Most of the other girls had dressed as we had, with their naked bottoms sticking out of ruined trousers, in most cases jeans, but corduroy jodhpurs for Carrie, and expensive-looking white cotton slacks for Natasha. Annabelle had chosen, or been put in, a catsuit that left both her bottom and breasts bare. Sophie, foolishly, had decided to go bare from the waist down. She was also the only one in heels, making me fairly sure that she was going to be the one who ended up with a cock in her mouth. Kay was like us, and other than my brief glimpse in the shower, it was my first sight of her naked bottom. Peeping out from her jeans it looked cheekier than ever, while she was deliciously self-conscious about having it bare, which made her all the more appealing. Unfortunately, everything was so rushed, and everybody so charged with adrenalin, that I barely had a chance to talk to anybody, least of all Kay, who was the last of the girls to turn up.

The last of the men were the three from Razorback, arriving on the same train as Kay. All three were in near identical military battle dress, complete with polished boots and presumably phoney insignia of rank. There the resemblance ended. There was Andy, a nondescript, rather shy man who talked in a nervous, high-pitched squeak. There was Jeff, a tiny, wiry man, who reminded me of a weasel. There was another Jeff, a huge, shambling bear of a man, heavily bearded, and with a round, red face from which tiny, piglike eyes peered, flicking quickly from one bare female bottom to another. The others were staring too. None dared to talk to us.

Bulmer had had the necessary legal papers drawn up for the transfer of the land if I was successful. I read them carefully, to his irritation, as he was desperate to start, and we signed the agreement with Michael Scott and Henry as witnesses. That left us ready to go. The men went into the HQ shed to draw lots, leaving us in a group, fourteen women, every one with her bottom bare behind her, nervous, excited, a little scared. Most of us were more than used to being naked, but all seemed self-conscious.

I had more reason to worry than any, and the butterflies were dancing in my stomach, even though I'd already been to the loo three times since getting up. Some of them were discussing tactics, others whether being hit with a paintball hurt more or less than a stroke of the cane. Only Penny had had it done to her, and she was very much the centre of attention, telling the story of how Marcus, Annabelle and others had hunted her down, and making it as dramatic as possible. Vicky stood to one side, limbering up.

The men emerged from the HQ, waving cheerfully or leering at us as they trooped past and on into the Strip. We watched them disappear down the paths, growing more jittery than ever, despite the half hour we had to wait before we could set off ourselves.

We could go singly, or in groups, but it was against the rules to shield another girl's bottom too closely. The four of us who'd stayed over at my house had discussed it. Vicky simply intended to sprint each territory and hope her speed and the winding tracks made her hard to hit. Ginny and Penny had agreed that the best thing to do was work together. That way one could cover for the over, but never close enough to be accused of deliberate blocking, and even if it proved impossible to avoid the snipers neither was likely to be hit by more than five of them. For them it was sensible.

It was no good for me, five was five too many. My tactics were simpler. Each sniper had one hundred paintballs. That meant just seven or eight per girl. I would therefore wait until most of the others had gone, and hope that some of the men had either run out of balls, or were conserving the ones they had left. I could also face them, and with heavy denim jeans and my jumper over my heaviest bra, I was sure I could take it if anyone did fire. I could also count on half of the men to either miss deliberately, or at the least allow me a sporting chance. They had to try, or Bulmer was likely to start whining, but only shots on bare bottom flesh counted. We had also agreed that if I did get hit, I became fair game. With the other five I would just have to take my chances. Bulmer at least would be really determined.

The time came soon enough. Vicky was already at the entrance to the Strip, and ran off immediately. The others followed, Carrie, then Ginny and Penny together, the twins and Annabelle, several alone, until I was left with Sari and Kay, both hanging back nervously. Sari shook her head and ran off, Kay shrugged and followed and I was alone.

I waited ten minutes. With fourteen girls, it was entirely possible that some of the men wouldn't realise how many of us had passed. I had to be in by six, so there was no rush at all. By the time I moved forward, I had already heard several paintballs pop in the woods, some quite distant, some followed by an indignant and girlish squeal.

It felt eerie in the Strip, with the noises ahead of me muffled by the foliage and the knowledge that between me and safety were ten men intent on shooting me. Bulmer's paths were simply packed earth, and it had rained the night before, leaving muddy puddles drying in the sun. I saw footprints as I had my eyes on the path, looking for signs that someone might be hidden ahead among the bushes. When Henry stepped casually from behind a big oak, right beside me, I nearly jumped out of my skin.

'There you are, my dear, I was wondering what had become of you.'

'Henry! You made me jump.'

'Terribly sorry. Now, that dreadful Bulmer fellow seemed to think I was rather elderly for this game, and insisted I take the first territory. The dull sort, Andy, is next, then Morris, and the fat fellow. I think Bulmer comes after him, and the last is the ratty one, Jeff.'

'Thanks. Any tips?'

'Not really. Vicky came past me so fast I missed her completely. I bagged Ginny though, and . . .'

'You'd better take a shot at me.'

'I suppose so, for form's sake. Stand behind that bush so I don't make a mistake. It's not like a shotgun, this thing.'

I nodded gratefully and jogged to the bush. It was gorse, and there was another one beyond it, prickling my bottom and tummy as I squeezed between. I expected Henry to say something, but before I was even ready there was a pop and something jolted me on one shoulder. It stung, but not as badly as the bit of gorse which stuck into my bottom as I jumped to the shock.

Henry chuckled, clearly enjoying himself, and I ran on, feeling a bit sorry for myself, but happy I'd passed the first territory. It had also been an easy one. Next came Andy. I stopped to listen at the boundary post, just in time to hear the pop of a gun and an immediate yelp of pain. I winced, but it had seemed to come from a fair way in front and to the side of the Strip. I ran immediately, and cannoned straight into Andy as he stepped from behind a tree.

He hadn't even been looking in my direction, and went down, his gun flying from his hand. I nearly lost my balance, hopping and flailing at the air before I caught myself, and just ran. He cursed. I felt a jolt of sick fear. The gun popped. Pink paint exploded among the bushes to my side, on the path ahead of me, on the back of my knee, to send me sprawling, off balance.

I went down, landing on a stone, which I barely felt. A ball flashed past me, and another, lower, to burst on the ground inches from my exposed bottom. I rolled, frantically, and caught the next on my chest, which hurt like mad. Cursing bitterly, I wrenched myself in among the bushes, staggered to my feet, and ran again, still expecting shots.

Nothing happened, and when I risked a glance back it was to find Andy still visible, gun in hand, but making no effort to aim. He shrugged, and I realised that he had expended all his shots. I gave him a wave and jogged on, pleased that my tactic seemed to be working, although it had been a close thing. He'd had six shots at me, and he was experienced, his last six, and he was a friend of Bulmer's.

Morris was next, and I was pretty confident he'd let me by. After all, it was in his interest for me to buy the land. Sure enough, he was waiting, leaning on a tree and smoking a cigar. He raised a hand in greeting as I approached.

'That sounded lively. Did he get you?'

'No.'

'Close?'

'Very. I'd better get on.'

I'd reached him, and he slapped my bottom as I passed, speaking again. 'I've one ball left, and I'll give you twenty yards, no, thirty, then go for your back.'

'Fine, just don't miss.'

I ran forward, fast, hoping he'd miss completely. The gun popped, I flinched, and yelped in pain and shock as the ball struck home right between my bottom cheeks. It hurt like hell, but it wasn't the pain that drove my anger as I rounded on him.

'You bastard! What the hell did you do that for? Damn you, Morris!'

'It was an accident, I swear!' he answered, trying to cover his laughter as he came towards me.

'The hell it was an accident. Why on –'

'Sorry, Amber, but it was, really. I tried to aim high. I'm actually rather a good shot, but I've never used one of these things before.'

'It's not like a real gun, you idiot! The trajectory drops. Wasn't Bulmer supposed to tell you at his briefing or whatever he called it?'

'I'm afraid I wasn't really paying attention. I was –'

'Looking at us out of the window, I suppose?'

'Well, yes. Fourteen bare-bottomed girls? Who wouldn't be?'

I sighed. It was hopeless. He'd got me and that was it. I turned to inspect myself, finding both cheeks spattered with gold dye. I could already feel the bruise coming up too, right at the top of my crease, in the little V of flesh. Rathwell shrugged as I gave him a last dirty look and ran on.

I didn't know if he'd done it on purpose or not, but I was suspicious. I was also wishing I hadn't been quite such a smarty-pants when I'd visited him. A few strokes of the cane, even a cock up my pussy and my tongue in Melody's bumhole would have been worth it. Then again, it might really have been accidental, and I'd have humiliated myself for nothing. I'd never know, which was typical Rathwell.

Any girl who felt she really couldn't take it was supposed to walk back. Nobody wanted to, even if it meant avoiding having to suck cock, and I certainly wasn't going to be the first. Melody would never have let me hear the end of it, especially if she took a lot of hits herself. Vicky and Carrie would be disappointed in me. Even Penny was bound to tease.

So I pushed on, hoping at least to keep my hits down and maybe get to take my frustration out on a male backside with the cane. The man Bulmer called Fat Jeff was next, and it looked like being an easy one. Certainly he wasn't going to outrun me, while it was hard to see him as anything other than a bumbling oaf.

I was wrong. About half-way through the territory he got me on my right cheek, from nowhere, then again, on my left even as I jumped and screamed in my sudden shock and pain. The third ball caught me between my cheeks and I was running, in blind panic, clutching at my hurt bottom to protect myself, only to catch a fourth, low, right under the tuck of one buttock. It hurt crazily, and sent me stumbling and gasping into the bushes. I kept running, scratched, dishevelled and scared until I'd passed his boundary marker. I'd never even seen him.

Kay, Harmony and Natasha had stopped on the next bit of neutral ground. They too had suffered the attentions of Fat Jeff, Natasha worst of all, who had stumbled when she was hit and caught the next ball about an inch away from her fanny. I sat down with them, adding my complaints to theirs, and wondering if I could improve my chances.

My tactics were a mistake, stupid in fact. Penny had been right, and I could see that what I should have done was to choose a friend who was prepared to risk hits, also move behind other groups of girls. It was too late, but I still had just two hits. Maybe if I could team up . . .

Natasha had got to her feet.

'I'm just going to run, sod them!'

There was a note of panic in her voice, and she seemed to be near to tears. Even as she took off Kay was jumping up, to follow. I exchanged a look with Harmony.

'What shall we do?' I asked. 'How about –'

'Run like hell, girl,' she broke in, and she was gone, following the other two, with her bare black and yellow bottom wobbling behind her, providing the same juicy target as I would. I had no choice but to follow.

I wasn't panicking, not really, at least until I reached the next territory. I saw a burst of scarlet paint on a tree, and knew it was Bulmer's. It was his pet colour, the one nobody else in his club was allowed to use, as he'd told me with pride. Seeing the splat on the smooth grey bark of a young ash just broke me. Immediately I was running blindly along the path, really afraid, with only a tiny, rational voice still telling me not to be stupid.

When the paintball hit me, that went. I never even saw him, just felt that awful jolt and the stab of pain, low on one cheek, again, higher, and again. Then I was really running, with all my speed, indifferent to gorse and the brambles beside the paths, indifferent to the sweat streaming down my face and plastering my hair to my forehead. Even the misery and humiliation of having to suck men's cocks in public had gone. I was thinking only of the pain of my bare, vulnerable bottom, of the balls hitting me.

I didn't even find out who was in the next territory, but they got me, full between my cheeks, to put tears in my eyes and a self-pitying whimper in my throat. The next was Anderson, visible through a haze of tears, sitting calmly on his shooting stick. He would have held me, but I didn't want him to see me in such a state, and ran past, to catch his ball full on the fattest part of my bottom just yards further on. I jumped and screamed, clutching at myself as I came down, to stumble on.

At the edge of his territory I fell, panting, against a bank of ferns and leaf mould. I lost count of the number of times I'd been hit, not just on my bum, but on my back and legs. All three had got me, and as I lay there gasping for breath the thought of what I was going to have to do if I lost came back with a vengeance. They'd be watching, the other nine men, and all thirteen girls, as I got down on my knees to suck on a man's cock, my nude, bruised, paint-spattered bottom stuck out behind me, sucking on his big, dirty penis, until he came in my mouth.

Sitting up, I forced myself to think sensibly and consult my list of sniper's colours. Five of them had hit me, and I had three to go. The splat between my cheeks was deep blue, which meant Marcus. So Michael was left, and Bart, who would spare me if I begged. Jeff wouldn't, but even if he hit me, six might, mercifully, be enough. I got up, to wipe my eyes on my top and the leaf mould and soil from the revolting, slimy mess on my buttocks. It felt awful, and had even run down between my cheeks to wet my bottom hole, which felt itchy and loose.

I moved on to the next territory slowly, peering in among the foliage as I went, only to find Michael standing calmly where a short path joined the two main ones. He grinned and raised his gun, but I put up my hand.

'Don't, please. I've taken five, and I'm scared I'm going to lose.'

'Oh, I haven't done too well myself. I was rather hoping you'd give me an easy shot if you'd already been caught.'

'I would, but I daren't. I have a horrible suspicion one of Bulmer's friends is going to win. Please, Michael?'

'Fair enough, I shall risk six of the best to spare your maiden modesty.'

'I'll make it up to you if you do lose, I promise.'

He smiled and I moved on, confident in his case that he would not shoot me from behind. He didn't, but as I reached the edge of the territory I heard the pop of his gun and a squeal. I'd thought I was the last but didn't wait for whoever was behind me to catch up, running on instead. Henry had said Jeff was last, but I wasn't certain, and moved forward cautiously, keeping off the paths as much as possible.

There was no sign of anybody and as I saw the boundary marker ahead I ran forward in relief. Immediately a sharp stab of pain caught me in my left cheek and I was sent stumbling forward, off balance, to land on my knees in the dirt. Looking back in shock, surprise and anger, I found Bart grinning at me, just his head showing from the dense holly he had hidden in. There was nothing to be said. I simply threw up my arms in a gesture of despair.

I wanted to go last, hoping Jeff would exhaust his paintballs, and tumbled down among the long grass in a clearing of the last bit of neutral ground. I needed to think too. Six hits and there was one sniper to go. It was not good.

I could still see back down the path, and turned at a noise. Kay appeared, at a run. Bart emerged on the path behind her, very coolly lowered his gun, and fired. There was a snap. Kay jumped, squealing and clutching at her hurt bottom, almost falling, to stagger past the boundary and collapse, right into my arms.

She was shaking, genuinely scared, and I held on to her, patting her back and soothing her. For a moment she clung on tightly, like a drowning kitten might do, making me feel so protective, and full of sympathy too.

It also made me feel a great deal braver. Then she had pulled away and was looking at me with an embarrassed smile.

'Are you all right?' I asked.

'Sure,' she managed. 'This is scary though. Shit, I'd never thought it would be so scary, and those paintballs hurt!'

'How many have hit you?'

'I don't know! Dozens! I know I'm going to lose, and end up sucking some bastard's cock. It'll be Bulmer, I know it will!'

'Maybe not. Six have hit me, out of nine. Can I see you?'

She turned with only a moment of embarrassed hesitation, sticking out her glorious bottom and looking back shyly over her shoulder. Her rear was a mass of splats, with coloured vegetable dye just about all over it, and running down the crease. I could smell the scent of her sex, which grew abruptly strong as her cheeks peeled apart with a sticky sound, exposing the tiny, deep brown dimple of her anus, into which a stream of dye immediately ran. Her fanny showed too, and my heart was hammering in my chest, and I was struggling to keep my voice level as I counted the different colours decorating her bottom.

'Let me see,' I managed.

The dye in her bumhole was brilliant yellow, which meant Fat Jeff, who had really plastered her with at least five hits. Bart's single purple ball had caught her full on the crest of one cheek, the dye mingling with Bulmer's scarlet from two or maybe three shots. Anderson's deep red also showed, low on one fleshy cheek, with Michael's leaf green just above, and more higher. A pink ball had caught her right on the turn of the other cheek, splashing her fanny with colour.

'Six,' I told her. 'I'm the same.'

'Oh God. Who's last then?'

Henry had said it was the weasel-like Jeff, and I was sure I'd had every one else. My mind didn't seem to be working properly though, as if I was drunk, and I pulled out my list, to hold it with trembling fingers as I read. Between us, we had every colour but dark green, which was Henry, and turquoise.

'One of Bulmer's friends, Jeff,' I said.

'Shit! They're good, and they're real bastards. They try to get as close as possible, and I'll swear that little shit Andy tried to get me in the pussy when I stumbled.'

'It looks like it.'

She moved quickly into a less revealing position at the rustle of foliage. A moment later Harmony appeared across the Strip, running, only to stop as she saw us. She was panting as she pushed through the bushes, apparently indifferent to scratches.

'Hi,' she puffed, 'how bad am I?'

She turned, presenting us with her bare black bottom, only not so very black any more, rather rainbow coloured.

'Ow!' Kay answered her. 'Bad, very bad.'

'A lot of hits, but not all that many colours,' I added. 'Stay still.'

There were only five colours, although she had suffered badly with Bulmer, and really badly with Fat Jeff, her whole bottom running with scarlet and yellow dye, while her legs and back had also taken hits.

'That big bastard really let me have it,' she went on. 'I tripped, and went down. He'd already hit me, but he just kept on shooting, six times! Bastard!'

'He got us too,' I said, 'but with five, at least you can't lose, or you're not likely to.'

She nodded gratefully.

'You coming then? One last dash . . .'

'I'm not sure I can take another hit,' Kay interrupted. 'It hurts so much!'

'Come on, girl, where's your fire? It's not so bad as the cane now, is it?'

'I've never been caned!'

'Never been caned? Where d'you get her from, Amber?'

'It's a long story,' I answered. 'Look, Kay, I'll help. You come thirty or forty yards behind me but on the other path. When you hear the pops from his gun, keep moving and I'll try and draw him on. With luck he won't even know you're behind him.'

'That sounds sensible, but . . . what about you?'

'Don't worry about me, Kay. Anyway, it will only be seven out of ten if he does get me. All ten have probably hit Sophie. She can hardly walk in those silly shoes, never mind run. Ginny's probably got eight or nine hits too.'

I finished with a smile. It was bravado, but not entirely. After the trouble I'd had, it was hard to see either Sophie or Ginny doing better. She smiled back, and took my hand as I reached down to help her to her feet. I could feel my panic coming back. Harmony laughed and ran on, Kay looking after her with a strange expression, fear, maybe envy too. I set off before my feelings could get the better of me.

If Jeff saw me, I would face him and take the hits on my front as I'd intended before losing my head. Then I'd be in with six, and someone was bound to have done worse. Or I could take the hit, and spare Kay on purpose, saving her even the risk of having to suck cock in public.

I never got the chance to choose. He'd been right at the start of his territory, hidden beneath a mat of leaves and twigs. As I crossed the boundary the mat lifted. I glimpsed the gun barrel. A jolt of panic hit me, then the ball, up under the tuck of my cheek, to send me hopping frantically about on one leg, clutching at my bottom, even as Kay made a frantic dash for the entrance to the other path. Jeff tried to roll, but too late, his first ball hitting a tree, the second too high. When he pulled the trigger again there was only a click.

Ignoring the temptation to kick him, I staggered on, my teeth set against the pain of the last shot, which had been from just feet away, and hurt far more than the others. Still, from the angle he'd been at, it might have caught my pussy, even gone up the hole, which didn't bear thinking about.

Kay had kept running, and I was the last girl to reach the end of the Strip. There was a sharp feeling of relief as I crossed the last few yards on to Henry's land and could at last pull off my protective headgear. It was short-lived, my trepidation rising as I walked through his woods and down across the meadow to the stable yard.

All the other girls were there, along with Henry and Morris, who must have driven round. Penny was the first to see me, and waved, then turned to show off her paint-splashed bottom. All I could manage in return was a shrug. She ran to cuddle me with a word of sympathy before she began to describe her own run in a voice full of excitement. She seemed proud. Sophie certainly was, doing handstands to show off to Morris, and giggling almost hysterically. Her bottom was a mess, but as she wouldn't stay still, it was impossible to judge how many colours there were.

Some of the other girls looked happy, some excited, others crestfallen or angry, but all but one had colourful bottoms. The exception was Vicky who, to my immediate astonishment and envy, had a pristine pink bottom, with only two splats on her whole body, a yellow one on her back, and Anderson's dark red on one calf. Clearly she would be the one wielding the cane.

By the time I'd reached the yard, men were coming out of the woods across the meadow, Bulmer with Jeff, then Anderson, Michael, Bart and Marcus. The first of them had reached us before Andy appeared. Bulmer was grinning and rubbing his hands. He knew I'd been hit, but not how badly.

'Come along, girls, line up for the Bottom Inspectors,' he called cheerfully.

It seemed to be some sort of in-joke, as several of the others laughed. It was all I could do not to cry. Morris and Bulmer had started to herd us together, so I quickly joined the line, my head hung in misery, too broken to really worry about the humiliation of lining up to have our bottoms inspected. It was what came next that hurt. Several of the others had taken a lot of hits, but I wasn't at all sure if any had more than seven. Kay was next to me and took my hand, squeezing it. I returned the pressure, and managed a weak smile as she looked up at me.

Andy reached the yard, grinning as he admired the line of girls. Glancing up the meadow, I found the last of them approaching, Fat Jeff, who looked like a walking bush, with bits of foliage stuck into the camouflage netting in which he had rolled himself. Even his beard had fern leaves stuck in it.

'So?' he demanded as he came up to us. 'Who gets to suck the big one?'

'Not so fast,' Bulmer answered. 'We haven't counted yet.'

'Thirteen out of fourteen,' Jeff answered, 'and I can see one clean arse. That makes me a winner! Winner!'

He threw up his arms and gave a yell of triumph, then began to swivel his enormous hips in a grotesque victory dance. I shut my eyes to mumble a quiet prayer, imploring any deity or saint who was listening to make it untrue. None intervened, but Bulmer did.

'Thirteen? No way!' he retorted.

He was already behind us, and I turned to find him frowning at our messy bottoms, like a baker inspecting an unsatisfactory batch of iced buns. Fat Jeff waddled up to join him.

'I got the fat bird,' Jeff announced, pointing at Ginny's ample bottom.

'Who didn't?' Bulmer answered, making me feel hopeful, then immediately a complete bitch.

'And both the black bitches,' Jeff went on.

I glanced at Melody, half expecting her to hit him. She was wearing a look of patient resignation and didn't move.

'Well, you didn't get what'sname ... Annabelle.'

'The bald bit? I did!'

'You did not!'

'I did!'

'You did not!'

I hid my face in my hands, shutting my eyes in pure shame. These were the men whose cocks I might shortly be obliged to suck, and they were bickering like schoolboys. Henry's deep, level tones cut through the argument.

'I shall judge, if I may, as I am clearly not a contender.'

'Fair enough,' Bulmer answered. Fat Jeff grunted.

I looked again, to find Henry squatted down, peering at Annabelle's bottom. There was certainly yellow dye on her skin, high on one cheek, but the centre of the splat was on her bodysuit. All three men peered closely, Henry rubbing his chin. Bulmer spoke.

'Yup, off target. Close, Jeff, but no cigar.'

'He's right,' Henry announced. 'No hit.'

'Shit!' Fat Jeff swore. 'Still, I reckon –'

'Let us do this properly,' Henry interrupted. 'I have a notebook here, and a pencil. Michael, you seem to have rather few hits, and ... Morris. Will you join me as judges?'

Both agreed, and there was more than one sigh of relief among the girls.

The inspection was still utterly humiliating, with them poking and prodding our bottoms, and the others watching from just feet away as we were forced to stand still and endure their remarks and jokes. At last the three men stood to confer in whispers. It was Henry who spoke.

'After careful consideration, we feel that your score, er . . . Jeff, is eleven.'

'Eleven?'

'Eleven. Your hit on Penny is definitely on the hip, a glancing blow only, and it would have caught her jeans but for a fold.'

'Yeah, but . . . I win, yeah?'

'Yes,' Henry sighed.

Jeff immediately went back into his victory routine, turning to wobble his vast and flabby bottom at us.

'You are in fact an equal winner –,' Henry went on.

'I still get my blow-job?'

'You do . . .'

There was a chorus of demands to know who the other winner was. Henry raised his hands and peered at his notebook.

'With eleven hits each,' he said, 'we have Anderson Croom, Jeff er . . . Bellbird, Jeff Jones, and er . . . Gavin Bulmer.'

'Nice!' Bulmer crowded. 'Fucking nice! Are Razorback the boys, or what!'

He and his friends went into what seemed to be a well-known routine, consisting of a lot of hand-slapping and variations on Fat Jeff's victory dance. My stomach was knotting so badly I was beginning to feel sick.

'So who's the lucky girl?' Bulmer demanded.

'Let me see,' Henry answered, running his finger along the rows of the matrix he had made in his book. 'The numbers are remarkably consistent . . . Ginny, you're on six, and Natasha . . . and Kay . . . and . . . no, there's seven here, for Amber, and . . . ah.'

He stopped and looked round at me. Morris Rathwell peered at the notebook.

'Seven. Yes, Amber it is.'

My mouth had come open and I turned, breaking

line, with a strange numb sensation creeping over me as his words sank in.

'Are you sure, Henry? I mean . . .'

'I am sorry, Amber, but I am sure that you will appreciate the need for fair play.'

'It's got to be done,' Rathwell stated. 'I mean, how do we look if you back out?'

'I'm afraid I'm forced to agree,' Anderson added.

'Best get sucking those cocks, girl,' Melody said, turning to grin at me.

'Yes, but . . . but all four!'

'Those are the rules, Amber.'

Everyone was looking at me. Most of the girls and some of the men looked sympathetic. Not everyone did. Sophie and Jade were giggling, and even Penny was struggling to keep a straight face. The only person who actually looked shocked at what I had to do was Kay, who spoke.

'But she's a lesbian!'

'Bisexual,' Morris Rathwell corrected her. 'Don't allow her air of martyrdom to impress you, my dear. It won't be the first time.'

I gave him a filthy look, but he was checking his watch and appeared not to notice. I paused, wondering if I dared back out, or argue. I was not happy with Henry, but I understood his reasoning. It wasn't Penny's fault either, or at least I was trying to tell myself it wasn't. Yet if she'd had a marginally bigger bottom or just been bigger full stop . . .

I'd still have had to suck Fat Jeff's cock, but not Bulmer's, or the weasel-like Jeff Jones. Anderson I didn't mind, normally. Unfortunately, there was nothing to be done.

'Oh, God, OK, willies out. Just never let anyone say I don't keep my word.'

Fat Jeff gave his gross body another wiggle. Jeff Jones licked his lips. Bulmer laughed. Anderson spread his hands in sympathy, but then put them straight to his fly. I watched, trying not to scowl too openly, as they pulled out their cocks. Anderson's was as ever, large, smooth, actually rather a lovely cock, while he somehow managed to still look elegant and formal, even with it, and his balls, hanging from his fly.

Henry had gone into one of the stable buildings, and came out with a squat stool. He placed it at the centre of the yard. I stepped forward and knelt down, feeling as if it was an executioner's block and I the victim. The others moved into a loose ring, watching.

'Anderson first, please,' I said, and heard the weakness and uncertainty in my own voice.

Rathwell was right. I am bisexual. I don't mind. Show me the girl who can still look confident when she has to suck off four men in front of an audience. An experienced porn star, maybe, but she wouldn't have Bulmer, or the two Jeffs.

Anderson sat down on the stool, his legs apart, his naked cock and balls just a couple of feet from my face. He might be trying to be considerate, but the idea was arousing him, his cock already half stiff. I swallowed, bracing myself to take him in, only to be interrupted.

'Tits out, Amber.'

It was Rathwell.

'Yeah! Tits out for the lads!' Fat Jeff added in glee, causing another burst of laughter from his friends.

I looked up to Anderson, hoping for sympathy.

'I would be honoured, naturally,' he said.

I tried to return a dirty look, but it just didn't work. My hands went to the hem of the jumper. It came up. My bra was showing. That followed and my boobs were bare, showing to all of them, with my hard nipples betraying my involuntary reaction to the prospect of sucking cock, and a round bruise, just above one nipple. I looked up.

'Not in my face, please, Anderson. I'll swallow for you.'

'Whatever you like, Amber.'

He reached down to tousle my hair, only to suddenly take a firm grip and pull me in. Then his cock was in my mouth, hard, and salty, and male, as I began to suck on him. It was the kindest thing to do, to make me do it and so spare me the shame of having to take him in of my own accord. I shut my eyes, pretending I was just giving him a friendly suck in my kitchen, as I have done before, and not performing for a crowd as the loser in Bulmer's sadistic game. It was no good. I could not push away the thought of their eyes lingering on my body, my naked, dangling breasts, my nude, colourful bottom, the rear view of my fanny, my dye-smeared bumhole, the junction of my mouth and Anderson's cock.

That was what really made the humiliation sink in, the thought of them watching me perform, sucking on men's penises in public, until my mouth got filled with thick, salty sperm. Anderson at least I knew would be mercifully quick, and he had already begun to fuck my mouth, pushing in short urgent jerks. I pursed my lips, making a fanny hole of my mouth, to let him get the friction right, and suddenly he was there, giving a low moan as my mouth filled with sperm, down my throat, spurt after spurt. I struggled to swallow, with that awful slimy texture catching in my gullet, fighting to hold it down as he used my mouth, his hand twisted hard in my hair, his cock head jammed down into my windpipe . . .

It was over, Anderson gently pulling my head up from his erection, to leave it glossy with my saliva. I swallowed what was in my throat and looked up, grateful despite the sick feeling in my stomach. Anderson gave me a pat on the head and stood, to nod politely to Bulmer and his friends.

I'd thought Bulmer would want to go next, but he gave Jeff Jones a slap on the back, propelling him forward. Jones was smirking as he took his seat. His legs came apart, to reveal a long, skinny cock, very pale, and a bit crooked. I had sat back, and as he began to tug on his penis his eyes fixed to my chest.

'Nice tits, nice,' he drawled, 'and your nips too, like little puppy-dog's noses.'

'Yeah, Dalmatians,' Bulmer cut in. 'Who shot you in the tit?'

'Your friend Andy,' I mumbled.

'Crap shot, Andy,' Bulmer answered, 'or are they so big you thought they were her arse!'

There was a burst of crude laughter. I found myself blushing and completely unable to go down on the stiff little cock Jeff Jones was now wanking directly in front of my face.

'What do you reckon, boys?' Bulmer demanded. 'Do we give her a facial, or make her swallow the lot?'

'I want to give her a pearl necklace,' Fat Jeff answered. 'I love it on their tits, and she's got nice fat ones.'

'Facials, then make her scrape it up and eat it!' Jeff Jones crowed, and his cock simply erupted in his hand.

I'd been coming forward, forcing myself to get on with my dirty task. The first of his load went right in my eye, more on to my nose, then in my hair. I squealed in shock and disgust, only to have my mouth filled with slimy, sperm-soiled penis as he forced my head down on to his erection, cursing even as he finished his ejaculation into my gullet. I was desperately trying to blink the mess out of my eye, and could only let him casually fuck my head until he had finished, totally out of control. When he was done I was forced to swallow, and came up feeling sicker than before, with my head spinning.

I was blind in one eye, a thick clot of come rolling slowly down my face. More was hanging from my nose, and bubbles of it were coming out from around my lips. I was in a real state, and badly in need of help. Jeff Jones didn't even seem to notice, but sighed in contentment and got up. It was Anderson who passed me a handkerchief.

Bulmer and Fat Jeff were laughing together as they watched me clean up what their friend had done in my face. I ignored them, wiping away enough sperm so that I could see properly, but really only smearing most of it in my face. If I swallowed any more sperm in the next few minutes I was going to be sick, and I needed a moment to let my stomach settle. Turning my head, I took a look at my audience.

Most of them were thoroughly enjoying my degradation, even my own girlfriend. She and Jade had their arms around each other, and while she gave me a sympathetic smile, there was no mistaking her excitement. Jade was as bad, and Sophie, who was cuddled into Harmony's side with a look of unmistakable arousal. Both the twins wore identical sneers of amusement, while Annabelle was at Melody's feet, holding tight to one leg.

Some of the girls had begun to wash down at the pump, with Vicky applying a stiff horse brush to Ginny's bottom. They'd been watching though, and Ginny gave me a happy smile, which was typical of her. Natasha was beside them, ruefully inspecting the mess of her bottom. Sari had washed, but had her back to me, showing her bottom, spotty with the round paintball bruises, which Susan had ducked down to inspect. Carrie was talking to Henry, but managed a weak smile. The remaining men were intent on my body, even my friends behaving exactly as if they were at some sort of peep show. Kay alone actually looked sorry for me, standing alone and biting her lip, with her hands folded in her lap.

Fat Jeff was settling himself on to the stool and I turned back to my task with a sigh. Of the four, he was undoubtedly the grossest, the least appealing, physically. He was not the worst. That was to come, with the humiliation of having to suck Gavin Bulmer's penis far outweighing any lack of appeal on Jeff's side. It was still going to take a lot of doing.

He had spread his thighs and pulled up his gut to let me get at his genitals. He had pulled it all out, a great, fat, wrinkled cock, with a thick, meaty foreskin, lying on a big, hairy scrotum, with his balls moving sluggishly inside. As he'd said he wanted to come on my breasts I cupped them, holding them out in the hope that he'd sacrifice his right to a suck in return for fucking me between them, or even coming over them.

'Suck on my balls, first,' he demanded. 'I like that.'

I made a face, but I went down, to kiss the wrinkled, hairy skin of his sack, once, twice, before I could screw up my courage and take a ball in my mouth. He gave a satisfied grunt as I began to suck. I could taste him, oily and male, not too clean either. I tried to push it out of my mind, but there was no good pretending. As my mouth came wider he pushed the other ball in with one grubby finger. I was sucking his balls and that was that.

He began to masturbate, right in front of my face, his hand knocking on my nose as I mouthed on the full, fat bulk of his scrotum. I could feel his balls squirming in my mouth, a truly disgusting sensation, while he had begun to push himself into my face. His breathing was getting harder, and I was wondering if he would just come over my head when his hand closed in my hair.

As I was pulled off his balls I was praying it would be his cock and not his anus he wanted attending to next. It was, and I actually felt relief and even gratitude as the thick, stubby erection was pushed into my mouth. I began to suck hard, eager to get him off before he made me do anything else dirty. He began to fuck my mouth, hard, jerking my head up and down by the hair, forcing me to make a fanny of my mouth, as I had for Anderson. I could barely breathe, and struggled to pull back, only for him to wrench my head back, grab his cock, and ejaculate full in my face and over my boobs.

I was still holding them, and it was only then I realised I had been playing with my nipples as he amused himself with me. He came across both, spattering them, in thick, cream-coloured blobs and streaks, spurt after spurt. I just let him do it, emptying himself over me, until both my boobs were slimy with it. A fair bit had gone in my face too, catching my other eye, with a streamer lying across one cheek.

He finished off between them, sticking his cock into my deep, slimy cleavage as I pressed them together to fold them in, and fucking briefly to milk out the last few drops on to his cock head and over my skin. When he at last pulled back, it was to wipe his cock on my jumper.

I look down in disgust, close to defeat. I was filthy, my cleavage a slimy mess of well-rubbed-in come. Both breasts were spotted and streaked with it too, an extraordinary volume for one man. A piece even hung from my nipple, stretching as I watched, to break and land on my stomach. It was nearly too much. It disgusted me, utterly, but I wanted to play with it, to rub it in, to masturbate with it. I wasn't going to, not in front of everybody.

Even as Fat Jeff climbed to his feet, still puffing, Gavin Bulmer was jostling in to take his place. I looked up, peering from eyes soiled with his friend's sperm. He grinned. Suddenly I was close to tears, but as his thighs came open I just went down to take his already erect cock in my mouth, as I was supposed to. My resistance was gone, broken. So many times I'd told myself that I would never, ever have anything to do with him. Here I was, regardless, down on his penis with my naked, dirty bottom stuck out behind me, my bare, filthy boobs swinging under my chest, cock sucking for him, like the dirty slut of his imagination.

He was really enjoying himself, making queer gulping noises and giving little chuckling laughs as he watched the shaft of his cock slide in and out between my lips as I struggled to control my feelings. My body was telling me one thing, to play with my breasts, to touch my sex. My mind was telling me something very different, not to give him an inch, not to show pleasure at all, to do what I had to, and no more.

I never did give in. Not that he cared, using me as if I were no more than an aid to his masturbation. What was it he'd called me when we first spoke? A fuck-toy. Now I was, and as if reading my mind, he added one more humiliation.

'Turn over, I'll give it you up the fuck hole.'

I shook my head, despite a sudden, awful need to lift my hips for entry. I sucked harder, imagining it, me, bum up, everyone watching, willingly letting him into my body from the rear . . .

Even as that awful, utterly humiliating thought hit me, he came in my mouth. It was sudden, unexpected, his cock tightening, and the next instant my mouth was full of his salty, slimy sperm. He held me tight by the hair as he milked himself out down my throat, and I just let him, unable to breathe, barely able to see for his friends' mess. Only when I started to choke did I try to pull back, but he held on hard, his hand locked in my hair, until a great, bubbling mass of sperm and mucus erupted from my nose, into his pubic hair and over his hand.

'Ah shit! Fucking gross!' he swore, and let go, allowing me to jerk myself off his cock, panting for breath as I sat back.

My nose and mouth were still full of come bubbles. All I could do was squat, coughing and gasping on the ground, with the mess running down my face and falling in sticky clots on to my boobs, belly and legs. Only when I was breathing properly again did it really sink in. I'd done it. I was utterly soiled, the whole front of my body filthy with men's come, but I'd done it, all four, and I didn't have to take any more cocks in my mouth.

It wasn't the end, not quite. I stood slowly. I was shaking, hard. I could feel the mess running down my body, slow and thick. I looked round. Penny stepped towards me, but I waved her back. I needed to be alone, badly. The back of the stable block was the place, quiet, sheltered, unseen. There I could do what I had to, what I had been driven to. I went, catching a last exclamation of disgust over what I'd done on his hand from Bulmer as I turned the corner.

My friends knew better than to disturb me. The others wouldn't, I was sure. I pulled off my jumper and bra over my head, my fingers slipping in the sperm Fat Jeff had wiped on them. My shoes were kicked off, my socks with them. My cut-out jeans stayed on. I wanted to keep the feeling of having my bare bottom sticking out of the hole in the back, to feel the bruises.

I sat down against the wall, on warm, soft grass, opening my thighs. It took a lot of coming to terms with, and I lay there for simply ages, my eyes shut, just playing with my breasts, and trying to turn my great headful of humiliation and self-pity into erotic pleasure. I knew Penny could have done it, easily. I couldn't, I had too much pride, but I needed to.

I listened as Vicky dished out six of the best to whichever luckless man had scored the fewest hits, full of envy for her natural athleticism. Even Fat Jeff hadn't been able to hit her, and he was good, cunning, deceitful, a near perfect shot, for all that he looked like a lump of dough. He was good when it came to humiliating girls too, coming in my face and over my breasts, fucking my mouth, making me suck his balls . . .

I was going to do it. I couldn't stop myself any more. The slimy mess they'd made over me was in my hands. I was smearing it over my belly, my boobs, up under my neck and into my face, rubbing it in, fouling myself deliberately. Reaching down, I gripped my jeans and tore, exposing myself, showing off my fanny, my fuck hole, as that horrible, crude bastard Gavin Bulmer had called it. Whatever, it was showing, open and ready, wet and willing. My self-pity was burning in my head, and it grew stronger as my thighs slipped fully apart. I was going to do it. I had to.

The scent of sperm was thick in the air, that and my own fanny, mingling with the smells of grass, and horse dung, and sweat. Four men had come over me, down my throat, in my hair, in my face, over my breasts, and I was rubbing it into myself. A finger went up my fanny, deep in. A second went to my bumhole, to tickle the slippery little ring, and ease open the hole. My thumb found my clitty and I was masturbating, already breathing hard as my dirty thoughts started to run wild.

I was wishing all ten had spunked on me, to leave me soiled and filthy on the cobbles, masturbating in their mess, rubbing it into my boobs, eating it, pushing sperm-covered fingers up my bumhole. I was wishing they would come round to take turns with me, all ten, with me on my knees, using each other's come to lubricate me and humiliate me. I was wishing they'd fuck me, make me suck, bugger me. The girls would come too, to make me lick the mess from their bottoms, and to swallow it, even to lick their bumholes clean, one by one, the way I had made so many of them lick me ...

I heard my own cry as I started to come. My fanny and bumhole tightened on the intruding fingers and I was there, imagining myself punished, degraded, used by all of them, thirteen girls and ten men, all making use of my body. I'd have to make everyone come, the way he or she wanted. There would be cocks in my mouth, up my fanny, up my bottom. My tongue would be poked deep in the girls' holes, fannies and bumholes too. I'd end up covered in sperm and juice, as I was, but worse, far worse. When they were done with me, they'd piss on me, piss over my boobs and my bum, in my face and in my hair, up my fanny and in my mouth, as I lay masturbating in it on the ground ...

I really screamed as the peak hit me. I was trying to get my fingers up my fanny and my bumhole, and still frig at the same time. I couldn't and then I didn't want to, as a great wave of shame hit me. As I slumped down in the warm grass, I burst into tears.

It was too much. I just lay there, big, oily tears running down my sperm-smeared face, to splash on my soiled breasts and filthy belly. I pulled my fingers out and stuck them in my mouth, too far gone to care, sucking, until a noise to one side made me look up. Kay was standing not five yards away, looking at me.

Five

Kay knew I had masturbated. To my surprise it didn't seem to make her less sympathetic, but she did seem to want to talk to me. There was no chance for anything in the way of intimate conversation, with everybody around, even when most of the others had drifted away. Finally Kay herself had to go, catching the last train back to London.

I was still at Henry's, along with Penny and Jade, who were getting on like a house on fire. I knew they'd had sex after my public degradation, and that it was what had happened to me which had aroused them, as much if not more than playing the game. I also knew that Penny, at least, would feel guilty, so I didn't push the issue.

All of us were exhausted, and we went to bed as soon as Henry had returned from taking Kay to the station. We used his spare room, the three of us in a huge four-poster, but even with the two of them snuggled into me from either side I was asleep within minutes. We did have sex at some point in the early hours, with the two of them suckling me and our thighs intertwined to rub our fannies, but in the morning it seemed more like a dream.

Everything in fact felt oddly detached, and walking back down the strip was a very strange experience indeed. Each of what had been the men's territories was spattered with dye of a single colour from missed shots. Each told a tale, and as we walked, we compared notes. Penny and Ginny's tactic of covering for each other had worked well. Jade had stuck close to Melody and Annabelle, always on the alternative path, in the hope that each sniper would choose to go for the pair rather than the single. Only three had hit her, including Fat Jeff, who was clearly the most skilled of Bulmer's friends.

They'd both done better than me. In fact, everybody had done better than me, which was really galling. I suppose I was sulking, but then I had every right to sulk, and when Penny asked what we were going to do with our Sunday I really couldn't find the enthusiasm to give her the answer she wanted. Jade had no such reserve.

'How about playing the piggy-girl game, with one of us as the greased piglet?'

'Yes, please,' Penny answered immediately. 'I want to be the piglet.'

'No, let me!' Jade demanded. 'Please, I've only just got my snout and tail, you've done it loads of times.'

'Not greased piglet,' Penny answered, 'but let's not argue, we can both do it, and Amber can catch us. She's got these great switches made out of plaited apple suckers she uses for piggy-girls. They sting like crazy!'

'Yes, please!' Jade answered.

'Come on, Amber.'

'I . . . I'm not really in the mood,' I answered, despite immediately feeling like a spoilsport. 'You two play.'

'But, Amber, we need you to catch the piglets!'

'I know, but . . .'

'Come on, Amber,' Penny urged. 'You're letting that prat Bulmer get to you. That's not like you.'

'I am not! Well, maybe I am a little. Anyway, we never did get the grease.'

'What about butter?' Jade suggested.

'Lard would be better,' Penny answered her.

'Lard? Yuck!'

'What do you mean, yuck, silly? It doesn't have to taste nice. I mean, it's not as if we have to eat it!'

Penny had opened the fridge as she spoke, and was peering in among the food. On the middle shelf was a five-hundred gram bar of lard, barely touched since I'd bought it a month or more before. Penny pulled it out, her eyes lighting up in pure mischief, and held it up. Jade took it, squeezing the packet with her face set in an odd mixture of disgust and delight.

'You two, that's perfectly good lard!'

It was too late, Jade was already out of the door, laughing.

'I'll buy you some more, I promise,' Penny called back as she followed Jade. 'Oh, keys, please. I wish you'd come and play with us.'

I shrugged and threw her the keys, feeling really bad, but just not able to raise any enthusiasm. I couldn't even tell myself that she would have been the same in my shoes, because I knew full well that it wasn't true. If she had lost she would not only have sucked the four men off, but masturbated as she did it, openly and joyfully, not shamefaced behind the stables as I had done.

She caught the keys and ran outside, to plant a resounding smack on the taut seat of Jade's jeans as she caught up. I watched, my chin in one hand, as they walked over to the old forge. Inevitably, once inside, Penny was going to have to give Jade a tour of the pony-girl gear, bondage and corporal punishment equipment and so forth, so it was no surprise to me when they didn't come out immediately.

I sat thinking, running over the events of the day before in my head. Really, I'd never had a chance, and I'd been fooling myself to think I had. Ten men I'd had to pass, three of them determined to get me, four if Marcus was counted, and all experienced. I lacked the experience, the fitness, and any specialist knowledge. It was hardly surprising I'd failed.

That left a question, a very nasty question. Had I wanted to lose? Had what I really wanted been the public humiliation of taking Gavin Bulmer's cock in my mouth and sucking him to orgasm? Rathwell argued that I was submissive at heart but had difficulty in expressing my needs, like Annabelle. Was I fooling myself to think that I was any different? Maybe I did need a master, to keep me in my place, to punish me now and then, the way Morris himself punished Melody, who was so similar to me in so many other ways.

I was still frantically trying to find a good reason to deny it when the girls came out of the forge. Both were naked, their skin pale in the sunlight, their breasts topped with proud nipples, Jade's wet, presumably from being taken in Penny's mouth. Both had changed, in so far as a piggy-girl need bother, with little upturned snouts over their noses, and curly pink tails bobbing above chubby, girlish bottom cheeks. Despite myself I smiled. Even if the men were right, and I ultimately needed to be mastered, there was no denying the effect that pretty, naked girls had on me, let alone when expressing such a divinely humiliating fetish.

Penny was holding the lard, now unwrapped, and I heard her giggle as they disappeared through the gap in the hedges. Jade had one of the apple switches. Suddenly I was wondering what the hell I was doing. I had two absolutely gorgeous young women just about begging me to play erotic games with them, and I was moping indoors. They were right. It was stupid to sulk. It was letting Bulmer win.

I went straight upstairs. I still wasn't feeling like it, but I was telling myself I was going to do it anyway, and damn Bulmer. From my window I could see over the hedge to the paddock. Penny had her bottom stuck out, wiggling it to make her piggy tail shake, and as I watched Jade gave her a cut with the switch. I heard the squeal and saw the thin line of Penny's new welt spring up, white, then red as the blood came in.

Jade ran but got caught before she had reached the middle of the paddock. She didn't put up much of a fight either, but went down, laughing and struggling as Penny twisted her ankle to force her on to her front and straddled her back. Penny began to spank, her face set in an expression of comic determination as she laid into the wobbling bottom beneath her as hard as she could. Jade just laughed, kicking her feet, but making no real effort to unseat Penny.

Penny stopped and reached for the lard, which she had dropped on the grass. It was muddy now, with brown bits on the glistening white as she squashed the bar in one hand and slapped it hard on to Jade's bottom, full between the cheeks. Jade's response was to push up her bum and spread her thighs, showing off the rear of her fanny and the deep crease between her ample cheeks, both filthy with lard and mud. Penny grinned, held up a single finger, and pushed it into Jade's lard-smeared anus.

That made Jade react, bucking in sudden shock. Taken by surprise, Penny fell off with a squeak, to land on the grass. Jade grabbed Penny immediately and they went over together, rolling on the muddy ground, and grappling each other, both trying to get on top, and to land spanks at the same time. Jade had scooped most of the lard out from between her cheeks, and it was going everywhere, plastered on to Penny's breasts and back, then on her bottom.

I wanted to watch, but I wanted to be there too, my sulky feelings pushed down. There were special jeans in my wardrobe, a design I've always been pleased with, with a wide brass ring sewn into the crotch, so that a dildo can be slid in, to make a very effective cock. The jeans provide support, so that I can fuck a girl properly, or in this case a greasy piglet, which was exactly what I intended. I changed quickly, my top as well, and hurried downstairs. The forge was open, with the girls' clothes hung over a whipping stool I'd been making, and the familiar scent of leather strong in the air. I picked a good-sized dildo and slid it into place, so that it protruded from my zip, an ever stiff erection.

Jade had lost, or rather given in. She was stood against the post at the centre of the paddock, her hands reached up to grip the wood, her feet planted well apart. The position left her bottom stuck well out, and her big breasts spread to either side of the pole. She had been well larded, and her skin glistened with it, except for the streaks of mud marking her in places, and whip marks.

Penny had the switch, and had been using it with a will. Jade's bottom was a mess of thin red lines, and so were her breasts, both great fat orbs slippery with lard and criss-crossed with welts. Her eyes were closed, and her breathing deep and even, so turned on that each time the switch cut in she merely jerked and gasped. Penny grinned at me as I came close, a big, happy smile. Dropping the switch, she sank to her knees, and took the dildo straight into her mouth.

Jade looked back, her eyes half-closed, her face slack with pleasure. Her tongue flicked out to wet her lips as she saw what Penny was sucking on, and she moved, shuffling back as her hands slid down the pole, to stick out her bottom.

'Fuck me then . . . come on,' she breathed.

Penny pulled back to take the dildo in her hand, tugging on it as if she was wanking a real cock. She spoke, her voice hoarse with arousal.

'Up her bum, Amber. Go on, bugger the fat little pig.'

'Pussy, first at least,' Jade groaned.

'You mind your own business.' Penny laughed. 'OK, Amber, fuck her first if she's going to be wet about it.'

Jade groaned and hung her head, obviously accepting Penny's filthy suggestion. Penny jumped up, laughing, and ran to Jade, her fingers going straight between the fat bottom cheeks, and up into the dirty hole between. Jade began to moan as her bumhole was lubricated, Penny squashing lard-smeared fingers in and out of the gaping anus, deep in. Jade had had her fanny stuffed too, with a fat plug of the lard oozing slowly back out in response to her contractions.

I moved close, squatting down to get the head of the dildo between Jade's cheeks. Penny giggled and took it in hand as her fingers left Jade's bumhole, to guide it down, pushing the head of the dildo to the soft, fleshy fanny hole. I pushed, watching as Jade's body took it, her vagina opening to accommodate the full, fat head, then the rest, smooth and easy with the lard to grease her passage. I took her cheeks, spreading them to watch as I fucked her, the ring of her pussy pulling in and out on the dildo shaft, her bumhole dribbling molten lard to add to the lubrication.

It was hard to get a grip on her slippery bottom, but she was clinging tight to the post. I managed to get a rhythm up, pumping into her until she was gasping and tossing her head from side to side. Her fat breasts were quivering and bouncing beneath her, her bottom wobbling with every push. Small, plump girls are so adorable, and the sight of her was really getting to me, and made all the better by the little pink tail shaking to and fro above her bottom. I wanted to come myself and Bulmer, and everything else bad, was forgotten as I eased the thick rubber shaft out of her sex and put it to her anus.

Jade gave the most beautiful little sob as she realised she was to be sodomised. Penny put an arm around my waist, her hand on my bum, her eyes fixed on the junction of bumhole and dildo as I began to push. Jade let herself open, the pink, lardy ring of her anus spreading, wet and ready to the cock head, wider, straining, at last to take it in. Again I pushed, and watched a little more of the thick black shaft slide up into the straining ring, and yet more. Jade began to pant as her rectum filled with dildo, and to stamp her feet on the ground in little, urgent treading motions. Her hand came back to rub her sex, and she began to talk.

'Hard, Amber, really hard. Smack me, Penny, smack me hard . . .'

Penny slapped out at the upper curves of Jade's bottom, all she could get at.

'No . . .' Jade babbled, 'my boobs . . . my face . . . in my face.'

I exchanged a look with Penny. She was biting her lip in hesitation, but stepped forward as Jade turned her face, her eyes imploring, in obvious ecstasy. With a last, doubtful shake of her head, Penny swung her palm in, to catch one wobbling breast, then again, harder, and again, full in Jade's face. Jade squealed, and gasped, the red print of Penny's hand already showing as the slapped skin coloured up.

'Again?' Penny asked.

'Again, more, harder . . . do it while I come. Hurt me, use me, both of you.'

I took her by the hair, twisting my hand to hold her on to my dildo as I began to pump it roughly up her bottom. She cried out in pain, but began to rub harder, making her whole body shake. Penny put another slap in, across Jade's other cheek, then another to one fat boob, and more, all reluctance gone as Jade began to gasp in her ecstasy. I jammed the dildo in, wrenching at Jade's hair as she began to come, Penny slapping out at the same time with all her force, hard across Jade's cheek, to spray spittle and bits of lard to the side. Jade screamed at the top of her voice and she was there, coming on the big rubber cock as Penny let go a flurry of hard slaps, full in her face.

She was embarrassingly noisy, but I let her do it, holding the dildo well in as Penny attended to her face and breasts. Only when she jerked suddenly away from a blow did I know she'd had enough, and I went down with her as she sank to her knees, the dildo still up her bottom. I pulled out gently, easing the thick shaft clear, to leave her bumhole open and oozing fluid. I needed to come myself, and glanced up at Penny, only for her to giggle, and run.

I gave chase, in play, but determined she would pay for making me wait. It was not easy, with her darting among the jumps and doing her best to always keep something between us, always laughing, and flaunting her bottom and piggy tail at me as she dashed from one safe place to another. I quickly realised I couldn't do it, with real frustration, until she ran past Jade, who stuck out a leg.

Penny went flat on her face in the mud, squealing in surprise and shock. She was struggling to rise immediately, but I'd been close, and caught her by the leg, only for her to wriggle free, her skin too greasy to let me hold her. She rolled, laughing, and I snatched down again at an ankle, gripping hard. She squealed, struggling and kicking, but I had her, and dragged her towards me through the muddy grass, until I could get the grip I really wanted, in her hair. Her eyes came wide as I squatted down, then wider still as she found herself looking right at my dildo.

'Suck it!' I ordered.

Her eyes screwed up in humiliation, but her mouth had come open. I was grinning as I fed the dildo in, with the most delicious wash of pure sadism coming over me as I watched her suck on the dildo I'd so recently had up Jade's bottom. It was wonderful. Her whole face was screwed up, with the rubber snout making her cuter still and her mouth wide in utter submission as I fed the thick rubber shaft in and out.

Jade crawled over to watch. She was in a fine state, her body filthy with lard and mud, her breasts stripy with whip marks, her face red from Penny's slaps. She was happy though, giggling in disgusted delight as she saw what I was making Penny do. Her hand went to Penny's bottom, burrowing between the cheeks, and into both vagina and anus, molesting her. Immediately Penny's sucking became more eager and her thighs spread to let Jade's hand in properly.

'Oh no you don't,' I said, 'not until I've come.'

I pulled out, leaving her looking up at me, mouth still a little open, with a ring of dirty lard around her lips.

'On your knees, Pinky,' I ordered, using her piggy-girl name to really rub her condition in. 'Bum in the air, it's feeding time.'

Her look immediately changed to real worry. It was a game we'd played before, and I knew just what she would eat if she was high enough on her submission. She obeyed though, scrambling into a kneeling position with her bottom well raised, her tail shaking to the trembling of her body, her eyes turned up, wide above her snout, a look of the most glorious consternation.

The look became stronger still as I began to scrape the lard from her body with my hands. Jade caught on immediately, and crawled quickly around Penny and started to clean up the mess from her fanny and between her buttocks. Penny just watched, her apprehension growing stronger and stronger as we collected the dirty lard. At last I had a good handful, which I showed to her, right under her snout.

'What was it you were saying about not having to eat it?' I asked gently.

She looked up imploring me with her eyes. Jade laughed.

'Come on, Pinky, feeding time,' I urged, 'or do I have to hold your nose and have Jade whip you?'

She shook her head frantically.

'Then open up.'

Again she shook her head.

'Come on, Pinky, I want to watch you eat it out of my hand, now!'

'Not that, Amber, please?' she said suddenly.

'Yes, that. You have a stop word ...'

She shook her head, her body now shaking hard as she struggled with her feelings, bringing my sadistic pleasure higher, and higher still as she once more began to babble.

'No, Amber, please ... that's not fair ... it's not ...'

Her stop word was 'red' and protests ended in a muffled sob as I pushed the handful of lard firmly into her face. Her eyes shut, screwed up in utter disgust as I rubbed it well in. At last her mouth came slowly open and she began to eat the mess.

I needed to come while she was doing it, just watching the utter disgust on her pretty face as she struggled to swallow down her feed. As I began to wrestle with the popper of my jeans, Jade realised and came to help. I lifted my hips, letting Jade push down my jeans and knickers, all the while holding out my hand so that Penny could feed. Air touched my bottom as I came bare, cool between my cheeks and on my hot fanny. Jade's fingers slipped down between my cheeks, to start tickling my bottom hole even as my own fingers found my clitty.

'Now eat up, Pinky,' I ordered. 'I want to see you swallow.'

Her face went down again, into the filthy mush in the palm of my hand, mouthing at it, to take it in. I began to masturbate, my sex and bottom cheeks already starting to tighten as Jade slipped the tip of one finger into my bumhole and two more up my fanny. Penny looked up, her eyes full of shame, her face filthy with dirt and lard. For a second her mouth came open, and I saw the ball of off-white muck inside, and then she was swallowing, her throat moving as it went down, her face screwing up in absolute, perfect revulsion.

I was coming, on a high of pure, undiluted sadism and control as I watched my girlfriend swallow down the filthy muck I had made her eat, made her eat as a pig, as a grovelling, naked, filthy, piggy-girl. It was truly glorious, an orgasm in the style I like, with my bumhole and fanny attended to, and something really, deeply sadistic to hold in my head. A piggy-girl made to eat dirty lard was perfect, and as the second peak hit me I slapped the rest of my handful into her face, to feel her mouth open for it, sucking it up from my hand, to swallow again, to suck again, and once more to swallow . . .

She came as I did it, although I hadn't even realised she'd been masturbating too. That made it just perfect, and disposed of the guilt I felt for what I'd made her do the moment my orgasm had begun to fade. After all, it was her fantasy as much as mine, and the first thing we did when we had both come down was share a long, lard-sodden kiss to reinforce our feelings for one another.

We retired, all three thoroughly satisfied, to wash and clean up. I was nearly as filthy as them, with my clothes in an appalling state, while it took ages to get the lard off. Of the three of us, Jade was in the worst state by far. She was covered in whip cuts, and her cheeks were bruised, all four, while her bumhole was an angry red ring, as she proudly demonstrated after washing, grinning happily and immensely pleased with herself despite everything.

Once properly scrubbed up, we settled down to share a bottle of wine and start lunch. Neither piggy-girl bothered to dress, save for pinnies to protect their fronts, Jade slipping into the servant's role Penny likes to take without hesitation. I dressed, knowing they'd prefer it, and sat down to sip my wine as they worked, now pleased with myself, and with the memory of Gavin Bulmer no more than a nagging irritation in the back of my head.

It was only when we were actually eating lunch that the talk came around to what we'd done, and in particular to Jade's need to have her face slapped. We'd been talking about her lifestyle, and the hardcore lesbian domination clubs she frequented, which made the sort of thing I like seem very tame indeed. Being tied up for torture by all comers was the least of it, and it turned out that she found us refreshingly light and playful.

'You let me call the shots,' she explained. 'A lot of butch dykes resent that, and won't even play if they think a bottom will try to top from the bottom ... if that makes any sense at all.'

'Enough,' I answered. 'For me the knack is just finding someone compatible. I'd feel really bad if I found out she'd only done something because she thought she had to, or that I wanted her to.'

'I know,' Jade answered. 'I like that, and the way you don't try to be hard. You're dominant, yes, but cuddly, sort of motherly ...'

I opened my mouth to threaten her with going back over my knee, welts or no welts, but she went on, so I let it be.

'And I adore a spanking the way you do it, sort of old-fashioned style. It's great, but what really gets to me, in my head, is sort of more general ... you know, being slapped around, but in a sexual way. Obviously it has to be by the right person.'

'Obviously.'

'How about you, Penny?'

'Not really no, or not much, maybe gently, on my tits, my thighs perhaps ... OK, maybe even in the face, but not hard, never hard enough to bruise.'

'So everything's centred on your bum?'

'Yes, I suppose so.'

'Do you like it up the bum then, being bi?'

I laughed. I know I'm bad about wanting my bottom hole attended to, but Penny is obsessive. When she masturbates it is the usual first place her fingers go, or one finger anyway. Not only that, but she had been sodomised before she lost her virginity. She gave me a playful slap as she answered Jade.

'Yes,' Penny answered, blushing slightly. 'And you're one to talk, Miss Amber bum-in-the-face Oakley!'

'You two are going to be in major trouble in a minute,' I answered.

Ten minutes later, with lunch finished, they were: across my knee one after the other, to have their bare bottoms spanked to rosy pink. It was the first spanking of many that afternoon, all playful, none hard, and several followed by the girls' attention to my fanny and bottom with their tongues. We even continued into the evening, and when we did finally go to bed, it was very different to the previous night, all three of us naked on the bed, cuddling and enjoying each other as we pleased.

Both Penny and Jade had to get back to work, and they left before I was properly up, saying goodbye at my door with hugs and kisses while I was still in my robe. Afterwards I was tempted to go back to bed, but didn't, making coffee instead. Before five minutes had gone I was feeling lonely, and by the time I'd had breakfast my black mood had come back with a vengeance. My bottom was still spotty with bruises, keeping me in mind of my failure every time I sat down, and of how I'd sucked cock in public.

The day was slow, with just a handful of customers, and I tried to busy myself with paperwork, not very successfully. The weather had turned too, a mirror to my mood, and making it worse. By closing time I was thoroughly depressed, and I really could not bear the thought of an evening alone. So I put on a souwester and started off up the Strip, hoping that Henry would be able to cheer me up, and maybe even provide some advice.

It was windy, with showers blowing in from the north, and cold for summer. The dye from the paintballs was beginning to dissolve, and running slowly down the trees and foliage where it had hit. Thinking back to it, only without the great rush of adrenalin that had seen me through, I began to feel ever more small and vulnerable. It seemed amazing that I could have done such a thing.

I had, and rationally I knew that much of my weakness came from what had happened afterwards. Emotionally it was very different, and I was extremely glad to reach Henry's. As I approached the house I caught the scent of roasting meat, then the sound of voices, his own, and another, almost equally familiar: Morris Rathwell.

Despite a pang of irritation, I went in anyway, finding Henry just dishing up a dinner of chicken roasted on a bed of peppers and mushrooms. I was invited to join in, and found my spirits lifting with the conversation and the wine.

Rathwell had come up to collect Henry's pony-girl cart for an event at his club and asked me the same favour. I agreed but declined his invitation. I was still glad to be treated as a fellow dominant, and to stay off the topic of Sniper's Alley. The dinner over, Rathwell suggested driving me down to my house to collect the cart, which was only sensible.

'Nice move, nice move,' he remarked as he turned out of Henry's drive.

'Nice move?' I queried, not at all sure what he was talking about.

'Very nice,' he answered. 'Now he's sure to go for it when you ask for a return match.'

'A return match?' I demanded as it sank in. 'With Bulmer? What are you talking about? I am not going through that again!'

He was going to say something, but paused, looking at me in apparent surprise before speaking again.

'You did it on purpose, didn't you?'

'On purpose? What, lost?'

'Yeah. You don't have to bullshit me, Amber. Come on, this is Morris you're talking to. Harmony said how you took a hit for little Kay.'

'Well, yes, but . . .'

I trailed off. He obviously thought I really had lost on purpose, to make Bulmer overconfident and so take on a more realistic bet. It was typical Rathwell, who firmly believes that all women are sluts at heart, but also sticklers for social convention, constantly needing to find excuses for indulging in sexual pleasure. I shrugged. He laughed.

'That's my girl! So what are you going to do? Train up and take him at his own game? Try and trick him into playing on your terms?'

'I don't know. Not Sniper's Alley, or not as a mark. It really panicked me.'

'Yeah, it even got to Mel a bit. Good game. I'm having it at the club.'

'There wouldn't be space.'

'Not for Sniper's Alley, no. I'm going to have a military environment, like the dungeon environment Mel does for the subbie boys. Bulmer says he'll throw the gear in for free if . . .'

'You've invited Bulmer to your club?'

'Sure, why not? Yeah, he's an arrogant little shit, but he's got ideas. I need new stuff all the time. You haven't been in ages, you really should come.'

'As I said, it's not really my cup of tea, especially with Bulmer and his ghastly friends running around with paintball guns.'

'We'll keep them in their area, but it's a good idea. Military stuff is always popular, uniforms and that.'

'True.'

I went quiet, thinking of what he'd said, and of his arrogant, masculine confidence. Bulmer had the same, to a lesser extent, but he lacked Morris's experience. An idea occurred to me.

'Look, could you do me a favour, Morris?'

'Sure.'

'You know your theory about women having to have an excuse for sex?'

'Fact, most of the time.'

'Regardless. Do you think you could explain it to Gavin Bulmer, and basically make out that I need the excuse of a game, and a significant bet, in order to swallow my pride for him?'

'No problem.'

He was already pulling the Rolls into a lay-by, the lights illuminating a huge pile of concrete blocks dumped by some fly-tipper. There was nothing to be said, and as he pulled his cock free of his trousers I simply leant down and took it into my mouth.

I felt a little better on the Tuesday morning. I might have sucked Rathwell's cock again, but at least I was doing something and for me. There is nothing worse than feeling I've given in.

Succeeding was a very different matter. I needed to outwit Bulmer, and creep though he might be, he was not stupid. Even if Morris managed to convince him that I deliberately wanted to lose in order to find my 'excuse', I still had to win.

I was scared of Sniper's Alley, but I knew I could do it again if I had to, or something similar. Looking back, I hadn't had a chance. Even Vicky had been lucky. So it was pointless anyway. I needed something different, something which allowed me to make the best of my own skills, although obviously also something that Bulmer would think he could beat me at, and would want to play. He also knew that I really did want the land, which made it that much harder.

I mulled over my options as the morning went on, rejecting one after another. There were a fair number of customers, but I was running very much on autopilot, with my mind elsewhere, at least until shortly before I was due to break for lunch. The door went, and I glanced up with my usual smile, to find it was Kay. My smile immediately became a great deal more sincere, also nervous. Her reaction was much the same.

'I er . . . didn't really get a chance to say thank you,' she said as she approached. 'I wanted to.'

'To thank me?'

'Yeah, for Saturday, for taking the hit for me. I mean, if you hadn't, then it would have been me . . .'

'Well, yes, but we didn't know that. It's OK, really.'

'You're not angry with me?'

'Angry? No, of course not, why should I be?'

'Well, I thought . . . maybe I should have taken your place, you know, with Gavin Bulmer and the other men, and, well . . . you seemed a bit cold that evening.'

'No, no, not at all. I was just fed up.'

She nodded, her lips pursed, and turned to inspect the rack of dressage and carriage whips, running her fingers up the long nylon shafts. Finally she spoke again.

'I was wondering if you'd like lunch together?'

'Fine. I was just about to go.'

'Great. My treat.'

'Not at all . . .'

'No, I insist.'

I shrugged and smiled.

No sooner had I locked the door behind us than she took my arm. My hopes rose, only to be dashed as she spoke.

'There's something I wanted to ask you about.'

'Go ahead.'

'Gavin Bulmer has asked me out.'

'Bulmer?'

My heart had dropped to my boots. The thought of Bulmer with Kay was awful, unbearable.

'Are you going?' I asked.

'I'm not sure. I mean, he's an arrogant git, but . . . I don't know, he's got . . . confidence I suppose. I like that in a man ... I don't know. I've always been a bit like that, you know, going for the wrong type of guy.'

'You and half the other women on the planet. I know the feeling, Kay, but Bulmer ...'

'You don't think I should, do you?'

I wanted to say that I didn't want her to, but I couldn't. It was impossible to know what I should say, without revealing that I was desperately keen on her. It seemed very likely that she thought of me only as a fellow female in whom she could confide, and not sexually at all. In the end I came out with the only thing I could think of.

'Well, it's just that, is it really sensible? I mean, you know what he's like, and if you feel bad about what might have happened on Saturday ...'

'That was four of them, in public! I couldn't have handled that at all.'

'No, and remember it was Bulmer's idea, Bulmer's rule. We would have stuck up for you, by the way, if it had been you and you'd wanted to back down, Kay. The men would just have to have chosen one of the girls with six hits. It's like that sometimes, when someone gets a bit more than they bargained for. At the end of the day, everyone knows it's just a game ... Well, maybe not Bulmer's lot, but ...'

'No, that's not it, Amber. I wouldn't have backed down. I wanted to do it! I wanted to do it, Amber, but I know I couldn't have handled it afterwards. That's why I'm considering accepting Bulmer's date, to sample a bit of it, but no more than I can handle. I'm not tough like you, Amber.'

'Tough, me? The tough ones are girls like Penny and Sophie and Jade. Submissive girls are always the stronger.'

'I don't understand. Don't they need the strength and protection of a dominant, like yourself?'

'Yes, in an emotional sense, sometimes in a physical sense, but it is having that protection which allows them to express their sexuality so openly. Penny knows that I'm always here to cuddle her, no matter how deep she goes.'

She nodded, biting her lip. I went on.

'That's the thing, Kay, if you want to try that sort of thing, you need someone who understands. There are plenty of men I could introduce you to if you want to experiment, or ...'

I went quiet as we passed a trio of women from the village, nodding politely and smiling. Kay gave me a bright-eyed, conspiratorial look as they drew out of earshot, and spoke before I could pick up the thread of my conversation.

'Could you explain something, anyway, something very personal ... if you don't mind?'

'I'll try.'

'Well, you really seemed to hate it, but you did it, and as you said, you didn't really have to, not really really, and afterwards, you ... you played with yourself.'

I felt the blood rising to my face as I sought for a convincing answer.

'Well ... I don't know really. I'm not even sure if I understand myself, entirely, but everything about kinky sex is full of contradictions. Some are simple, like dreading a spanking at the same time as wanting it with all your heart. Vanillas – people who just like straight sex – can never really understand, because it's not part of them. It does make sense though. I mean, your feelings aren't always the same, are they? Everyone knows that, but it doesn't mean you can't acknowledge the way certain things will change your feelings.'

'Well, yes ...'

I was babbling, but there was nothing to do but keep going, interrupting her.

'It's all in the way your body reacts, chemically. Think of PMT, or just getting turned on for that matter, or hungry, or thirsty. I mean, when you've eaten so much you couldn't take a mouthful more, you still know you'll be hungry the next day, don't you? No, that doesn't explain it at all . . . What I'm trying to say is that I can get into a really submissive state, sometimes, just because . . . because of the way my body reacts, but I don't like to, because it spoils my sense of dominance. I can't help it though, any more than I can help feeling hungry. All my friends, the ones who're into that sort of thing, they all know me well enough to know that once I get really turned on to submission, the best thing is to let me be, to let me work it out of my system. To do that, I have to come.'

She nodded, pursing her lips in thought. I went silent, wondering if I'd said too much, how much she knew, what had been said between her and the others on the Saturday. It also occurred to me that if she was likely to be seeing Bulmer, then it was a really stupid confession to make. Altogether too many people know the state I can get into, or be put into. It was foolish to risk adding Bulmer and his cronies to that list. He already had a hold on me, and if he came to understand me, there was no question that he would take advantage of it. Finally she spoke.

'So what you're saying is that sometimes you have to put yourself into a situation you're scared of, in order to get what you really need? I can understand that.'

It wasn't at all what I'd expected her to say, and it took me a moment to answer.

'Well, yes, I suppose so. If I want to feel like that I have to put myself in a situation where it will happen, yes. OK, sometimes I do it on purpose. Do I need it? I don't know, sometimes I wonder . . .'

There was another group of people, coming down from the station, and we went quiet again. Kay stayed quiet even after they'd passed, and in the Coach we had little chance to talk, other than of mundane things, with the wind too chilly to sit outside and indoors crowded.

I did learn a little about her, that she was a Londoner like myself, twenty-three, and worked with charities, which was what had led her to get her rickshaw troupe together. That at least gave me a chance to ask the question I had wanted to the first day we met, whether the idea had been influenced by pictures of girls in harness, but not until we had left the pub.

'Yes,' she admitted. 'I was going to do it with a real pony, but when I fed a few keywords into a search engine to look for somewhere I could hire things, half my results were about girls being used as ponies! I was a bit shocked, but intrigued. You do that, don't you? I mean, I'm not trying to be intrusive, but Penny and your friend Ginny Scott were talking, and –'

'That's fine,' I cut in, 'just as long as you're not shocked. I've been doing it for years, since just after I left school. Henry taught me.'

'Henry, the big old guy whose house you got made ... we ended up at?'

'Yes. He's my godfather. He used to run a pony-girl club. Morris Rathwell still does, but it's really big now, and more a sort of free for all SM club. He's doing one next weekend, with Bulmer running some sort of military thing.'

'Are you going?'

'Yes ... I thought I would.'

'Can I come?'

'Yes, of course ... if you really want to.'

'I do, sort of, and I don't. Like we said, sometimes you have to put yourself into a situation you're scared of, in order to get what you really need. I'm not sure what I need, but I do know it's more than the odd shag in a club toilet, or joining the search for Mr Right.'

'OK, great.'

'There's something else, too ... What I meant to say earlier, was ... not that I wanted your advice on Bulmer, really, but ... well, if you'd rather I didn't. At the club, if you like, I'll tell him no. Maybe say I'm your girlfriend?'

She went on before I could reply. 'Penny wouldn't mind, would she?'

'No, we have a completely open relationship, except in that . . .'

I stopped, thinking of some of Penny's other relationships, with Melody, with Annabelle and Marcus, with her own cousin. There was no except. There had been, but not any more.

'Fine,' I finished, 'but we do need to establish a few ground rules.'

I was going to do it. If she was coming to one of Rathwell's clubs, I had to know how she felt, how she really felt.

'How do you mean?' she asked.

'If you are with me as my girlfriend,' I explained, 'it will be assumed that you are submissive. Other people will want to play with you, and they'll ask me. Now, I don't have to let them obviously . . .'

'Yes, that's best, I think.'

'. . . but I don't want to stifle you.'

'No, that will be fine. Just say I'm yours, the way Melody treats her slave.'

'OK. Then there's Rathwell. There's pony-cart racing, there's a show, some sort of competition. I'll be straight here. He's not going to pass up the chance of getting a girl as cute as you to play.'

'How do you mean, play how?'

'Well, at the least to take a spanking up on stage where everyone can see. He tries to get all the new girls to do that.'

'Oh, right . . . what, with their pants down?'

'Usually, yes. Look, I can say no if . . .'

'Maybe. I'm not sure. You'd do it, yes?'

'Yes.'

'Well, OK then, if it's you.'

I had to ask. It was too much.

'Do you want me to spank you, Kay?'

'I . . . I don't really know. I've never tried . . . Maybe you should . . . you know, to practise.'

It was almost too much for me. My heart had begun to hammer in my chest, and I could feel a hot flush suffusing my skin. She wanted me to spank her, to spank her lovely bottom, maybe even with her jeans down, maybe even bare. Struggling to seem calm and dominant but feeling anything but, I took her hand. She gave no resistance, but let me lead her, back towards my house.

She had offered, and I was not going to lose the moment, not now. Indoors, I went straight to the dining room, pulled out a chair and sat down, still holding her firmly by the hand. As I looked up I met her eyes, patted my lap, and down she went. Her jeans tightened as she bent, bringing the glorious globe of her bottom into full prominence, with both meaty little cheeks sheaved in tight blue denim, and the crotch pulled tight against the swelling lips of her fanny. Her hands met the floor, her head hung down, and she was there, across my lap, ready to be spanked. My urge was to give her a few solid swats on the seat of her jeans and then make her take them down, spank her until she howled and make her lick me to heaven, but it was no time to hurry, or for clumsiness. A girl's first spanking is a very important moment, and not one to rush.

'All right, Kay,' I told her, as I took her gently around the waist. 'I'm going to spank your bottom, and I'm going to have to do it quite hard. If you really can't bear it, use your stop word, which is "red". If you need me to slow down, use "yellow". I would much rather you said neither, but simply let me take control.'

She nodded, looking back from among the tangle of her fallen hair, her eyes full of apprehension, but also excitement.

'Also, I'm going to take down your jeans, and your knickers, and do it on your bare bottom.'

Again she nodded, and swallowed hard.

'Good,' I stated. 'I'm glad we understand each other.'

Once more she turned her head to the ground, and obligingly lifted herself on to her toes. She was shaking, and so was I. I slid my hand under her tummy, groping for the button of her jeans. They were tight, and I was forced to tug it free, but as it came, so did her zip. I took hold of her waistband firmly, and began to pull, jerking her jeans slowly down, around her hips, and lower, to pull out her bum and expose the high-waisted, sheer black panties beneath. They were well up her bottom, and her cheeks spilt out as I tugged her jeans lower, most of each cheeky, creamy globe bare, with just the upper part of her divine rear covered. To spank her I didn't really need to take them down at all. To spank her properly, there was no question of leaving them up.

'Do you understand that your knickers have to come down?' I asked as I settled her jeans in a tangle of blue denim at knee level.

She nodded, her hair tossing around her head. She knew, she was for real. Nobody who was just curious would have responded so promptly, and without question.

I took hold of the back of her knickers, lifting them off the pale, smooth skin of the small of her back, savouring the moment as I began to peel them slowly down, and watching the subtle quivering of her bottom cheeks as she was properly exposed. Her shaking grew harder as they came down, and as the gusset pulled free of her fanny she gave a low moan. I assumed it was at the knowledge that everything was now showing, although some women just don't seem to realise how rude they look from the rear.

'There we are,' I said happily, 'bare bottom, as every girl due a spanking should be. Now, look back between your legs, and you'll find you can see yourself in the mirror.'

She moved, just a little, and I knew she was watching. I let her, and turned to admire the same view. It was the most beautiful sight. She lay bare bottom across my lap, her cheeks a little apart. Her fanny showed in the mirror, her lips pouting out provocatively from between her thighs, so, so sensual, with their little puff of dark gold hair and the wet, pink centre. Her cheeks were just that little bit too chubby to really let her bottom hole show, but a few fine lines were visible, running down to a darker area, which I soon intended to have on full, rude display. Her head showed too, between her spread arms, with her hair hanging down and her mouth and eyes wide in anticipation of what was about to be done to her.

'This is what you will be showing if I spank you at Rathwell's,' I said. 'Everything, in front of men as well as women, men who may well want to masturbate over the memory, as may the women. You realise that, don't you?'

Again she nodded.

'Very well . . .'

'Go on then, do it to me. Spank my bottom.'

She sounded breathless, and her voice caught on the word 'spank', as if she could barely bring herself to say it, as if the waiting had finally become too much, and she had been forced to ask for it.

I began gently, using just my fingertips, to plant quick, precise slaps to the crests of her bottom cheeks. Her flesh had a wonderful texture, resilient, not too soft, but not too firm, as a woman's bottom should be. Each little smack sent a tremor through her, and left a faint pink imprint, which began to merge as I enlarged the area of my operations.

She stayed quiet, only the depth of her breathing betraying her emotions as her bottom slowly warmed. I held back, forcing myself to be patient, and admiring the view of her naked rear end in the mirror, also watching to see how her fanny juiced, and the way her bottom came slowly open as she relaxed to the spanking.

Only when her whole, chubby seat was an even pink did I change my style, using my palm to plant firm, even swats on her bottom. She gasped at the first, but went quiet again, so that the only sounds were her breaths and the rhythmic slap of my hand on her bare bottom cheeks.

She was juicing, her fanny slowly, surely changing, the lips opening as the blood came into them, a bead of white fluid forming at the entrance to her hole. The temptation to slide a finger up was close to overwhelming, but I resisted. I'd said I'd spank her, no more, just to let her know how it felt, but it was very, very hard not to see what we were doing as a prelude to sex.

Her bottom was coming open too, as she slowly gave in to her rising excitement, with her thighs slipping apart and her cheeks lifting to the smacks. Unable to resist, I lifted my knee, to hump up her bottom and make them spread properly. Up she came, to reveal the deep crease between the two meaty little buttocks, and her darling little bumhole. It was tiny, and tight, a dark brown ring of flesh in a star of fine lines, with the actual hole a tiny wet cavity at the centre, closed by four little pieces of flesh set in a perfect cross. I had to tell her.

'Your bottom hole is showing, Kay. You have a very rude bottom hole, don't you?'

She responded with the sweetest little sob. I began to spank harder, my arousal now rising steeply with her so blatantly exposed in front of me. Again she gasped at the first smack, but this time kept on, until her breathing had changed to a fast, rhythmic panting and her bottom cheeks were bouncing and wobbling to the blows. She began to wink too, her anus pulsing to the same lewd rhythm and, as I laid in harder still, the first drop of fluid was dislodged from the mouth of her fanny.

She began to moan, suddenly, then to kick, one calf tensing to thump her shoe on the floor, then harder, her leg lifting in her pain. The other came up fast, and she was kicking freely, giving in to her feelings, both legs pumping as I finally applied the full force of my arm to her glowing bottom. At that she began to squeal, little, high-pitched cries of shock and pain, one to each heavy slap on her bottom.

Her kicking legs flew wide, stretching her lower jeans and panties open between them, to spread her fanny and her bumhole, her pain too great for her to care any more. Then she had given in completely, bucking and thrashing over my knee, squealing and gasping. Her bottom was rich pink, her skin prickling with sweat, her fanny wet and open, as if she'd been masturbating, her bumhole winking to a fast, urgent time.

Still I spanked, with all my force, ignoring my stinging palm and aching muscles, now full across the fat of her cheeks, making her meat bounce and shake, and spattering drops of sweat across us. Her skin was a full, deep red, and glossy, truly, properly spanked, and from her urgent, frantic bucking I was wondering if she would come simply from the spanking. With that I realised that I was going to have to touch her.

I stopped, panting slightly, Kay gasping for breath. She made no effort to rise, and with a quick prayer, I put my hand back on her bottom, no longer to spank, but to caress. Still she made no move to get up. I grew bolder, more hopeful, stroking her hot cheeks, even between her open cheeks, just short of the puffy, sweat-slick hole of her anus. My heart in my mouth, I let my fingers slip lower, gingerly, expecting rejection at any second. I touched between her thighs, the puff of hair that covered her sex, her flesh, and I was masturbating her, rubbing between the pretty, pouted lips.

She moved, but not to get away, to lift herself, and turn, into my arms. I cradled her, still busy with her sex, not daring to stop for an instant. She was clinging to me, as she had on the Strip, shivering, only now with arousal, and that wonderful feeling that really only comes with a good spanking, and can only be given to the spanker. Her thighs came wide, cocking apart over my lap, to open her bottom for me, surrendering her sex as she began to kiss my breasts, my neck, my mouth.

As our tongues met the last shred of reticence went. My thumb went to her bottom hole, to rub the tight, wet ring even as I was rubbing her clitty. It was intimate, dirty, maybe a liberty, but her response was a strong shiver and her arms flung around my neck, to pull herself hard into me, her mouth wide, pressed hard to mine, hard enough to bruise. I cupped her bottom, feeling one hot, rough cheek, her plump, firm flesh so womanly, juicy and round, a truly glorious, utterly female bottom.

She was coming, her bumhole tightening on my thumb, her fanny squirming against my hand, spanked and rubbed off, and in response kissing me, cuddling me, holding on as if she would never let go as she went through orgasm. I just held on, very tight, until she collapsed against me, gasping, her anus still in spasm, squeezing over and over on my thumb. Her heated moans of pleasures stopped, to be replaced by sobs. She was crying, but still clung on with that same urgency, letting all her emotions out against my neck. I slowly pulled my fingers from her body, but still held on, one hand supporting her under her smacked bottom. Neither of us said a word. It had gone far, far beyond where we had intended it to, I was sure beyond what she had expected.

I was desperately aroused. If it had been Penny, I'd have pushed her down, and she'd have known what to do. With Kay I couldn't. I might have spanked her, but

I needed to let her make her own decisions, to give me what I needed because she wanted to, and not because she knew it was what was expected of her. Not that she even knew, and all I could do was hold on, with little pulses of ecstasy running through me, just stroking her hot bottom and her back. Finally she spoke.

'Thank you, Amber. That was . . . that was the most wonderful experience I have ever had, thank you so much!'

She kissed me, on my lips, but briefly, and pulled back, to stand, slightly unsteady. There was a smile on her face, combining satisfaction, excitement and a fair bit of embarrassment. Her back was to the mirror, and she giggled as she looked over her shoulder to inspect her bottom, her mouth coming in a pretty O of shock as she saw how red she was. Reaching back, she began to rub at one cheek.

'Look at my poor bum! It does feel lovely though.'

She leant forward, on to the table, still looking back as she stuck her bottom out. I had two views: side on, with her back arched elegantly down to make the best of her tiny waist and cheeky, swelling bottom, and in the mirror, with the full red moon of her smacked bottom and the lips of her fanny between her thighs. It was too much. She liked confidence. She was going to get it.

'Stay like that,' I ordered as my fingers went to the buttons of my jeans.

'Have I turned you on?' she asked, in what sounded like genuine innocence.

I just shook my head in disbelief as I peeled open my zip. She watched, her mouth a little open, her lovely bottom still pushed well out, as I pushed down my jeans and knickers, to my ankles. It was not a dignified position, but I needed to come too badly to care. My fingers found my fanny, I took hold of one of my breasts and masturbated as I focused on her beautiful body. Kay giggled, her eyes fixed to my fanny.

'Do I look sexy then, to you?'

'For God's sake, Kay, you look too sexy for words, so beautiful, so alive . . . and spanked too.'

She giggled, looking pleased, and stuck out her bottom still further, really flaunting herself. The pose spread her cheeks, showing her bumhole in the mirror, the little ring still wet and open. I began to rub harder, my clitty bumping under my fingers, my climax starting to rise, and with that all my caution, all my reserve just went.

I reached out, snatching at her wrist. She squeaked as I caught her, but came down, clumsily, to her knees, squeaked again as I took her hard by her hair, and went silent as I stuffed her face unceremoniously into my fanny. She licked, immediately, looking up from above the thick golden bush of my pubic hair with surprise and shock, but licking.

It was that look of shock which took me over the edge. There she was, a spanked girl, bare red bottom stuck out behind, her face well in my sex, licking, yet vulnerable, unsure of herself as she tongued my fanny, maybe even licking another woman for the first time, but licking. I just came, almost immediately, holding her firmly in place to make sure she did it properly, with wave after wave of ecstasy going through me as her half-eager, half-reluctant little tongue dabbed and lapped at my clitty.

Six

It was sensible to go to Rathwell's club, and I was glad I was not going on my own. That allowed me to make my position very clear to Gavin Bulmer and his cronies, and to Morris himself. Because they were introducing Bulmer's military environment, they'd made it a uniform night, which was fine by me. A bit of effort allowed me to convert a male dress uniform from an army surplus store into a really worthwhile cavalry officer's uniform. It was nearly all black and very smart, jodhpurs, jacket, cravat, peaked cap and riding boots, along with a horn-handled whip. Only the starched blouse was white, which set everything else off nicely.

The overall effect was extremely Germanic, but I held back from adding any insignia that might give offence, or medals. I know Morris's line, that Hitler and company would have been incandescent with rage to know that their uniforms had become associated with sexual fetishism, but I don't entirely buy it. Clean lines look better anyway, and I didn't want to end up looking like a colonel from a banana republic any more than a Nazi. Sometimes there is a fine line between dominant and comic.

There is often no line at all between submissive and comic, something Rathwell loved to exploit. The ridiculous maid's outfit he'd put Sophie in at the dinner was only one of his imaginative and cruel costume ideas, and there was nothing he liked better than to see a girl looking sexy, yet faintly ridiculous. So in advising Kay on what to wear, I steered her firmly towards elegance. Nor did she feel ready for more than a touch of nudity.

Despite what had happened between us, I was a little cautious in my approach to Kay. She was full of enthusiasm, but obviously nervous, calling me every few hours to ask questions about what was likely to happen. We had stayed together on Tuesday night until the last London train left, kissing and cuddling, but I did have the impression that she could have stayed the night if she'd really wanted to. It was just nerves though, or I sincerely hoped so, and she had promised to give Bulmer the thumbs-down, which was immensely satisfying.

She came up on the Saturday in the early afternoon, immediately showing me what she'd bought, a simple black leather dress, short, tight on the bust and waist, but flared over her bottom. She also had ankle-length boots with four inches of heel, which were both sweet and submissive, but still left the top of her head three inches below mine with me barefoot. I donated wrist cuffs and a collar to complete her look, and to my delight discovered that she wanted to go bare under the dress, to tease both others and herself.

I did want to develop my relationship with Kay, quite strongly. Strongly enough, in fact, to feel bad about Penny. So I called her, telling her we were going to Rathwell's and asking if she wanted to come. She agreed, and to my complete surprise turned to call to somebody else in her flat, asking if they wanted to come too. As the answer came, I recognised the voice – Jade.

It didn't surprise me, but it was a little irritating. There I was getting myself into a state in case the intimacy between Kay and me hurt her feelings, and she was happily playing with Jade. She hadn't even told me, and while she was in no sense obliged to, it still hurt a little, if only because she was so casual about it.

The club was being held in an abandoned church Rathwell had purchased, well out in the East End of London. I had no idea if it was even a legal venue, but it was certainly impressive, with the nave cleared to make an excellent dance floor and pony-cart track, one aisle as the bar and the other as Bulmer's military zone. The choir and altar area had been converted to a stage, with the base of the tower as perhaps the most atmospheric dungeon space I had ever seen.

Kay and I met Penny and Jade there. They were full of excitement and had really dressed the part. Both were in army uniform, identical to all intents and purposes, and very smart indeed, save the difficulty Jade was having in keeping her abundant figure inside hers. Even their stockings matched, tan nylon with seams at the back, and underneath their smart green skirts they had 50s-style girdles and big white panties. They'd been there for a while, and knew the itinerary, which consisted of pony-girl racing, a dressage show, then some sort of competition.

The first thing I did was check that my cart and tack were being looked after properly. Melody was in charge, as beautiful as ever, in full riding gear, scarlet coat and all, the image only slightly spoiled by the fact that she was holding a clipboard and a biro instead of a riding whip. She grinned as we approached, her eyes flicking over my companions.

'Three? That's just plain greedy, Amber.'

'You're one to talk, Mel. Where's your pet?'

'Hitched up in the vestry. So what formation are you driving them in?'

'I'm not.'

'No? There's two-fifty and a Salmanazar of champagne in the kitty.'

'And for the loser?'

'Nothing heavy, stripped and hung up on the bell ropes in the dungeon for a flogging. That or an OTK from me and Morris gets to fuck the ponies. Anyway, you're not going to lose, Amber!'

'That's what I thought about Sniper's Alley. No, thank you, Mel.'

She laughed, which was intended to gall me into taking her up on it. I simply wished her luck and moved on. It was typical Rathwell, a nice big prize to tempt competitors, and serious punishment for the loser. In some ways he and Bulmer thought alike, which gave me food for thought.

'A piece of advice, Kay,' I said as we made for the bar. 'Never take anything Morris Rathwell says at face value, or Melody for that matter.'

Kay nodded. At the bar Penny took out a note, holding it between her fingers. I scanned the church as we waited to be served. It was crowded, with everything from hardcore SMers in their immaculate black leather and rubber, to blatant dirty old men. Among the latter was Mr Protheroe, the man who had spanked me on the bare bottom at the party Penny had dropped me into, and worse. He, at least, was fully dressed, even if he did seem to have come as Winston Churchill in old age, with his great flabby body concealed beneath a heavy overcoat. Nearby was a man no less old and only a little less fat, in nothing but a nappy.

We were being served before I saw Rathwell himself, dressed in the uniform of a full army colonel, with a swagger stick under one arm. He did look wonderfully severe, just the sort to spank an insubordinate girl, an embarrassing thought I pushed quickly down. As soon as he saw us he started over, grinning, and obviously highly amused by something, although nothing to do with us. As he approached he jerked his thumb over his shoulder, towards the arches draped in black cloth and camouflage netting which concealed the Razorback aisle.

'Looks like your friend Bulmer's a bit out of his depth,' he said laughing.

'Please, Morris, he is not my friend! How?'

'Well, he thought he'd be getting a lot of pretty girlies to play with, not submissive men!'

I laughed, imagining Bulmer's irritation as he discovered that helping out at an SM club was not all to do with molesting girls.

'It's a bit of a pain, as it goes,' Rathwell went on. 'He's not up for it, and the bloke he's brought with him isn't either. I need a dominant woman to shoot the male subs. How about it?'

'Me?'

'Sure, why not? No strings and a fifty in your pocket at the end?'

'Well . . . What about Melody, or Harmony?'

'Mel's running the pony show, Harmony's racing for me. You're great, Amber, and you've got the look!'

'Maybe, Morris, but –'

'But nothing, Amber, you're perfect for the job!'

'Morris, you know I don't get anything out of dominating men –'

'You get fifty quid, can't be bad! All you've got to do is shoot the fuckers, girl, I'm not asking you to make them lick your cunt. Come on, Amber, I need help here.'

The temptation to simply unzip my jodhpurs and point down to my fanny was considerable, only I didn't actually like the idea of him licking me any more than the submissive men. He went on.

'Then there's the revenge! Come on, girl, after Sniper's Alley, you don't want to plug a male backside?'

I made a face. Put like that, it was tempting. I could leave Kay with Penny and Jade safely enough. I nodded.

'OK, never mind the money, some champagne will do, and only until the racing starts. I take it Bulmer's there?'

'Yeah, with the fat one, Jeff Birdbrain or whatever his name is.'

'Did you speak to Bulmer, as we agreed?'

'Yes, of course.'
'What did he say?'
'He told me he already knew.'
'He already knew?'
'Yeah, like, he'd already figured it out for himself.'
'The arrogant little shit!'
'Hey, don't knock it. You've got him where you want him.'
'Yes, or I would have if I could think of a convincing game to challenge him to. It's not easy, because he knows I really do want the land.'
'You'll think of something. Now if you wouldn't mind? Hey, Penny darling, I'll get that.'

He had pulled a note from his pocket, waving it at the barman and still talking as I walked away. I was telling myself that Penny could look after herself and Kay, while I couldn't imagine Jade having any difficulty, but I still found myself glancing back. Rathwell had his hand on Penny's bottom and she was saying something to him, but I didn't catch what. I shrugged off my immediate irritation, and crossed to where Fat Jeff was standing at the opening in the curtains. He grinned as he saw me.

'Hey, cool! I do like the uniform.'

He began to walk round me, shaking his head as if in disbelief, and making a grunting noise when he came in view of my bottom.

'Fucking nice!'
'Quite. Morris said you needed help?'

At that moment Bulmer himself appeared, pushing through the inner section of the curtains.

'Amber? Fuck, am I glad to see you! There are all these blokes, and I don't know what the fuck to do! They all say they want a Mistress . . .'

'How many?'

'Twelve so far! Some of them want this, some of them want that . . . I've never heard of half the fucking stuff, and I'm not a poof anyway, but they don't seem to care. What's urolagnia?'

'Drinking piss.'

'Fuck that for a laugh! That's what one of them wants done to him, to be shot, then pissed on, in his mouth! Can you fucking believe it!'

'I've seen worse,' I answered, picking up one of the paintball guns. He was in a fine state, totally out of his depth, which was immensely satisfying. I might not have been quite in my element, but at least I knew what I was doing.

'So what's the set-up?' I demanded.

'They're in there, five of them just now,' he said, cocking his head toward where the inner curtains shut off our view. 'I liked the churchy look, so we got some of the old seats and that, and set it up so it's like the marks are after sanctuary, and we're the secret police . . . They'll love you!'

'I bet they will. So what am I supposed to do?'

'Simple. Catch 'em, drag 'em out of wherever they're hiding, tie 'em to a pillar, and bang, you shoot 'em in the arse. If they want more, give 'em more.'

I nodded, putting the gun down to select a face mask.

'Some of them are in gas masks,' Bulmer commented.

'And not a lot else,' Fat Jeff added. 'Watch what you're doing, yeah?'

'Buttocks only, count on me,' I promised, and pushed through the curtain.

I'd expected a row of eager submissive men waiting for someone to tell them what to do. There was nobody, only the high, empty space of the aisle, brilliantly lit near me, but stretching into shadows. The curtains were supported on a frame of scaffolding, completely blocking off the aisle. With the high, stained-glass windows to one side, the dust rising in the spotlight beams and the old high-backed pews, it might almost have been real, the curtains contributing little more than blackness, while the thump of some Gothic music outside just added to it.

I set my legs apart, sure I was being watched, and brought the gun up. Immediately there was a flicker of movement in the shadows. A figure darted from behind a pew, male, hooded, two thin legs and a flat backside on view. Indifferent to Bulmer's instructions, I brought up the gun and fired. Scarlet paint exploded across one scrawny buttock and the man shot up into the air with a pained squeal, to come down clutching at his bottom and crawling quickly away. Under my mask I was grinning.

It was like shooting pheasant, only without letting them out of the enclosure first. They wanted to be shot, obviously, and made it ridiculously easy. I'd shot three of the five before another man came in, but he was quickly joined by two more. Word was clearly getting around that there was a Mistress in the military zone, and I could here Bulmer and Fat Jeff giving instructions behind me as they issued masks. Three more came in, in quick succession, then a fourth, who asked if he could lick my boots while I played. My response was to threaten to shoot him on the spot if he didn't hide. He moved, and I shot him anyway, full on one fat cheek as he struggled to get in between two of the pews.

Feeling thoroughly pleased with myself, I stepped forward, screaming orders as I walked down the length of the aisle, and threatening various painful fates to those who didn't obey. They did, all of them, getting into a ragged line against the end wall, their hands on their heads, their backs to me, and twelve pairs of male buttocks presented. Ordering them to stay put, I walked back, to seat myself on a convenient pew and cross my legs in my best sadistic officer pose.

I was still grinning, and it grew broader still as I began to pot them off, one by one, in line, so each could get the full benefit of the apprehension of knowing what was coming. They jumped and squealed as the balls burst on their buttocks, showing no more reserve than I had in Sniper's Alley, or the other girls. Rathwell was right, it was revenge indeed, the only shame being that Bulmer and Fat Jeff were not among my targets.

Despite that, I was absolutely in rapture by the time the music faded for Morris to announce the pony-girl racing. All twelve pairs of buttocks were comprehensively spattered with scarlet dye, especially those of the men who had tried to take their hands off their heads so that they could masturbate. I even blew the tip of the gun barrel after firing off my last shot, a pointless but satisfying gesture.

Inevitably they clustered around me as soon as I declared the game over, most wanting me to be their Mistress for the rest of the evening, a few demanding more specific favours, including Bulmer's urolagnia enthusiast. He was really begging, but so were several others, mainly to lick my boots. I did not want spittle all over my beautifully polished boots, but what went on the men was nothing to me. With the beer Rathwell had bought me I knew I could manage it, and it was tempting, too tempting.

Shaking off one who was clinging to my leg, I ordered the rest back to the end of the aisle, snapping out what was going to happen to them at the top of my voice. Five fled, seven stayed. Again I screamed at them, ordering them into a line, and to drop when hit, even as I brought the gun up and fired. Scarlet paint splashed across an already messy buttock and one dropped. Another followed, beside the first, and a third, each paintball exploding on target. The fourth I caught on the leg, but he went down anyway, quickly joined by the fifth, and the sixth as I started to walk forward. The seventh fled, losing his nerve, to dash between the curtains to the sound of my derisive laughter. The others stayed down.

They were out on the open floor in a pile, but too spread out to stand over. A pew was near, and I hauled it close, climbing up with my adrenalin singing in my veins. My jodhpurs came open and down, my knickers followed and I was standing over them, my hips pushed out, all six pairs of eyes turned up to watch. I smiled back, a grin of pure sadism, which was exactly what I felt.

Erotic it might not have been, but it was still good, so good, as I simply let go, spraying out a great fountain of rich golden urine over their recumbent bodies, to splash over their paint-soiled buttocks, their backs, their legs, their hair, even their faces. One opened his mouth, and I peed right into it, moving my stream to catch him properly, and laughing as I watched the piddle bubble out at the sides.

I just left them like that, with my pee dripping down their bodies to form a wide pool on the floor beneath them. One tried to crawl up to kiss my boots, but I pushed him down and quickly rearranged myself, then walked away, twirling the paintball gun and grinning like a maniac.

Fat Jeff was standing by the entrance, staring at me and shaking his head from side to side, clearly hardly able to believe his eyes. I was going to say something, but Bulmer spoke from inside the little cubicle of curtains and he turned, then leant in through the curtains.

There it was, his enormous backside stuck out, right towards me. It was too good, far too good. I brought my gun up, took careful aim at one huge buttock, and fired.

He went down, forward, into the cubicle, with a yelp of pain, clutching at the curtains in a desperate attempt to keep his balance. It didn't work, the curtains quite unable to take his weight. Down they came, the entire cubicle collapsing around them, Bulmer cursing, Jeff also, but with a lot of panic in his voice, as his backside was still showing. I just laughed, put the gun down on a pew and walked back the way I had come, to escape by the same gap in the curtains my seventh victim had used.

I was now extremely glad I'd come. The paintball game had put me on a natural high, made better by revenge on Fat Jeff, the attentions of my girlfriends and the admiring looks I was getting from all sides. I was really strutting as I walked down towards the doors, to find a good place to watch the racing from, and look out for the others. I couldn't see the girls, but Melody was already marshalling the teams into place, four pony-carts, which was going to make it pretty tight on the turn.

Rathwell's cart had been repainted, his blue and gold colours absolutely gleaming. The rider was some woman I didn't recognise, tiny, in immaculate gold leather with a blue trim, more exotic than dominant, with a little tail coat that only half covered a cheeky bottom squeezed into blue fishnets. She was cute, but it was not her who took my eye. Annabelle was between the shafts, stark naked but for her harness and boots, the bit already in her mouth, her little round bottom red from spanking, her pert breasts the same colour, slapped up to a rich pink, with her nipples achingly erect. They'd kept her bald, but blue and yellow ribbons trailed down her back from the top of her harness, which was itself in the same colours. Nor was she the only one, with Harmony standing at a hitching rail behind the cart, and I realised that the race was going to involve a swap of ponies at the midway stage.

None of the other teams were quite as spectacular as Rathwell's. Trisha Ellis was hitched to Henry's cart, with her glorious red hair caught up in bright green ribbons and nothing on but her harness and a minuscule pair of panties, which did very little to conceal the evidence of what must have been a severe caning. I didn't recognise her driver, or the exchange pony, a lightly built girl with dyed blonde hair. The others I didn't know at all, although I was pleased to see the team using my cart was all-girl, and that the pony-girl in harness had a full, sturdy build, bottom and all, which was going to be needed.

One of Morris's friends was running a book as usual, and I put twenty on my own cart, getting the bet in only just in time. Even as I turned back Melody was dropping the pair of bright pink panties that served to signal the start, another of Morris's tasteful touches. As I screamed out for my team a hand closed on my bottom, and I turned to find Penny beside me, holding out a fresh beer. I took it, calling out again in delight as the big girl pulling my cart cut in front of Annabelle, almost unseating Rathwell's driver. She got a cut of the whip across her legs for the trouble, but had made the end first, and turned in the lead.

We were screaming encouragement as she came back down the nave, coming in neck and neck with Trisha. There was a frantic scramble for buckles and poppers as the teams began to switch ponies, and experience told, with Annabelle out of the shafts and Harmony between them so fast that they made up the time they had lost. There was still nothing in it as they left, but with Harmony as big and strong as the second girl on my cart, I was sure we were going to lose. It was one or the other anyway, as Trisha's replacement simply didn't have the muscle, while the fourth cart had made a total mess of switching ponies.

Harmony got the turn first, by feet, and the two carts came back, side by side, bumping, Rathwell's open wheel catching the housing of my own cart, the two swinging together, Harmony staggering off balance, their wheel springing loose, and my own cart ploughing through the wreckage as their driver sprawled on to the floor.

I was laughing so hard I think I would have wet myself if I hadn't just been. Rathwell's cart lay in a heap at the centre of the nave, one wheel gone, the frame visibly bent. Harmony was down on one knee, shaken but not hurt, while the little domina who'd driven was sitting on the floor ruefully nursing an ankle. My own cart romped home, well ahead of the others.

The crowd began to break up, with just a few of us heading for the bookmaker's little stall. Melody and Morris had come out on to the floor, but could hardly claim it had been unfair, and I soon had my winnings, a hundred pounds, Rathwell's team having been the firm favourite to win.

It was impossible not to tease, and I went over to give a few tips on pony-cart construction and racing technique. Morris was none too happy, or Melody, but as she bent to inspect the damage with the well-rounded seat of her jodhpurs stuck out towards me, it was more than I could resist not to lift her coat tails and give her a cut of my whip across her cheeks. She gave me a filthy look, but I just stuck out my tongue and walked back to the girls.

Penny had some tickets, which meant she had entered something, making me instantly worried.

'What are you three up to?' I asked, leaning close to make my voice heard above the music. Kay answered.

'We've put our names into some sort of prize draw.'

'What for?'

'All sorts! There's one of those huge bottles of champagne, and a whole hamper of chocolate and stuff . . .'

'And for the losers?'

'Losers?'

'The usual,' Penny cut in. 'Fancy spankings, pony-girl play, bondage. Doms pay a tenner to put their suggestion up on a list, and the losers have to choose. It's quite clever, because –'

'And you put our names in, ours?'

'Not yours, Amber! Just the three of us.'

'Fair enough, but you should have asked. In fact, young lady . . .'

I reached out to take her by the ear. She squealed in delight, putting up no resistance whatsoever as I dragged her down on to her knees. There was no question in my mind that she was the one who deserved the whipping, because she should have known better than to enter anything at one of Rathwell's parties, let alone allow Kay to do so. So I pushed her right down, her face to the floor, and held her by the scruff of the neck as I busied myself with her army skirt.

It came up easily enough, allowing me to get at the big white panties underneath and tug them open at the back, and down it all came, her bare pink bottom exposed as she squeaked in alarm. Standing, I placed a foot on her neck and lifted my crop, glancing at the others and the rapidly gathering crowd, to discover Jade staring at Penny's bare bum with what could only be jealousy.

'OK, miss, if you're so eager, get down there!' I barked.

She went, fast, down on her knees, tugging her shirt up to her hips to expose identical panties to Penny's, but rather than just tight, absolutely bulging with fat, girlish bottom. I took my boot off Penny's neck, and gave Jade a gentle kick on the leg.

'Get them down, all the way!'

They came, pushed down off her lovely chubby bottom, exposing the big cheeks with her crease spreading as the tension of the over-tight panties went. With the panties around her knees, she put her head down, and her cheeks opened fully, to show off her bumhole and the rear of her fanny in the same rude show as Penny was already giving.

I glanced up at Kay. She was biting her lip, but as our eyes met she gave the tiniest nod. I pointed to the ground with my whip, and to my utter delight she went, slowly, obviously seriously apprehensive and also embarrassed, but obedient nonetheless.

Her little skirt came up as she got into position, half baring her bottom. A minor adjustment and it was all showing, her cheeky buttocks quivering slightly, closed, but they spread as Penny's arm came around her.

I swallowed hard. Kay's bottom hole and fanny were on show, to me, to the crowd, between lush cheeks raised for punishment. Maybe she didn't know how rude she looked. More likely she did, because her muscles were twitching in reaction to her feelings. She had her arm around Penny in turn, as had Jade, the three of them hugging to give each other comfort as they waited for punishment.

Even for Rathwell's club, a line-up of three bare females bottoms was unusual, let alone with three such pretty girls. Everybody was staring, the crowd thick around us, and leaving only just enough room for me to dish out the punishment. I was also worried someone might try to touch, or join in without permission. I had to do it though, for my own pleasure, for theirs, and to see it carried through.

Penny was in the middle, and I lifted my foot on to her back, pressing the toe to her neck gently, but enough to force her head right on to the floor. Her bottom came up in response, her cheeks flaring, to make a full show of her little dark bumhole and hairy sex and crease. I knew just how humiliating it would be for her to be forced to show it off, with so many men, and women, peering at the most intimate details of her body.

'Think about it, Penny,' I called out, 'they'll all go home and masturbate over you, thinking of what you're showing, or your hairy little fanny and your dirty bottom hole, and how they'd like to fuck you, to bugger you . . .'

On the word 'bugger' I brought the whip down, hard on one cheek, making the flesh bulge out as she screamed her reaction into the floor. I laughed, pressing her face down with my boot, and put in a second cut, to the other cheek. Again she screamed, and I bent down, to rub at the welt I had put across her pale flesh and watch it turn from white to red. She was panting, her pussy already juicy, her bumhole winking at me, her emotions as open as her body. I gave her a third cut, this time horizontal, and a fourth, higher, to leave a checker pattern on her whipped bottom, for all the world like a noughts and crosses board.

Somebody laughed, and I realised I wasn't the only one to appreciate the joke. I had a lipstick in my pocket, deep red, a shade or two darker than Penny's welts, but not much. Keeping my foot planted firmly on her neck, I took it out, bent down, and placed a lipstick X across the middle of her crease. There was more laughter, and I looked up, trying to find a familiar face. Harmony was watching, still in her pony-gear, and I held the lipstick out to her, above the heads of those nearer.

She took it, pushing through the crowd, to mark an O at bottom centre, making a target of Penny's bumhole and drawing fresh laughter from the crowd. I took the lipstick and put my X at bottom right. Harmony blocked me at top left and I had won, putting a cross in the mid right and smiling as I passed back the lipstick. She marked top right, leaving me to complete a line across the middle of Penny's bottom, and mark my victory with a hard whip cut, full across the three Xs.

Penny was sobbing with humiliation at what had been done to her, but she kept her bottom up, flaunting the way she'd been used for all to see. Harmony had stepped back a little way, but as I pointed to the floor she went down, giving me a last, resentful look before turning her face to the tiles and lifting her bottom into line. That made four, three white, one black, only bigger, and dark, her shaved fanny the colour of the darkest chocolate and pink in the middle, her anal ring near true black, fading to a rich purple in the actual hole.

I wanted to top my little noughts and crosses game, but it was not easy. Then there was the question of who to do. I knew Jade could take it, and Harmony, but I was worried Kay might have had enough of flaunting her bottom and fanny to a crowd, so chose her. She was already shaking, and it grew harder as I settled the instep of my boot carefully on to the back of her neck. Her bottom came up, spreading wider, and her pretty little bottom hole was on even more blatant display than before. She was certainly turned on, her fanny moist and puffy between her thighs, the hole open enough to slip a finger into. I began to smack, just gently, tapping her buttocks to leave faint pink marks, which grew slowly richer as I increased the force.

Her breathing was inaudible beneath the music, but I could see it in the way her torso moved, growing slowly deeper as the warmth in her bottom increased. With Penny I knew the key – humiliation. With Kay I could only guess, and from her reaction to the spanking it was possible she could come as she was beaten, as Jade could. If she did, it would be her first time.

I made my flicks harder and faster, slowly increasing the severity of her beating, and keeping my own needs well held down. Her bottom had begun to glow, sweat prickling up on the hurt areas and blending to make her skin shine. A drip grew and broke away to trickle down her crease, pooling in her bumhole. Like Penny before, she had begun to wink, her ring tightening over and over, and now open enough to show the fleshy pink hole at the very centre. I wanted to bugger her with my whip handle, to push it well up into her bottom and make her suck it as I masturbated her to orgasm. I couldn't, not with Kay.

She was going to come though, I was determined, to come in front of everybody, under my whip. Her fanny was juicing so well I was sure she could have taken a fist with ease. White juice was running from the hole, which had begun to pulse in time to her anus. I smacked the crop down harder, on one fleshy cheek, the other, then gentle, on her sex. She gasped, but she was sticking it out, dirty, wanton, indifferent to or even eager for the display she was making of herself. I repeated the sequence, cheek to fanny, cheek to fanny, and again, as she moaned in response, loud enough to hear. She was going to come, soon.

Again I smacked her, harder still, to leave a trace of purple bruising on each chubby bum cheek. When I caught her fanny she screamed, and I hit again, and again, unleashing a rain of slaps, each bringing the wide leather sting of the whip directly on to her clitoris. She came, screaming and thrusting her bottom up, bucking frantically and yelling out my name at the top of her voice, her head shaking, her smacked buttocks wobbling crazily from side to side. I kept hitting, until the ecstasy of her voice changed suddenly to pain and she cried out 'red'.

An instant later she was in my arms, trembling against my body, and babbling out thanks and more, crying freely, the tears running down her face to soak into my jacket. I held her, stroking her hair, doing my best to soothe her and wishing the crowd would just go away and leave us in what was obviously an intimate moment not intended for show. Not one left, and at last I was forced to kiss Kay and tell her to hush.

I stood up, intent on resuming my role as domina. Jade was looking up, her mouth wide, the full lower lip pushed out, her eyes lidded. She was masturbating, her fingers working in the mushy flesh of her fanny, which was open and ready. As I stepped across to her I was forced to bring my whip down on a reaching hand, and turn my eyes to the crowd. The offender backed away and I turned my attention to Jade.

She was nearly there, rubbing hard, her fat bottom jiggling to the movement of her fingers. I wasn't so very far off myself, and if I had to be careful with Kay, I did not with Jade. I brought the whip down on her bottom, the leather snapping on to her flesh, and again, as I began to beat her hard, a real thrashing, the whip rising and falling on to the fat, bouncy ball of her buttocks, to leave her screaming and snatching at her sex.

I saw her bumhole tighten and I knew she was coming. Instantly I reversed the whip, put the smooth, horn tip of the handle to the little pink hole and pushed. It slipped in, lubricated with her own sweat, and up, deep into her rectum. I began to sodomise her, in a series of sudden pushes, making her cry out as she went into orgasm. Her cheeks clenched, trying to keep the whip inside herself as I pulled, but I already had her hair and out it came, sticky and glistening, put straight to her mouth, to be taken in and sucked, with her face set in the most sublime look of humiliation as she came slowly down from her orgasm.

The crowd burst into applause as Jade slumped slowly down on to the tiles, her knees coming apart to leave the gaping pink hole of her fanny on show to all, with her fingers still between her lips. Her fanny was bubbling fluid, and her bumhole too, a thoroughly dirty display, but no more so than the way she was still sucking on the thick shaft of smooth horn which had so recently been in her rectum.

I let go of her hair to look down on Harmony. I needed to come, and I didn't much care how, or who saw. She was ready too, wide-eyed and expectant, with her hand between her thighs to keep herself ready for whatever I had planned for her. Penny and Kay had rolled back clear, and Jade joined them as I was twisting my hand hard into Harmony's hair and brought the whip down across her glorious black backside. She cried out, but she was crawling to me as I squatted down, my thighs spreading, until I could pull her face into my crotch.

She knew what to do, her hands scrabbling at my jodhpurs button even as I began to whip her. Down came my jodhpurs and panties, baring my bottom beneath the tails of my jacket. Another tug and she had my knickers down too, and as I twisted her hair she rolled, lying to let me settle on to her face. Her tongue went to my anus and I was in heaven, my bum licked as I used the whip sting on her big, firm breasts and the mound of her fanny. She took hold of my hips, feeding on my bumhole and I began to whip her sex, as I had Jade, eager to see her flesh jump as I came...

The others closed in, Penny cuddling me, her mouth opening to mine, Jade taking Harmony's legs, to roll them high and wide for the whip. Kay came last, behind me, supporting me with her hands cupping my breasts through my blouse. Penny's hand slid between my open thighs and I was being masturbated, brought off in a pile of wriggling, squirming girls. Still I smacked the whip down, Harmony's bare brown fanny mound shivering to the strokes as Jade pushed two fingers into her. My hand slid under Penny's bottom, a finger into her anus, the hole moist and open with the juice from her sex. Her kisses became abruptly more passionate, her rubbing more eager.

Harmony's tongue burrowed deep up my bottom hole, sucking and licking eagerly as my muscles tightened in her face. The crop slipped from between my fingers as I started to come. Jade went down between Harmony's thighs, burying her face in plump, dark fanny flesh. Kay's fingers found the hard buds of my nipples, Penny began to slap my fanny and I was there, coming under their hands and mouths, totally in charge, with three, whipped, eager girls attending to my body.

It was one of the best, and broken only by the sudden uproar from the audience as they broke into clapping and cheering. Even then I might have come again had not some oaf chosen to slap Jade's upturned bottom. She squeaked, turning in anger at the unwelcome touch, and spitting out a string of expletives as she realised it was a man. He gave back, but the moment was broken, Jade already tugging her skirt down to cover herself, then fumbling for her panties.

I stood, slightly unsteady, but determined to speak to him about etiquette. He had already gone, and as we covered ourselves the others began to melt away too, interested only so long as there was plenty of naked female flesh on show. Penny hadn't come, nor Harmony, and both looked irritated. It took only an instant of eye contact between Penny and me and she was gone, holding Harmony's hand, with Jade quickly following.

Personally, I was more in need of a wash, with my bottom sticky between the cheeks and just generally uncomfortable. Kay stayed with me as we went in search of the ladies', and we helped each other to clean up, now sharing a casual intimacy which would have been unthinkable before, even after I had spanked her. We talked as we tidied up and corrected our make-up, Kay eager and excited in a way I had never seen her before. She was also very cuddly, clinging to my arm as we left the loos, and insisting on buying fresh beers, which were very welcome indeed.

I was feeling good, despite the display I'd made of myself. After all, I'd come with more people than I cared to think about looking on, but I'd shown almost nothing. I'd been in control too, which made all the difference, while the glances shot my way from those who had been among the crowd were of envy as much as lust.

We went to watch the pony-girl show as we drank our beers, with the pretty fillies being paraded in the harness, all beautifully polished and set off with ribbons, bells, rosettes, even ostrich plumes. Each Master or

Mistress used a dressage whip and single word commands to put the pony through her paces, demonstrating gaits, tricks and poise.

Harmony was acting as compere, still in her harness and otherwise bare, which looked a little odd. There was no sign of Melody, or Penny and Jade, and I was wondering if Harmony had tied them up in the dungeon or some quiet corner and gone for her sister once she'd come, when they appeared from the little area Morris had curtained off as an office, arm in arm, and giggling together. They made for the bar and I turned back to watch the ponies, satisfied that whatever had happened to them they weren't in trouble.

The show climaxed with a parade, all seven pony-girls put in line to perform a slow circuit of the ring, high-stepping as they went. This ended with them in a line, for Rathwell himself to come forward and award first, second and third prizes, pausing for a leisurely grope of each girl's boobs and bum before pinning appropriately coloured rosettes to their harness.

With the show over, Kay and I went in search of the others, finding them drinking beer on a pew Rathwell had had pushed to the side. We talked for a while, or rather shouted, as the music had been turned up once more, until it died again and we turned to see what was going on.

Rathwell had climbed up on the lectern, and raised his arms for silence with the microphone held in one hand. We turned to face him as the music died completely. Harmony jumped up on to the stage, now naked but for her boots and wrist cuffs, followed by Melody. Both went to an X-shaped frame of thick wooden poles which had been erected in front of the altar, Harmony going down on to her hands, and flipping herself over, legs wide, as her sister caught one ankle.

'Is she going to torture her?' Kay asked, pressing to my side.

'No,' I answered, 'it's the way they do the draw. You'll see.'

Melody had fixed one of her sister's ankles to the cross, and was working on the other. Morris watched, and just about everyone else, as Harmony was fastened in place, upside down, with her legs fully open, to leave her vagina agape. Only when she was firmly in place did Melody turn, to nod to Morris. He returned the nod, and spoke into the microphone.

'Ladies and gentlemen, Mistresses, Masters, slaves, perverts and playmates of every description. For the last event of the night, I give you our prize draw, and, with six prizes and just three losers, let it never be said that I am ungenerous. For those of you who don't know how it works, my wife is stuffing her sister's cunt with balls for a reason. Each is numbered, and those numbers correspond to the tickets you brave and hopeful girls and boys hold in your sweaty little palms. Melody will draw the six prizes first, starting with the least and working up. But if you don't win a prize, beware! That means you could lose, and tonight we have some very inventive perversions to punish you. So, without further ado . . .'

As he was speaking I'd been watching Melody feeding the little coloured balls into her sister's fanny. With the last in, she casually sucked her fingers, picked up her clipboard and reached up to take the microphone from Morris.

'I'll say this now,' I whispered to Kay, 'I'll eat my cap if the winners aren't friends of Morris's, and the losers aren't all girls and among the prettiest in the club.'

'You think it's fixed?' Kay asked.

'Of course it's fixed!' Penny laughed. 'This is Morris Rathwell, Kay, don't be silly!'

'So you know who's going to win?'

'We know who's going to win the chocolate. Jade and I just gave Mel a lick.'

'Rathwell's wife? You licked her pussy, both of you?'

'No, Penny licked her bum!' Jade laughed. 'Dirty slut!'

She slapped Penny's bottom, a blow immediately returned, and as the two girls began to fight playfully I shook my head in despair. Kay was visibly shocked, but not actually repelled, and it was impossible not to wonder if I could make something of the suggestion later.

'Do you two mind?' Melody's voice rang out suddenly from the speakers.

'Sorry, Mel,' Penny called, waving as she disentangled herself from Jade.

'I should think so too,' Melody answered. 'Amber, if I might?'

'Help yourself,' I called back, knowing it was what Penny would want.

There was a ripple of laughter, then quiet as Rathwell raised his hands.

I'd seen it before, but I was still staring as Melody reached out and pushed her hand into her sister's vagina, to pull out a ball.

'If it's fixed, how does she know which one to pick?' Kay asked in a whisper.

'She doesn't have to,' I answered. 'Think about it, only she gets to see the balls. The whole drawing business is just for show.'

Kay nodded and turned, her eyes fixing firmly on Harmony's naked body. Melody was holding up the ball, and had put the microphone to her mouth. Briefly she consulted her clipboard before calling out.

'For our sixth prize, kindly donated by Scorpion Whips, a fifty-pound shopping voucher! And the winner . . .'

She paused, and called out a name I didn't recognise. A man stepped up, one of those who'd been in the military zone, still with a scarlet stain on his bare buttocks where they showed through his chaps. He took the prize and kissed Melody, every bit as if he had been collecting an award on TV. I half expected him to make a short speech, but he stepped away, leaving Melody to pull another ball from her sister's fanny.

Again the prize went to a man, as did the third. Penny and Jade got the basket of chocolate, as promised, and went to collect it. Melody immediately took me up on my offer, opening their clothes to show off their breasts and sending both to stand to attention at the altar. Second prize went to a girl I didn't recognise, although from the warmth of the kiss she gave Melody it was obvious they were no strangers. Trisha Ellis then took the grand prize, which explained the state of her bottom.

Melody had been pushing her hand in pretty deep, and I knew that there weren't that many balls left. Not that it made much difference, with Melody able to cheat at will, but I was praying she would consider the services of Penny and Jade for a punishment session to be enough, and leave Kay be.

After a lengthy, open-mouthed kiss with Trisha, Melody once more passed the microphone to Morris and went to stand by her sister. I felt my stomach tighten as her hand went back into Harmony's fanny hole, and Morris began to speak.

'And so to our losers. As most of you will know, each loser must choose a punishment from the board, and take it on stage. Each punishment has been selected by one or another of our dominant men and women, who may decline the right to punish if they wish, in which case, the loser goes free. So, Melody?'

Mel pulled out her hand, glanced at the ball and spoke to Morris quietly, to leave me biting my lip as he chuckled and made some equally inaudible remark back before turning to the audience once more.

'Sophie Cherwell,' he called out.

I joined the others in a round of appreciative clapping, although it was hardly surprising Sophie had lost. As one of their closest friends and a born exhibitionist, the whole thing had probably been arranged in advance, including her punishment. Certainly I could be sure that among the punishments on the board would be something from Melody, and it was entirely like the Rathwells to ensure that whatever happened it would make a good display.

That was one down. Again Melody dipped in. Again she drew out a ball and spoke to Morris. This time his grin was positively evil.

'We have . . . Mistress Angelique.'

Across the room a girl looked up from where she was sitting on a man's back as another sucked on the toe of her boot. It was the girl who had driven my cart. She seemed surprised, and pointed at herself as she stood up.

'What, me?'

'Is there another Mistress Angelique?'

'No, but . . .'

'Then it's you.'

'But . . . but, I thought it didn't count for dominas?'

'It counts, girl, rely on it,' Melody called out

'What's the matter, Angel?' another voice rang out. 'You dish it out but you can't take it, that's what!'

Angelique turned, angry, but it was impossible to see who had spoken. I was smiling, thoroughly enjoying the thought of seeing a domina punished, even if she had won the race I'd bet on. She didn't answer, but sat back down, tight-lipped, only to suddenly stand and unleash a torrent of whip strokes across her slave's buttocks. Several people laughed, myself included. That was two down.

I crossed my fingers as Melody dipped again, the last time. With the ball in her hand she glanced at the clipboard. Her eyebrow rose a fraction and she spoke to Morris. My hopes rose as he gave a disinterested nod.

'And our third girl,' he called, 'is . . . Kay.'

191

My heart sank.

'Kay, who is Kay?' Morris asked innocently.

I let out my breath in a long sigh as Kay slowly raised her arm.

'Ah, that Kay, Mistress Amber's new playmate,' Morris announced as every eye in the room turned to look at us. 'How delightful. Well then, up you come, girls. First come, first served! First served, first come!'

He laughed, and stepped away from the board. Kay hadn't moved, and I urged her forward.

'Come on, if you don't hurry you'll miss all the easier punishments.'

'How do you mean?'

'Well, you don't want to end up taking an enema on stage or something, do you?'

'An enema! Shit! They can't do that!'

'They can, believe me, now hurry!'

She hurried, and I followed. The punishments were posted on a blackboard, as if it was a briefing, Rathwell using his swagger stick to point to each as the luckless girls gathered around him There were ten to choose from, ranging from the simple 'spanking, OTK and bare', to 'striptease on stage, into little white panties for a beer enema and expulsion into the panties'. The enema one had been there the last time I'd seen the game played, nearly two years before. Obviously it was the private fetish of some obsessive regular. It was also an absolutely disgusting thing to make a girl do, and it was very hard to imagine anyone actually choosing it.

'I'll take the spanking,' Angelique was saying as we stepped up on to the stage area.

Melody nodded and made a tick on her clipboard, then turned to talk to Sophie.

'So?'

'Caned and fucked,' Sophie said without the slightest hesitation, and I knew it was a set-up, doubtless paid for by one of Rathwell's spanking clients.

'Who gets to dish these out?' Kay asked, nervously scanning the board. 'Our dominants, yes?'

'No, whoever posted them. They're anonymous on purpose, so . . .'

'So I can't pick you to do it?'

'Well, no, not really.'

She turned back to the board, biting her lip as her eyes ran down the selection of painful and degrading punishments. Finally she spoke.

'I can't do this! What if it's some hideous old bloke?'

Her voice was rising in pitch, showing real fear. Melody turned to us.

'Problem, girls?'

'Look, Mel,' I answered. 'Kay can't really take this. She's a novice and . . .'

'She came under your whip, girl. That did not look like a novice thing.'

'That was different. That was me. She can't face the idea of being given to some guy at random.'

'Well, I'm not pulling it, Amber, someone's got to go down –'

'Penny will do it, gladly. Or perhaps Jade?'

'Not Penny, not Jade. There is only one person I'll accept.'

'And if I refuse?'

She merely gave a tut, a single motion of her lips, but it held so much contempt, so much derision that the blood came straight to my face. In my place she would have taken her medicine, and we both knew it.

'OK,' I sighed. 'I'll do it.'

'Cool. Choose mine, yeah? We'll have fun.'

It was the last thing I was going to do, but I had to choose something, and as I turned for the blackboard I could feel my panic rising. With two punishments gone, I was left with eight choices. The enema was out of the question, just too humiliating, just too dirty. The same went for eating a can of beans off the dominant's flesh.

It was meant to tempt, hoping a loser would think she might get to lick the beans off another girl's chest. I knew better. If I picked it I'd be sucking them off some dirty old bastard's cock and balls, or worse. Another definite no was one for anal fisting. It almost certainly had been posted by a gay male dom, who might choose to reject me. If he didn't, I would end up with half his arm up my bottom, looking like a ventriloquist's dummy.

That left me with five to choose from. Melody's was hard to pick out, and I couldn't even be sure if there was more than one, or if it had gone. The first to catch my eye was 'Spanking: bad language style'. It was not likely to be Melody's. She swore like a trooper, and a straightforward spanking was a bit simple for her. It suggested an old-fashioned spanker, probably a man, probably middle-aged or older, hardly ideal, but then a quick OTK from some old buffer was one hell of a lot better than having to expel an enema into my panties. The 'style' meant some sort of ritual, having to stand against the wall with my hands on my head or something. I had no idea what 'bad language style' might be, but I was fairly sure I would be able to take it.

Another which seemed unlikely to be hers was spending the rest of the evening with the handle of a feather duster stuck up my bottom. The duster was propped against the choir stalls, a huge thing with the feathers dyed brilliant pink. Mercifully, the handle was smooth and rounded, so it would be painless going up and in place, but incredibly humiliating. I'd either have to slit my immaculate jodhpurs at the back seam to push up the stick, or go bare from the waist down. In either case I was going to look completely ridiculous, and the Rathwells could be counted on to sneak a picture and post it on the club website. Not only that, but people would be certain to tug it, which would hurt.

The third called for the victim to fill a pint glass with pee, and drink it in front of everyone. It tempted, because there was no contact with the dominant, and it was really no more humiliating than a panties-down spanking. After all, I'd shown my fanny to the slaves I'd peed on earlier, so the only real problem was actually drinking it, or rather, it looked that way. What it didn't say was who got to fill the glass up if I couldn't pee a full pint. Inevitably the answer would be the dominant who had posted it, and that seemed more than likely to be Melody.

The next also seemed to have her touch to it. To be put into harness and saddle as a crawling pony-girl, including a tail up my bum, and ridden, fed and watered. Again, it didn't sound all that bad, although having an audience watch as the plug on the tail was pushed up my bottom hole was pretty strong. It was the 'fed and watered' part I didn't like. Dry oats and tap water was hardly a pleasant combination, there was bound to be enough for a real horse, and Mel would undoubtedly beat me until I had eaten the lot. Worse still, I might not get oats and tap water at all, but something else.

Which left the last, something I might well have put up myself. It was to be a piggy-girl, tied, basted and put on a spit with an apple in her mouth, then roasted. Obviously I wouldn't actually be spit-roasted, but I'd be nude, in tight bondage and slippery with oil, while the 'put on a spit' bit might well prove to be a euphemism for sodomy, public sodomy. That implied the dominant would be male, or just as likely Melody with a strap-on dildo. After all, it was suspiciously close to what Penny and I had done to her.

Just reading them was doing terrible things to me. I could feel the need for submission rising up. I was lost, and could try to make myself choose something that would keep my humiliation to a minimum. Again I ran my eye down them, and again. All the while I was thinking more and more of how Penny had shaved

Melody's head, and how I was held responsible. Pigs don't have hair on their heads at all, not to speak of, ponies have manes. Either animal-play punishment might hide a trick to shave me. Just the thought made me feel sick.

So it was the pee, the duster or the spanking. I know myself, and if I let a duster up my bottom it was more than likely to have been replaced by a cock before the night was over. It made drinking my own pee look tempting, but to drink Melody's would mean utter surrender, and after that anything might happen.

Harmony had been let down, and came to join us.

'Any tips?' I asked.

'For the girls who just had me lick her ass in public? No.'

'Come on, Amber, or do I have to choose for you?' Melody said laughing.

'No, thank you, I've chosen,' I answered. 'I'll be spanked.'

'Yeah, but Angelique's being spanked, and Sophie's taking the cane. Be different, yeah? How about the pig?'

'No, thank you, Melody. I'll take the spanking.'

'You won't like it, Amber, I warn you. You will not like it!'

'I wasn't born yesterday, Mel. The spanking.'

'OK, but I'll catch up with you, Amber Oakley, you just wait.'

I stuck my tongue out at her, already feeling small and girlish, just at the prospect of what was to happen to me. Spanked across somebody's lap, my knickers down, everything on show, probably in tears . . .

I couldn't bear to speak to anybody, but went to sit in the choir stalls, near Angelique, joining the queue of girls to be punished. We shared a sympathetic glance, but said nothing. Sophie was up first, someone who I usually love to see punished, but I felt sympathy for her. It looked like I had reason, too. Her normally bright smile was distinctly nervous, and she was fidgeting badly as the Rathwells arranged the stage for her punishment.

It was soon ready, and Morris stepped forward to call for the dominant. Immediately a man pushed forward from near the bar. Sure enough, it was one of the men who had been at Morris's spanking party, where he had spanked Penny with a shoe, a Mr Judd. He was fifty or so, and very average, a bit flabby maybe, and with his hair slicked back around a bald spot. His sole concession to the dress code was a worn leather jacket, which he held over his shoulder. He also held a cane, a short dragon with a crooked handle, school style, the sting of which it was all too easy to imagine.

I'd expected her to choose something from Melody, and was sure that Judd would have paid quite a bit for the privilege. Melody had put out a whipping stool, over which Sophie had already bent, not waiting to be told. She was at an angle, making sure the audience got a good view of both her bottom and her face as she was beaten. Not just beaten, but beaten and fucked, I reminded myself, fucked by Mr Judd, a thought which added to the sick feeling in my throat. Head down, her blonde hair hung in a curtain around her face, while her army trousers were taut on her rounded bottom, showing her cheeks off beautifully, also her fanny lips. It was a good pose, a wonderful pose, and all the better for knowing that her trousers and the panties – the outline of which showed beneath – would soon be coming down. Unfortunately it was impossible to forget that I myself would soon be in a similar and perhaps yet more undignified position.

Sophie stayed very still, not even moving when he came up to her and began to fondle her bottom, his face split in a smug grin as he stroked and squeezed at her cheeks. He took his time, groping and teasing until a tell-tale patch of wet had appeared in the tight groove of material between her fanny lips. As he saw, he gave a cruel chuckle and pushed a hand under her tummy. Her trousers came loose, and she shut her eyes as his hands went to the waistband, to tug them low, showing soft pink flesh, then the navy-blue colour of a pair of traditional school panties.

Down came the trousers, to the level of her knees, where they were left, stretched taut. Sophie's bottom looked more enticing still in the over-tight school knickers, and my feelings were becoming ever more mixed as he began to feel her again, his fat, sweaty fingers loitering on her panty-clad cheeks as the wet patch over her fanny grew slowly larger.

By the time he decided to pull down her knickers I was beginning to actually want to be dealt with the same way. Not by Judd, but anyone attractive, even Melody, could have had me for spanking then and there. Watching Sophie's school knickers taken down made it worse still, with her lovely rounded bum in full view as Judd peeled them away. His eyes were fixed on what he was revealing as he did it, her deep crease, the rude star-shape of her bumhole, the pouted lips of her fanny, with the hole wet and ready between.

As with her trousers, he left the knickers at knee level, stretched tight. She had been spanked earlier, because there was a distinct pink flush to her bottom flesh, but it had been playful, no more. As Judd flexed the cane, with his eyes still feasting on her bare bottom, I realised that playfulness was the last thing on his mind. To him, her pleasure was irrelevant, she was simply a nicely shaped piece of meat.

He stood back, and tapped the dragon cane on her bottom. I winced, and so did she, her cheeks tightening as the cane was lifted, to spread again, wider, giving a full show of her bumhole, and coming suddenly together as the cane whipped down on her bottom. Sophie cried out, and went into a little dance, jumping up and down on her toes for a second before she managed to recover herself.

It had been a hard blow, on cold flesh, and left a twin set of scarlet tram lines on each chubby cheek, making me wince again. Judd once more brought the cane up, and down, laying another double line across her bottom, and once more setting her dancing. I could see Sophie's muscles starting to work, and could imagine exactly what she was going through, except that for her, it was everything she craved.

Judd laid the third stroke across her bottom, then paused, to adjust the lump at the front of his trousers. It looked like he was hard, or nearly hard, erect over her pain and humiliation, a thought which had me hoping fervently that my punishment would be from a woman. The fourth stroke came down low, catching Sophie's thigh to make her hiss in pain and kick out her hurt leg, then turn back a reproachful look. Judd didn't even acknowledge his mistake, but laid the fifth in harder still, low, to leave a vicious welt right where her buttocks tucked under to meet her thighs. Sophie was left gasping, but given no time to recover. The sixth stroke came in, full across her cheeks, delivered with all his force, to jam her forward as she screamed out her reaction.

It left her gagging and shaking her head, even when she had finished dancing up and down on her toes. Judd was red in the face, his fingers trembling with eagerness as he jerked down his fly, the cane forgotten on the floor. Sophie regained her composure just in time to look back between her spread legs and see not the cane, but his erect cock. An instant later it had been pushed up into her vagina, just stuck unceremoniously up her, and she was being fucked.

He was going furiously, holding her by the hips with his eyes fixed on her caned bottom, and pumping away with manic energy. She was clutching the whipping stool, and gasping, with her hair shaking to the thrusts and the meat of her bottom wobbling in time. It was so hard that the twins had to duck down to hold the stool, Harmony also stroking Sophie's hair to comfort her.

I knew Judd couldn't last, and he didn't. His face was red, with sweat running down over his cheeks and his bald spot glistening in the lights. I could see his cock, the shaft wet with Sophie's juice as it pushed in and out, and when it stopped suddenly and his mouth flew open, I knew he had come. Sure enough, he pulled slowly back, to take hold of his cock and milk out the last of the sperm over Sophie's bottom, even as she reached back to get at her fanny.

She began to masturbate, utterly wanton, apparently indifferent to the hundreds of watching eyes. I had to see, and moved a little way down the bench, to get a proper view of her fanny as she did it, a view both obscene and totally compelling. Mr Judd's sperm was running from the open hole of her vagina, thick and glistening, down to where her fingers rubbed frantically in the open, wet mush of her sex. Her bumhole was winking, and wet too, as were the angry red lines of her cane marks, aglow with the sweat from her beating.

When she came she really screamed, louder by far than she had under punishment, and she kept her fingers on her sex, dabbing and rubbing, dabbing and rubbing, until she was fully finished, only then letting herself go limp over the whipping horse. Morris began to clap, others quickly joining in, most just staring.

Sophie stayed down for a while, and shook her head as she pushed herself up, before turning to the crowd. Her cheeks were flushed and her hair in disarray, but she was smiling, not just happy, but proud, as she accepted her accolade with a little curtsey, before pulling up her panties and trousers, to skip cheerfully over to the choir stalls.

'That was nice,' she announced. 'He's a dirty old bastard, but it was still nice. You're up, Angelique.'

Angelique answered with a formal nod. She stood, to step forward, all poise and pride, her little pointy chin tilted defiantly upward, her back straight, her face showing only contempt. Melody smiled and stood up.

'It's yours?' Angelique demanded, in obvious consternation, all her poise just vanishing.

Melody's smile became broader still. I was right. She'd had two, something complicated, and a simple spanking, doubtless designed to draw Angelique in. That there was history between them it was clear to see, while with my own punishment drawing closer, I felt as much sympathy as pleasure as the unfortunate Mistress stepped uneasily forward.

As calm as ever, Melody sat down on the front rank of the choir stalls and patted her lap. Angelique hesitated, looking seriously worried, and perhaps unsure if she wanted to show her bum or her face to the audience. Melody didn't bother to wait, but reached out, to grip the little domina firmly by the wrist and pull. Angelique resisted, but she had no chance against Melody, and was drawn in, still fighting.

It was a big mistake. Had she been calm, she could have taken the spanking as calmly as her pain threshold allowed. By fighting, she made Mel fight back. So she was dragged over, held hard, kicking and squealing and flailing around with her fists, and forced down over Melody's lap, with her tight little bum stuck high in the air, her legs kicking wildly and her head almost touching the floor boards.

Her struggles became wilder still as Melody prepared her, jerking down the fine black leather trousers to expose a pair of white panties decorated with big pink spots. That had Morris laughing, and me, along with half the people in the hall, but Angelique just fought harder, holding on to the ridiculous knickers for dear life as Mel fought to get them down.

Mel won by twisting the unfortunate Angelique's arms up high, so that the panties were either going to be pulled up, or down. Angelique let go, and down they came. Mel held on easily with one arm and tugged off trousers, boots and all. That left Angelique in pink socks and the silly panties, which were hung on one foot, then off completely, flying high as the first hard smack caught her little bottom. Angelique squealed. Mel caught the panties, to take her victim by the hair and stuff them into the struggling domina's mouth, then set to work.

It was funny, a real brat spanking, with Angelique kicking and struggling as her bottom bounced to hard, purposeful slaps. Everything showed, and to make it worse, she farted several times, drawing laughter from the crowd and setting Melody's expression into disgust as the spanking redoubled in force.

At that the polka-dot panties fell out of Angelique's mouth, and she started to howl, really loud, her dignity utterly lost as she went into the sort of squalling, pathetic tantrum dominant woman so often do when they have to take a dose of their own medicine. That included me, as I was all too aware, with a huge lump rising in my throat as Melody finally slowed and stopped. Angelique got up, dabbing at one eye and rubbing at her reddened cheeks as she returned to the stalls, not even bothering to retrieve her panties. As she sat down she gave me a pained look. Melody beckoned, and I stood.

Morris had taken up the microphone once again, and spoke as I came down on to the stage area.

'A slight change here, as for our third victim we have none other than Mistress Amber, or possibly Obergruppenfuehrer Amber.'

He laughed at his own tasteless joke, gave me a wink, and spoke again.

'Who is to be a given a spanking, bad language style, from . . .'

Again he looked at me and winked.

'. . . from, Mr Protheroe.'

He gave a little satisfied nod towards the audience as my jaw dropped open. Melody laughed and slapped her thigh. Sophie giggled. Protheroe himself appeared, pushing through the crowd, his great flabby body wobbling as he came, his face already red and sweating.

I just stood there, staring at him and thinking of Rathwell's spanking party, how I'd gone down over his knee, how he had humiliated me, and afterwards, when I'd completely lost control...

'Ah, Amber, my dear, how nice to see you again,' he said, chuckling, as he mounted the stage. 'I must say that I am most gratified you chose me. You knew, of course?'

'No!' I answered, outraged by the implications of what he was saying. 'I did not! And what is that?'

It was perfectly obvious what it was. He was holding an enamelled bowl, full of water. Something was floating in it, a perfectly ordinary bar of soap, cheap soap, green with a disgusting fake-floral smell. It had begun to soften in the water, the surface soggy and flaking, making it look truly disgusting. The real question was what he was planning to do with it. Unfortunately, I could guess.

'No,' I stated firmly. 'Not up my fanny, that is not...'

'My dear girl,' he interrupted. 'I wouldn't dream of doing anything so crude. I intend to use it to wash your mouth out.'

'Wash my mouth out?'

'With soap. A traditional part of the punishment, I think, for girls who use bad language.'

Not for me it hadn't been, but of course I'd heard of it being done, and could only stare in horror as he calmly put the bowl down on a stall and turned to Rathwell.

'Might I have a chair, please, Morris?' he said. 'I always feel the audience should have a proper view. Top and tail, so to speak.'

'Sure,' Morris answered, 'but turn her a bit while you do it, yeah? Make sure they see the soap going in, but can get a good view up her cunt if they want.'

Protheroe nodded his understanding, and I was left to wait, shaking and biting my lip, as Harmony ran for a chair. In front of me was the audience, no more than a blur of faces, mostly men, and including men I had shot with paintballs, and peed on. Now they were going to see me spanked, bare bottom spanked, and have my mouth washed out with soap into the bargain.

My vision was already hazy with the gathering tears as Harmony returned, to set the chair up at centre stage, sideways, so that everyone would be able to get a prime view as I was methodically humiliated. The first tear dropped from one eye as Protheroe sat down, and I was crying. I went down anyway, feeling thoroughly broken as I laid myself across his lap, my head to the audience. His legs felt fat and soft, his belly pushed to my side, yet I could still feel the bulge of his penis digging into my flesh. Instinctively I hung my head in submission, but was taken by the hair and pulled up, forced to face hundreds of staring eyes.

'Who's been a bad girl then?' Protheroe drawled, his voice thick with lust and cruelty.

I managed a miserable nod in answer as Melody stepped close with the microphone.

'And what happens to bad girls?' Protheroe asked.

I shook my head.

'Now you do know, don't you?' he insisted.

'They ... they get spanked,' I answered, my voice weak and miserable.

'I didn't hear that very clearly,' he went on.

'They get spanked,' I repeated louder, and I could hear the resentment in my own voice.

'That's better,' he answered, 'and where do they get spanked?'

I knew what he wanted, and that resistance would only have painful consequences.

'On their bottoms.'

'Yes, but a little more detail, I think, don't you?'

'On their bare bottoms.'

'Certainly on their bare bottoms. Now, what else are their bottoms?'

'Um ... rude?'

'No. You know what I mean.'

'I don't, I swear ... Pink? Big? Fat?'

'Yours may be all of those things,' he chuckled, 'as we shall shortly discover, but it is not what I want to hear. Now come along, or I shall have to increase your punishment.'

'I don't know ... I really don't!' I wailed, fresh tears squeezing from my eyes at the ripple of laughter his little show of mental torture was causing. 'Dirty?'

'Well, you would know best about that, although I dare say the rest of us will find out ...'

'You bastard!'

It had just come out, the last of my self-control breaking the way he had twisted my words to imply that I wasn't clean. I was sorry instantly, but he had taken a tight grip on my waist.

'I beg your pardon, Amber? What did you call me?'

'Nothing ... I'm sorry ... I'm really sorry ... Look, just spank me, will you, I can't take this!'

My voice had risen to a squeal as I spoke, high-pitched and frantic, while the tears were streaming down my cheeks, making it hard to speak at all. He merely laughed and went on.

'Well, since you are obviously incapable of taking your punishment like a lady, I shall have to treat you like the impudent, mouthy little brat you are, won't I? All you had to say was the one word, 'naughty'. Now, will you or will Mr Shoe be paying a visit to your bottom instead of Mr Hand? Well?'

'Naughty,' I managed, choking on my tears. 'Bad girls get their naughty bottoms spanked.'

'Good,' he answered, 'that wasn't so very hard, was it? Now, as you are so naughty, and have used a nasty word in front of your elders and betters, do you know what else is to be done to you?'

I nodded miserably again.

'Say it!'

'I am to have my mouth washed out with soap.'

'Exactly. Now come on, again, all of it.'

'I'm to be spanked on my naughty bottom and I'm to have my mouth washed out with soap!' I wailed, really loud.

'Perfect,' Protheroe declared. 'So, Harmony, my dear, if you would be so kind?'

Harmony came over and held out the basin with the slowly dissolving bar of soap in a cloud of white at the bottom. I swallowed, feeling an edge of panic as the smell of cheap scent thickened. He released my waist, tightening his grip in my hair, and reached for the soap bar, bringing it up dripping, with soft white ridges squeezing from between his fingers, and flaking, like rows of maggots.

'Open wide, my dear,' he ordered.

My mouth came open, although my brain was screaming at me to keep it shut. I shut my eyes, though, in pure misery as the slimy soap touched my lip, and then it was being pushed in. A horrible taste filled my mouth, soap and cheap perfume, and it squashed as Protheroe forced the whole bar past my teeth, caking it into my mouth until I was choking and my cheeks were bulging out at the sides. My mouth was wide too, as he rubbed it all in, until he took hold of my jaw and forced it shut, squeezing more soap into my cheeks.

I was pop-eyed, streaming tears, hardly able to breathe, with soap and spittle running from the corners of my mouth. They were laughing at me, thoroughly amused to see me get my come-uppance, and one or two had already begun to call out for my knickers to be taken down. Protheroe gave my jaw a final shove and let go of my head.

'Patience, gentlemen, patience,' he stated. 'Please be assured that they will come down, but all in good time. Now, Amber my dear, you're to hold that in until I've spanked you and you're truly sorry. Now, turn about, and no mess on the floor, or Mr Shoe really will be paying a visit to that naughty bottom.'

He was enjoying himself immensely, his voice full of smug satisfaction. As I began to get up he patted my bottom, then pinched me right under one cheek, nearly making me spit out the revolting mess of squashy soap I was struggling to hold in my mouth. It tasted disgusting, sharp, with a horrible tang of synthetic fruit flavour, and felt worse, slimy, fatty, yet solid at the centre. My expression must have been a picture, and so many of them were laughing, Protheroe included.

'No, my dear,' he chuckled, patting his lap, 'it may not be very nice now, but you will thank me for it later, as we both know. Over you go, then, botty up . . . no, let's have those silly jodhpurs down first, shall we? And your jacket off. Really, you girls do like to dress up, don't you? And so severe, as if you couldn't be touched! I can't think why, when you know it will all be coming off anyway.'

He laughed out loud. My hands had already gone to the button of my jodhpurs, popping it open. I glanced around as I drew down my zip. Morris was watching, Melody, Harmony, Sophie, Angelique, Protheroe and the entire crowd, as I pushed down my immaculate jodhpurs to expose myself, and shrugged off the uniform jacket. It was an extra humiliation, but I was extremely glad that I'd had the sense to put on black silk panties. Not that it gave me any extra modesty, and they'd come down just the same, but I couldn't bear the thought of being laughed at the way Angelique had been.

The crude remarks and whistles of appreciation were little better, and as I once more bent down across

Protheroe's lap and felt the silk stretch taut across my bottom, my humiliation hit a new peak. I began to sob, little, choking gulps around my bulging mouthful of soap, and as he once more took me firmly around my waist, my tears started once more. His other hand found the waistband of my panties and I just gave in, blubbering miserably on to the floor. Again he began to talk.

'Now then, Amber, I think it would do you good for everyone to see these come down, don't you?'

I couldn't speak, and my pathetic attempt to answer him just made soap bubbles come out of my mouth, to send Sophie and Harmony into fits of giggles.

'What a crybaby!' Protheroe chided. 'Oh well, I'm sure she knows that naughty girls' knickers always come down, so down they come!'

They did, jerked down off my bottom with one, hard tug, and I was bare behind. Suddenly I was showing my bare bottom to the crowd, big and pink, no, fat, just as Protheroe had said, a great, wobbling rump, fit only for me to be punished on, to be spanked.

His foot moved, to push my legs apart, and show off my bare fanny, which I knew would be shamefully juicy and open. I was about to be spanked, and I was ready for fucking, and I couldn't help it, it was just too much, as I began to blubber incontinently on to the floor, gasping through my nose, with a froth of bubbles coming out of my mouth.

If he cared about the state I was in, he didn't show it. Instead he finished undressing me, casually pulling off my boots, my socks, my jodhpurs, and at last my panties, to leave me stripped from the waist down, my clothes strewn around me. When he began to pull up my blouse I let him, even helping with my bra, to leave my boobs hanging down, heavy under my chest, quivering with my sobs and gasps.

'Isn't she a fine one?' he said happily, and began to spank me.

It wasn't hard, not at first. It didn't have to be. I was broken already, snivelling miserably across his lap, my legs wide apart, as my bottom slowly warmed to the smacks. I knew what he was doing, warming me so I got turned on instead of trying to hurt me, and I knew what that meant, but felt only gratitude.

I was going to be made to suck his cock, or fucked, or had up the bum. I would do it too, I couldn't help myself, sucking penis like any other little slut, or bum up and fanny wide, offering myself for him to exercise his cock inside me. Only it wouldn't be that way. He didn't have the energy. So he'd lie down, and I'd mount him, not fucked, but fucking, in control, to make my fate more humiliating still, as I brought myself off on his cock with my smacked bottom to the audience.

As my bum cheeks began to bounce to yet firmer slaps I was shaking my head, trying to break away from the feelings being spanked and humiliated bring me. It was no good, I was over a man's knee, my bare bottom jumping to the slaps, my fanny on full, rude show, wet and willing. I was really going to do it . . .

The last of my pretension disappeared in a flurry of kicking legs and I had begun to push up my bottom. My cheeks were so hot, really glowing, with every spank making them hotter still. I wanted more, and I got it, my bottom brought up to a blistering, aching heat, which had gone straight to my fanny. My legs were wide, my bum up, both holes on show, in blatant display of my femininity and the female response of my body. It was right for me to be bare from the waist down, right to be spanked until I howled, right to have my mouth stuffed full of soap.

Protheroe was putting everything into my spanking, delivering great stinging slaps, which sent the tears and bits of soap spraying from my face, and sweat from my bottom as my cheeks bounced, faster and faster, wobbling crazily, at last to climax in a furious crescendo. He stopped. It was over. I'd been spanked, punished, and now I was going to be made to say thank-you.

It left me weak, and gasping, exhausted, limp, with my hair hanging down into the disgusting pool of soap and spittle beneath me on the floor. The bar, or what was left of it, slid slowly from between my lips, to splash in among the rest. Protheroe was panting too, and made no move to get me off his lap. I obliged, eager for my own degradation as I slipped to the floor, falling heavily on my hot bottom before crawling up on to my knees.

The front of his trousers was bulging with cock. I didn't wait to be told or further humiliated. Grabbing at his fly, I tugged it smartly down and groped inside, freeing his erection straight into my mouth. My fingers went back between my thighs as I started to suck, and I was masturbating, rubbing at my sodden fanny as I tugged his cock into my open mouth. Nothing else mattered. I was lost to the world, everything concentrated on my hot bum cheeks and the fat, soapy cock in my mouth, sucking the man who had had the courage to spank my bottom, to pull off my panties and spank me bare, bare and kicking with my bumhole on show, my mouth washed out with soap, my bottom spanked, spanked like a mouthy little brat, spanked bare, spanked ...

I came, and so did he. Even as my muscles locked a great gout of sperm erupted into my mouth, taking me totally by surprise. As he came, so he grabbed my head, forcing me down to fill my windpipe with bulbous, slimy penis head. My throat was full of soap and sperm and cock, choking me, making it impossible to breathe. I didn't care. I was coming, with my gullet in the same furious contractions as my fanny and bumhole, milking sperm down my neck, filling me, pumping into me as the dizziness rose up in my head.

I very nearly fainted, but jerked back at the last second, gasping in air, then choking. A great froth of soapy, spermy bubbles exploded from my nose, and more from around my mouth, all over Protheroe's lap. I went into a coughing fit, blind with tears as I bent double, muck spraying out of my mouth and dribbling from my nose, all over the floor, as Harmony came to help, pulling me upright and slapping me on the back.

I must have looked as if I'd got rabies. There were bubbles coming out of my nose and mouth, my eyes were red from crying, my cheeks tear-streaked. I was gasping for breath too, my throat still half clogged with soap and sperm, then spitting frantically to try to clear my airway and get the filthy stuff out of my mouth.

It came, suddenly, all over the floor, in an explosion of thick white muck which splattered out on to the tiles as if I'd been sick. Harmony moved quickly away, but Protheroe just laughed. I hung my head, defeated, broken, spanked until I'd willingly sucked a dirty old man's cock. I was stripped from the waist down, my bottom fat and rosy behind me, my boobs swinging bare, the mess I'd had put in my mouth now dribbling out, my fanny open and ready for a good fucking.

I got it. As I sank down in exhaustion, something wet and mushy was slapped between my buttocks: the soap. Strong, male hands took hold of my hips, and a cock was shoved rudely up my fanny. I didn't even look back. I knew it was Rathwell. Who else would fuck me from behind, so casually?

Besides, Mel and Harmony would have stopped anyone else, so it was Morris, enjoying my fanny as Protheroe had enjoyed my mouth. I let him, and when Melody took hold of my head and pulled my face into her sex I licked, willing and obedient, to make her come under my tongue. I was being fucked, in public, and I just didn't care. I could hardly even take it in, just lap up Melody's rich, musky pussy juice as Morris jammed his cock in and out of my fanny.

Melody came, and Harmony took her place immediately, even as Morris began to tickle my bumhole with a soapy finger. A moment later he had invaded me, creating a stinging pain as my anus was forced and soap pushed up into the hole. I thought he was going to bugger me, which would truly have been the final degradation, but he contented himself with fingering me. I was given another degradation anyway, Harmony coming under my tongue, to be replaced by Annabelle, her fanny pushed into my face, with the tattoo declaring her Melody's property right in front of my eyes as I licked. I was licking Mel's slave as I was fucked by her husband, and her laughter was ringing in my head as it was done.

Annabelle came in moments, and as she did, Morris pulled out. Immediately he stuck his cock into my mouth, adding the taste of my own sex to the mixture of sperm, and pussy, and soap. Behind me, my vacant fanny closed with a long fart, and then there was more sperm in my mouth. He'd come and it was done.

I collapsed as they let go of me, a mess of soap and sperm and tears, laid gasping on the floor, with fluid running from every orifice. The crowd was cheering and clapping, calling out Morris's name in appreciation, and Melody's, and Harmony's, but mostly mine. Finally I managed to look up, my vision still hazy with tears, but clearing slowly, to show those who had been witness to my utter degradation. There, in the front row, grinning like a demented Cheshire cat, was Gavin Bulmer.

Seven

They had set me up. OK, nobody had known I would pick Mr Protheroe, or how carried away I would get, but basically, they had set me up. Morris, Melody, Harmony, even Penny and Jade, had all played their part. Even Kay had helped, largely unwittingly.

Melody had been going to offer me the chance of taking Kay's place, pretty certain that I would accept after what had happened in Sniper's Alley. Unfortunately, I'd pre-empted her, and instead of choosing the spanking from her, which had been put there for that very purpose, I had gone for Protheroe, and suffered the consequences. The result – if Bulmer hadn't believed I liked to find an excuse for submissive sex before, he certainly did now.

That was Rathwell's explanation anyway, and if I didn't believe it, then it was impossible to be absolutely certain. That was the trouble with Rathwell. He always seemed to arrange things so that it was impossible to be absolutely certain. It didn't quite make sense either, because the spanking from Melody still looked like a trap for Mistress Angelique, but again, it was impossible to be absolutely certain.

What was certain was that it had worked. Afterwards, Bulmer had been teasing me mercilessly until I'd agreed to another bet. So it was on, and while I'd had the sense not to agree terms at the club, I had agreed to make an offer by the next weekend. Afterwards, Bulmer had been absolutely crowing.

Oddly enough, it was not the uppermost thought in my mind when I woke up the next day. That was of Kay, and whether I had pushed her too far by masturbating her in front of other people. Yet she was next to me, fast asleep, cuddled on to my arm, her mop of tawny gold hair spread over the pillow and my skin, her thumb in her mouth. She looked so content, so peaceful, that it was hard to imagine her as angry with me about anything. After all, to suck her thumb, such a vulnerable, childish gesture, surely she had to feel secure with me?

Truth comes out with drink. I'd been sober, after three small beers spread across several hours. Penny had not, nor Jade, nor Kay. So we had come back together, the three of them drunk and giggling, teasing me for the display I'd made, Penny trying to comfort me by explaining Rathwell's argument. She had succeeded, at least sufficiently to make me put the three of them in a line on my bed and spank them with a bath brush, naked.

Inevitably that had been the trigger for sex, but when we had all finally given in to our tiredness, Penny had taken Jade to bed and Kay had come in with me. That was the final intimacy, not the fact that it was Penny's face I'd been sat on when I came, not even that the others had made her kiss my bumhole and that she had done it with enthusiasm. Sure, it would have been very hurtful indeed to make Jade sleep alone, and four in bed was simply too many, but Kay and Jade could perfectly well have slept together. They hadn't, and it had been as much Penny's choice as mine.

I was still wondering whether we ought to talk about it or just let matters take their course when Penny's head appeared around the door. She looked sleepy, but smiled as she saw Kay was cuddled up to me, and if she felt any jealousy at all, it was not evident in her face. All she did was ask if we wanted coffee.

So that was it. I seemed to have swapped girlfriends. There was a sneaking suspicion that I'd been manipulated, or at least manoeuvred, but I didn't mind. There was a dependency about Kay which Penny had never had. Love, yes, but never dependency.

Sunday was very lazy, which was just as well, as I badly needed to think, and to try to come to terms with what had been done to me, or rather, with the way I had behaved. After all, there had been no real coercion, and by the end I'd been frankly showing off.

It still took me most of the week to acknowledge that I needed to take advantage of the situation. On the Friday night I sat down with a pad of lined paper and a bottle of Rioja. By the time the last of the bottle was in my glass I had three sheets covered in scribbles. Even with a bottle of wine inside me what I had written was terrifying, but a large glass of brandy dealt with that and I finished it off before going to bed to work off my drunken emotions with a finger.

Looking at the plan in the cold light of morning, with a mild hangover, I could hardly believe I had written it. Emotionally, it was insanity. Logically, it made sense. I emailed it to Penny for her opinion, praying that she would find some glaring fault with it and present an alternative which left me with my pride intact as well as the land. She thought it was great, and sent it back more clearly set out and annotated, also with an added detail that left me staring open-mouthed at the screen.

Penny's suggestion was that I go to Fat Jeff for training. Unfortunately, it made perfect sense. He was the best of the Razorback boys and there was no doubt I could learn a lot. He could also be guaranteed to report back every detail to Bulmer, in glowing colour.

I didn't really want to do it, especially after I'd shot him in the bottom, but a long phone conversation with

Penny ended with her persuading me that the benefit was worth the cost, even if that cost turned out to be yet another mouthful of sperm. She also pointed out that I would find life a lot easier if I acknowledged my need to submit from time to time, something she had never said before. When I put the phone down I was left once more thinking about my sexuality, but I couldn't accept what she had said. It was far easier to tell myself I was going to do it because I had to, or at the least because it made sense to do so in order to get what I wanted.

As was now normal, they were paintballing at the weekend. I was hopeful Fat Jeff would be there, and sure enough a stroll down along the Old Siding found him with the rest, unmistakable even in his combats and protective headgear. Bulmer was harder to identify, but I sought him out first, to take him aside and explain the idea of the game while his friends sniggered behind their hands and made coarse remarks. Only the ones who had played Sniper's Alley actually knew what I'd done, or at least I hoped that was the case, but I was red in the face with embarrassment by the time I'd finished.

Just going up to speak to Fat Jeff was out of the question, and I didn't want Bulmer to see anyway, so I went to work on the hedge for the Old Siding, and waited for my moment. It came sooner than I expected, Jeff detaching himself from the others to speak to me, presumably reasoning that any woman who would suck his cock once might do so again. It was pointless to dissemble, so I made my suggestion straight out, and found myself booked to see him the next day. From the grin on his face as he turned away, there was no question as to what he was expecting.

His address was in south London, a big house converted into flats with a security lock on the front door but no buzzer, so that he had to come down and let me in. He was in combats, which came as no great surprise, but also smelt strongly of aftershave. The stairs were steep, and as I followed him up my face was level with his more than ample behind, bringing back the image of how I had shot him. His flat was at the top.

'Don't be scared of the clowns,' he said as he turned the key in the lock. 'I use the passage as my shooting gallery.'

'Clowns?' I asked.

'Yeah, clowns. Never trust a guy who paints up his face so you can't recognise him and goes around in weird clothes . . .'

I just laughed. I couldn't help it. He understood immediately, and looked hurt.

'There's nothing weird about military uniform, Amber,' he said, absolutely serious. 'Remember who keeps you safe.'

I shrugged, not wanting to argue, or point out the difference between the genuine armed forces and his pseudo-military fantasies.

'Clowns are weird,' he insisted. 'There's this guy, a serial killer . . .'

'I don't want to know, thank you.'

'Suit yourself. Anyway, he used to be a clown and now he paints clowns in prison, really freaky stuff. I copied one for a target.'

He had pushed the door open, and there, sure enough, were the clowns. It was quite a shock, but mainly because I'd been expecting paintings, not mannequins, and if I'd never considered clowns as disturbing before, I could see that he did. There were three, two on the ground in postures of aggression, the third hung from the ceiling as if leaping at whoever had just come in at the door.

Both those on the floor were in harlequinade, one yellow and black, and the other white and a vivid magenta. The same colours were reflected in their faces, both made up into grotesque parodies of the smiling children's entertainers I was used to. The leaping one was worse, his baggy suit striped red and white, the face white, with his eyes picked out in vivid blue, and the painted mouth a great red slash, curved up in a travesty of a smile. All three held wooden knives and bunches of balloons, or rather, the tattered remains of balloons.

I cast a slightly worried glance at Fat Jeff, but he did nothing peculiar, and I followed him into his living room. It was normal, to my relief, or at least relatively so, a complete mess, and decorated with posters showing various military goings-on and a framed copy of a Second World War aircraft recognition chart.

'Get your butt down,' he said, giving me a momentary twinge of apprehension before I realised he was only offering me a seat.

He pushed a pile of magazines off a chair and I sat down.

'I was just fixing a sandwich, want some?'

'I'm all right, thank you.'

He disappeared, to return moments later with a triple-decker sandwich in one hand and a four-pack of beer in the other. Pulling free a can, he passed it to me. I hesitated, but took it.

'So you want to learn how to beat Gav, yeah?' he said, lowering himself into a chair.

'Yes,' I answered. 'Did he explain the game?'

'Sure, sounds great. We really get to fuck you, yeah?'

'If you can catch us.'

'Oh, we'll catch you.'

He paused to open a beer and take a bite from his sandwich, all the while his eyes never leaving my body. When he had swallowed, he spoke again.

'Gav's a good team player, and a good shot. What he doesn't have is patience. He doesn't prepare properly. Like in Sniper's Alley ... Yeah, sure, we drew, but everybody knows I got more shots on target.'

'That's true. You should have won.'

He grinned, presumably thinking I was flattering him when actually it was only that I'd have had to suck one cock instead of four.

'Yeah, dead right I should,' he said. 'So, yeah, if you're going to get past Gav, your best tactic is to wind him up. Get him riled, or horny, whatever, so he's in a hurry. Then get round the back, and you're in.'

He stopped to attack his sandwich and drink, his forehead creased in thought, then spoke again.'

'Another thing you've got to do is to learn to work as a team. Last time, that big fat blonde with the knockers and the little bird with the nice arse, they used teamwork, so they cut down their hits by maybe thirty, forty per cent. Now if you'd all worked like that, you might have made it.'

I nodded, knowing he was right, but it was not so easy.

'There's a problem there,' I stated. 'Melody and Harmony, the black twins, yes?'

'How could I forget? Fucking gorgeous! I love a bit of black skirt.'

'Well, there's a lot of rivalry between us, going back years, since just after I left school, as it goes. If I wanted to . . . Well, it's not easy to get them to work as a team.'

I'd been going to say that the price would probably be to have my head shaved, but that was not an idea I wanted to put in his head.

'Yeah,' he answered. 'It gets like that in Razorback. Still, you can get some of them together, your girlfriend, that little bird with knockers bigger than her head, the tall one, that bird with the red hair . . .'

'Some, maybe,' I admitted. 'OK, so teamwork.'

He paused, looking thoughtful as he munched on his sandwich, crammed more into his mouth before he had swallowed, then followed it with a great gulp of beer.

'Got it,' he announced. 'You've got to get to old man Henry's ground, get an apple, and get back to Razorback. So, you let the two black tarts go their way, along with any others you can't work with. That draws some of the hunters on. Your team comes behind, slower, so your mates can draw attention away from you. OK, they may get caught, but then they love all that stuff, don't they? You get round the back –'

'What about Bulmer? He's sure to single me out.'

'That's why you've got to get round the back. You need a foxhole – you know, a dugout you can hide in while we pass. Gav doesn't think that way. Gav thinks action, all the time. He'll think you're ahead, and reckon on catching you on the way back, when you'll be a lot more tired than he is. So he'll move on, and all the time, you're behind, just strolling. He gets all the way to Henry's, and some of our mates are there, a good way down the path. He goes to them, you come up behind, grab the apple and fuck off back, as fast as you cane. Odds are he won't even see you. If he does, I reckon you take him over the distance, starkers, and him with all his gear. He's not too fit, is Gavin, bit of a beer gut on him and all.'

Again he stopped, to push the last of the sandwich into his mouth and wash it down with beer, then adjust his huge belly over the top of his trousers. I could see the sense in what he was saying. It wasn't perfect, but it might work. If I could count on his help in the field, then it almost certainly would work. He opened a fresh can of beer before speaking again.

'So, what do you girls get out of it, all this spanking and stuff, like at the club? I mean, it's easy to see how the bloke gets off, with a nice bare arse to play with, but not the girl. Doesn't it hurt?'

'It's supposed to hurt, but it's a pleasant pain, an erotic pain, not like a headache or something.'

'Yeah?'

I always get defensive when I talk about kinky sex with someone who doesn't understand, and I began to explain, as best I could, about endorphins, and sexual submission, and how humiliation could be erotic, which was where he stopped me.

'So like when that bloke Protheroe made you say all that kinky stuff before he spanked you?'

'Yes, exactly. It made me cry, but . . . well, you saw.'

'Fucking right! That was nice.'

He nodded, grinning, and adjusted his cock in his trousers. It was coming.

'There's a problem here, isn't there?' he drawled. 'I know the plan.'

'Yes.' I sighed. 'I was wondering when you'd get round to that. Couldn't you be nice, for once, and just –'

'Look at it another way,' he interrupted. 'You've got my advice, and that's for nothing. If you want my help, you've got to be a bit more friendly. Think about it. I can say I saw you run past, or whatever it takes. I'm one of Gav's best mates, he'll believe me.'

'I admit that thought had occurred to me.'

'Yeah, makes sense. And you shot me in the arse. You've got to admit, I deserve a big sorry for that.'

'Sorry, I got a bit carried away.'

'That's not the sort of sorry I mean, Amber. More like – "I'm really sorry, Jeff, would it make up if I gave you a blow-job" – sorry. Yeah?'

I shrugged, too chagrined to speak. He went on.

'Anyway, you're well up for it. I mean, if you can do that bloke Protheroe.'

I nodded and blew out my breath, knowing it was pointless trying to explain.

'OK,' I sighed, 'you can spank me, on the bare, and I'll . . . I'll give you a suck.'

'That's nice, yeah,' he answered, 'but I want my own kick.'

'Which is? There are limits, Jeff.'

'Yeah?'

'Yes. No sodomy, no watersports, nothing which draws blood . . .'

'Hey, hey, be cool, babe! All I want is a bit of clown action.'

'Clown action?'

'Yeah, I really fancy that.'

'I'm sure you do, but what does it involve?'

'Nothing heavy, just dressing up, bit of girlie stuff, you know.'

'I'm not sure I do. Anyway, I thought you hated clowns?'

'Male clowns, sure. Girlie clowns are different. Take a look in my bedroom.'

He followed me as I rose, steering me towards the door with a pat on my bottom. I got another pat as we crossed the passage into another room, and this time his hand stayed in place, gently kneading one cheek as I surveyed his bedroom. It was a mess, and smelt of unwashed male. Clothes, magazines and all sorts of detritus was scattered over the floor, the magazines military, pornographic or both, one on his bed picturing a buxom blonde with her combats trousers pushed down at the back to show off her full bottom. Other than the garish make-up, she looked pretty much like me. There was other mess too, empty coffee cups, pizza boxes, bits of electronic gadgetry; and then there were the clowns.

As he'd implied, they were female. All but one were paintings, pretty girls in eroticised clown costume, either tight enough to show every detail of their bodies, including exaggeratedly fleshy buttocks, breasts and fannies, or cut to leave the rude bits bare. The exception was the real shock, a life-size plastic doll, complete with gaping mouth, spread legs, absurdly large breasts, face paint and a clown outfit.

It was truly, utterly disgusting.

For me, anyway, Jeff was grinning, entirely oblivious to my reaction as he pawed my bottom, his fat fingers now well down and cupping my cheeks. He gave me a smack, quite hard this time.

'Strip off, then. I'll paint you up. I reckon Mandy's gear will fit you.'

Mandy's 'gear' was another harlequinade suit, but in pink and green, and also tight. Just looking at it put a lump in my throat. Not only would it leave my breasts bare, sticking out of two holes in the front, but the lower part was designed like suspender tights, with two broad straps at either side and nothing in between, so that my bum, belly and, inevitably, my fanny would be left bare, just as were the obscene blow-up doll's. The sleeves were puffed at the wrists, with long ribbons hanging down, also at the ankles. There was also a ridiculous hat, with a double crown rising to points, each with a big, tin bell at the end. Lastly there were high heels, one pink, one green. Dressed up in it, I was going to look not only incredibly rude, but completely ridiculous.

I had begun to undress, mechanically peeling off my clothes as Jeff watched, grinning and occasionally reaching out to touch me, as if finding it hard to believe I was real. When my bra came off he made a strange gurgling noise in his throat and a comment about bazookas, then took hold of my breasts. I shut my eyes, letting him feel, with his hands underneath to support them and his thumbs on my nipples, rubbing. In no time both my nipples had popped out, drawing a fresh gurgle from him.

He let go, and it was time for my panties to come off. Down they came, my back to him, only for a hand to close on my bottom, low, and a finger to slip forward, and up, into my vagina with embarrassing ease.

'Fucking soaking!' he swore, and began to finger-fuck me.

I was still clutching my lowered panties, and clung on tight as he opened my fanny up, his fat finger sliding in and out until he had room to fit in a second, and a third. I was gasping, and wondering if he'd fuck me then and there, and so spare me the humiliation of having to show off to him in the ludicrous and indecent clown outfit. He didn't, but pulled out, to suck my juice from his fingers as I stepped out of my panties.

He had sat down, and was squeezing his crotch, so I was forced to get the clown costume off the blow-up doll, which I could not bear to think of by the name he had given it, or any other. It was not easy, the lycra tight on the plastic, and the huge breasts making it harder still. Finally I realised what to do and found the valve in the horrid thing's ankle. It deflated with a long farting noise and I quickly had the costume off.

I was already feeling humiliated, and it grew quickly stronger as I struggled to squeeze my body into the suit. It had been tight on the doll and was far too small for me, but it stretched, and I managed, pulling it up my legs and feeding my arms into the sleeves with great difficulty.

In it, I felt more naked than when I'd been starkers. Bare boobs, bare bum and bare fanny, I was concealing nothing, yet my sexual characteristics had been picked out in a way that left me looking both vulgar and foolish. The heels made it worse, tightening my legs and bottom, and leaving me tottering and unsteady. The hat added the final, excruciating touch, and I was a clown, or nearly.

'Right,' he said, 'make-up. Face first, then titties, then bum and cunt. Sit on the bed.'

I sat. He went to a drawer to take out a large box, which proved to be full of body paints, brushes, sponges and eye-liner pencils. Placing it on the floor, he pulled up a stool. I held still, trying to keep back my emotions as he took a pencil and began to draw on my face. There was a mirror opposite me, making me wonder if he made up his own face. It certainly showed mine, all too clearly, as he drew a pair of huge, pouting lips around my mouth. Ovals followed, around my eyes, before he began to apply white paint to my face.

Slowly I became unrecognisable as it was daubed on, first the white, then vivid scarlet for my lips and a circle on each cheek. My eyes were done blue, not unlike the hideous leaping clown in the passage, with black lowlights. With those done, he leant back to admire his work.

'Let's do a tear. I love the way you cry when you get your bottom spanked.'

Again he dipped his brush into the blue paint, to draw in a large, solitary tear on my left cheek. It made an absurd contrast with the grotesque, pouting mouth, yet still seemed entirely appropriate. He nodded his approval.

'Titties,' he announced happily. 'Stick them out.'

I put my hands behind my head and stuck out my chest. His eyes were almost popping out of his head as he began to work on my boobs. I like to think my nipples are a nice size, in proportion to my breasts. Obviously he didn't, drawing rings around them at least three times the size of my areolae. The rest of my boobs he painted the same glaring white as my face, along with my neck. With both boobs glossy and pale, like two big pillows on my chest, he switched to scarlet once more, to paint on the false nipples, and add crimson shading to make the straining buds even more prominent than they already were.

'Like fucking melons!' he said. 'Stand up, then, turn around, and stick out your arse. Hold your cheeks open, so I can do your chocolate starfish first.'

'Couldn't you leave that?'

'No way! Come on, spread 'em. I'll do the back of your cunt at the same time, I think.'

Reluctantly, I put my hands back, to spread my bottom, showing every intimate detail from about a foot.

'Nice cunt, very neat,' he commented. 'Nice arsehole too. Now let's see, red for your cunt, and a nice dirty brown for your arsehole. Here goes.'

The brush touched my anus, painting a circle, adding points to create a star shape, then filling in the middle, the brush tip going well up my hole. He laughed. I shut my eyes, struggling to hold in the tears. He knew full well what he was doing to me, he'd seen it with Protheroe. It didn't stop him, it just made him worse, chuckling to himself as he dabbed more brown body paint on to the sensitive flesh of my bumhole.

'There we are, nice and shitty,' he declared. 'What a laugh!'

I swallowed the huge lump in my throat, desperate not to start crying, but unable to thinking of anything except the state I was in, and most of all, the way my bottom hole would look painted brown. He was still chuckling, as he changed brushes and set to work on my fanny, daubing scarlet paint on to the rear of my lips.

'That's the colour a girl's cunt ought to be,' he said as he added a final stroke to where the knotted flesh of my inner lips protruded from between the outer. 'Now your bum. Red patches, I think, like you've been spanked, and they'll match your face cheeks, so you'll have a face like a smacked arse, and an arse like a smacked face!'

He laughed again, a coarse, braying sound, louder than before. A pencil jabbed at one bottom cheek and he had begun to do it, drawing circles on my bottom, at the crests of my cheeks, with the fingers of his free hand pinched tight in my flesh to stop it wobbling.

'I love a woman's bottom,' he said suddenly. 'I mean, a real woman, little waist, and then this great big arse, like a fucking pumpkin or something! Hold still. There we are. Now the paint.'

All I could manage was a resigned sigh as he began to smooth the white body paint on to my bare bottom. I had my head hung, full of humiliation, knowing how I looked, what I was, a girl clown, like the silly, smutty pictures on his wall, stripped and painted up for male entertainment, male amusement.

My bottom and hips and thighs were painted white, the crests of my cheeks filled in with scarlet, the sponge and brushes stroking my skin, to bring me slowly up to full arousal whether I liked it or not. By the time he'd finished I was wondering if I was juicing enough to leak, and if I did, whether it would make red streaks down my legs. I didn't look. I didn't dare, in case I was, but kept my hands on my knees as I tried not to think of the view I was giving him of my painted anus and sex. At least he had finished and gave me my next order.

'Stand up, turn around, let's see your cunt from the front ... get it, cunt from the front, it rhymes!'

He laughed again. As I stood straight I felt the greasepaint squash out between my buttocks, doubtless making the brown patch around my anus yet more obscene. I turned, opened my legs and stuck out my tummy, another silly pose, but one I did not want to give him the chance to tell me to get into, and so make more demeaning comments. Again he took a pencil, to draw a line around my sex lips, in a love-heart shape. White came next, coated on to my lower belly and the front of my thighs, finally my hands, to finish what remained of my exposed flesh.

I held my pose as the final humiliating detail was added, the V between my thighs and my pubic hair and mound painted scarlet, to transform my neat little fanny into a great, obscene, painted mouth ... No, there was only one word harsh enough for how he had made me look – cunt.

When he at last stood up he was grinning like an idiot.

'You are a fucking picture! Hey, can I take one?'

'No!'

'Oh, come on. I've got the new Ixus. I'll send you copies, hi-res, large format ...'

'I don't want a picture of me looking like this, Jeff!'

'No? Why not? I have never seen anything so fuckable, not ever!'

He ran from the room, ignoring my squeak of protest, and returning moments later with a tiny silver camera.

I threw my hands in the air in despair. The camera flashed.

'Cute! Now pose a bit. Stick those big titties out!'

I put my hands on my hips, determined to remonstrate. Again the camera flashed.

'That's my girl, stick 'em right up! Fucking nice!'

'Jeff! I am not posing for you! Now put it away.'

'Aw, come on, Amber, just a few, I don't get much, and . . .'

He was whining. I hate men who whine.

'Oh, OK!'

'That's the way! Titties out then.'

I stuck my breasts out, in a deliberately vulgar pose, hoping he would have the decency to sense my revulsion and stop.

'Fucking gorgeous! You are such a babe! Now turn, show us your bum.'

I sighed, resigning myself utterly as I followed his instruction, posing to look back coquettishly over my shoulder with my bottom stuck well out.

'Nice! Arse and tit and face all at once. Stay still.'

I held the pose as he moved to photograph me from different angles, realising too late that from behind the dirty brown smudge around my bumhole would be blatantly obvious. I stood up, but it was too late. I'd been photographed, not just as a girl clown, but a girl clown with a dirty bottom.

'Great,' Jeff said happily. 'I'll take some more while you dance for me.'

'Dance? I'm not really very good . . .'

'Come on, all girls know how to dance sexy, pole dancing and that . . .'

'I've never been a pole dancer, or anything of the sort!'

'It's easy. I'll show you.'

'No, no, really,' I said quickly, appalled at the thought of him attempting to give a display of erotic dancing. 'Just tell me what you want me to do, and I'll try my best.'

'OK. It's easy. Just give me plenty of bum and tit and cunt. Wiggle your arse around, make your titties bounce, and swing them down, so they hang under your chest. Cock your legs up too, like sumo wrestlers do as they warm up, so your cunt shows, and keep your arse out so I can see your brown eye. Most of all, keep moving, keep it all jiggling.'

I knew what he meant. I didn't want to, but I knew. He'd got me, worse than Protheroe, and I could feel the tears starting in my eyes as I went into the sort of prancing, bottom-wiggling dance he wanted, my bells jingling, my ribbons flying out around me. He photographed me, over and over as I twisted my body into one lewd pose after another, until finally he could hold off no longer and pulled his cock free of his fly. He began to wank as his eyes feasted on the obscene, clownish display I was providing for him to get off on, his cock growing quickly to erection, his voice hoarse with passion when he next spoke.

'There, you're a fucking natural. Go on, wiggle that big ass, babe! Fucking nice!'

I turned, shaking my painted bottom right in his face even as the tears streamed down my cheeks. It wasn't just my bum that was wobbling either. My boobs were bouncing crazily, flopping from side to side and slapping on my chest, with my real nipples shamefully stiff under the absurd red ones.

'Yeah, nice!' he crowed. 'I said you could do it. Go on, make that big arse move for me! Do the shimmy! Yeah! Stick it out more, show us your dirty hole!'

I did, my bottom stuck right out, my brown painted anus on show, also the scarlet cunt he had painted, painted to fuck. I wiggled closer, my bum right in his lap, his cock brushing my cheeks, between them, touching my bumhole, touching my fanny, and up, deep in my cunt as I sat myself down in his lap. I grabbed my breasts, squeezing, the greasepaint slippery under my fingers, my scarlet nipples taut and slimy.

Suddenly he was pushing me forward. I went down, on to the bed, his cock slipping from my body. I got in doggy, which just, somehow, seemed the right pose to fuck a clown, and up went his cock once more, deep in my sloppy scarlet cunt. I tried to brace myself as his fat belly jammed into my bottom, only to have him snatch at my arms. I grunted as my face went down into the bed, and again as my wrists were twisted up into the small of my back. I tried to pull away, but my ribbons had already been tugged together, and the next moment my arms were bound tight together. It was his turn to grunt as he took hold of them and began to fuck me again.

He had me hard, grunting and panting with effort as he fucked my bottom, with his great fat gut slapping on my buttocks, until he mounted me, his hand digging under my chest to grab my slippery boobs, his cock slipping out of my hole, and jammed hard back in as he came, right up me, sperm exploding from my cunt mouth as he spent himself deep inside me.

'Fuck!' he swore. 'Fucking wasted! I didn't even get it in your mouth. Oh, what the fuck . . .'

I was grabbed by the hair, my head twisted round, and his cock stuck in my mouth. I sucked, swallowing down the mixture of sperm and greasepaint, and still sucking as his cock deflated slowly in my mouth and his breathing returned to normal. At last he let out a long sigh.

'Shame,' he panted. 'I meant to come in your clown face and rub it in, still . . .'

He let go of my hair, dropping me to the bed. I rolled on to my side, looking round to find him with the camera in one hand, even as his fingers touched between my legs. The camera flashed as three fingers were pushed rudely up my fanny. It flashed again as they were pulled free, sloppy with sperm. The next showed the sperm being wiped in my face, then smeared across my features, to rub in the greasepaint, the last, his filthy hand stuck in my mouth.

With my face utterly soiled, his hand went back between my thighs, and to my horror I realised that he was going to masturbate me. Sure enough, he began to manipulate my fanny lips and clitoris, bringing me up quickly, until I was gasping, and all the while photographing me in my filthy, degraded ecstasy. His come was still dribbling out of my fanny, and down over his fingers. He began to rub it in, over my sex, smearing me with sperm and greasepaint right on my clitty and I was coming, screaming out my orgasm, cursing him, begging him to rub harder, cursing him again, calling him a bastard and an abuser and a freak, even as I rubbed my sopping, painted clown cunt on his hand in wanton, abandoned ecstasy . . .

When it was over I collapsed completely, to lie still and utterly spent, both physically and emotionally. He went to get the last beer, and drank it, sat beside me on the bed, only then untying me. I got up, my knees weak, unable to find words to describe my feelings, but staring blankly at the mess. The bed was filthy with greasepaint where my boobs had been rubbing and my face pushed down. So was he, his trousers and the part of his shirt where his belly had pushed against my bottom absolutely filthy, his hands and sleeves smeared where he'd been groping my boobs. Even the camera was covered in greasepaint.

It took me three hours and three baths to clean up properly, but when I left I had the solemn promise of his assistance. I didn't believe it for a moment.

The game was to be called Pig Sticking. The rules were straightforward and boiled down to piggy-girls being chased along the Strip. If we got caught, we got stuck, not with a real stick, or course, but with a cock, anyway they liked. It had to work, but it was impossible to rid myself of the conviction that I was doing it not to get the Strip, but to make Gavin Bulmer my Master.

Men were easy to get. In fact the only difficulty was limiting the numbers. The girls were not so easy. Even some of those who had cheerfully joined in to play Sniper's Alley were completely horrified at the idea, and in a couple of cases husbands put their foot down. I badly needed more women than men, and kept trying, until, with myself, I had Penny, Jade, Melody, Harmony, Annabelle, Sophie, Vicky, and Kay.

Kay was a bit of a problem, because while she had gained enormously in confidence since allowing me to masturbate her at Rathwell's club, I still wasn't sure if she could handle the game. Nor did I want her to. I was in love with her and, after a day and a night of almost continuous sex, she had asked to move in with me. The last thing I wanted was her getting put to the use of people like Bulmer and Fat Jeff, or even my own male friends. Yet she wanted to join in, and I was equally keen not to make my dominance over her extend beyond sex.

It took even more effort to keep the number of men down, but we finally agreed on Bulmer himself, Fat Jeff, Jeff Jones, Henry, Morris, Marcus and Anderson. That made nine girls to seven men, which was just going to have to do. I rang round on the Friday night, checking everyone was OK, and arranged for the girls to come to my house, and the men to go to the Razorback HQ.

All nine of us had gathered by eleven-thirty, and we took a light lunch together, discussing tactics. My utter surrender at the club proved more valuable than I had expected, with even Melody as keen as any to help me. Each woman knew she was likely to be fucked for my sake, and probably put through some heavy humiliation into the bargain, and each accepted it, making me feel proud, and very nervous.

We got ready in the kitchen, stripping and helping each other with the simple transformation to piggy-girls. I did most of the work, painting on the gum arabic to the others' faces and lower backs, and letting them hold on the noses and snouts I had made. That left me last, and I had to wait until Penny was ready before she could do me.

It felt odd, looking into her little piggy face and knowing I was going to be the same. So many times I'd done it to other girls, but never myself, and even as she painted on the gum I could feel my emotions change, from dominance to submission, from the desire to be in charge to that of being exposed, humiliated, punished. I was shaking so hard it made it difficult for her, but I couldn't stop myself.

With the snout in place over my nose and the little curly pig's tail bobbing over my bottom, my feelings became stronger still, almost overwhelming. The others were delighted, but Penny most of all, and I wondered if she had secretly wanted to see me as a piggy-girl for all the years we had been together.

Modesty was pointless, and we trooped out together, stark naked but for our trainers, walking up the Old Siding with me at the back, like a sow with eight girl piglets, each with her curly tail bobbing over her bare bottom. It was a wonderful sight, and even distracted me for a moment, until we reached the Razorback site.

All the men were there, in combats save for Anderson and Henry as usual, and the Rathwells' lawyer, Ira Edelberg. Apart from the lawyer, each had one or more hanks of rope at his belt, some had nets, others bulging pockets which I knew would contain all sorts of devices, both of restraint and outright cruelty. Yet those were the rules, catch as catch can, with our stop words to be used only if we were in more pain than we could take.

I knew Jeff had told Bulmer and Jeff Jones about the clown episode as soon as I saw them. I could see it in their faces, and while Jeff gave me a knowing wink the moment he could get away with it, I still didn't believe he was really on my side.

With Michael Scott disinclined to have Ginny fucked and possibly buggered by strange men, we had Ira Edelberg to oversee the legal details, along with Henry and Fat Jeff to act as witnesses. Edelberg was a dry, elderly man who seemed entirely unphased by having nine naked girls dressed as pigs around him. He was also meticulous, insisting that Bulmer acknowledge the validity of the contract verbally as well as in writing, and making him repeat his first, scribbled signature.

I had decided that putting the Old Siding up as part of the deal would make me look too eager, and held back, hoping that Bulmer would therefore assume I was content to lose and take whatever he had in mind for me with my 'excuse' intact. He certainly seemed cocky enough, barely glancing at the contracts before signing.

The formalities over, it was time to go. Just as before Sniper's Alley, I felt sick and shaky, with my stomach fluttering and a big lump in my throat. We had to get to Henry's, collect our apple, and get back with it. For three of them I would be the prime target, really the only target. If caught, I could fight but they'd work together, and I'd have no chance of escape. Then I'd be bound, molested, made to suck their cocks, fucked, maybe even sodomised if they got out of control. It didn't bear thinking about.

Ira had agreed to referee, and he kept glancing at his watch, making me more and more nervous. I needed to pee, but didn't dare, for fear of losing precious seconds but was going to anyway, when he called for our attention. One o'clock was the start, and he raised his hand as we padded across to the start of the Strip. Kay took my hand and squeezed it, then Ira's arm came down and we ran.

Vicky ducked down to lift a squat white and blue package from among the leaves and took off down the path like a sprinter, vanishing in moments, with the twins and Annabelle close behind. The rest of us followed, in a group, aware that we had just five minutes to do what was needed. As Jeff had explained, I had to get behind the hunters. That meant concealing myself, and well.

As soon as I was out of sight I ran ahead, as fast as I could, counting the seconds in my head. Two minutes gone, I pushed in among the bushes, to where a stand of ferns edged the Strip as it fell to a railway cutting, and in under the low boughs of a holly, wincing at the prickles. Underneath the tree was a rotting door, half covered in spiky, brown leaves, many reduced to skeletons. I tugged it up, to reveal the hole I had dug during the week, and slipped down into it, brushing away the traces of my passing.

The dank smell of earth and mouldering leaves assailed my nostrils, and I winced as I settled into the wet mud at the bottom of the hole. It had rained since I'd dug it, filling it with an inch of slimy mud and water. Forced to lie flat, my hair was in the cold, dirty water. I was earnestly wishing I'd dug it deeper, but closed the door carefully above me anyway, and lay still, listening.

I'd timed it carefully. There were two minutes to wait before the men started, no more. It seemed like an eternity, lying in the darkness, with only weak light filtering in from a few gaps around the door, with the chilly water seeping slowly in between my bottom cheeks to wet my bumhole and fanny. Then it came, Bulmer's whistle as Ira sent them off. My heart began to pound immediately. If Fat Jeff had betrayed me, they would be looking for a foxhole. If they found it I would be the first caught, probably to be given a quick fucking, then tied and left, maybe in the hole, or hung from a tree, buried in holly leaves . . .

Fighting down rising panic, I forced myself to lie still and listen. Voices came a moment later – Anderson's lazy, aristocratic drawl, Fat Jeff's squeaky piping – then footsteps, boots squelching in the mud of the path, coming towards me, closer, just feet away, and straight past my hiding place. I let my breath out in a long sigh, only to catch it abruptly as more footsteps sounded, drew close, and passed. Voices sounded again, from beyond where I was: Bulmer, Marcus answering him, then Jeff Jones. That put all three Razorback boys beyond my position. Still I waited, forcing myself to count off a full five minutes, before cautiously pushing up the door.

I half expected to find Fat Jeff and Bulmer waiting for me. Neither was, nor anyone else. I climbed out of the foxhole, to brush leaves and thick, black mud from my body. Feeling slightly foolish, I daubed some of the mud on my face, the way several of the men had done in an effort to break up their outline, only to realise that as I was nude it made little difference. A pig is a pig, so I squatted down by the hole and scooped out two good handfuls, which I plastered to my tummy and smeared up over my breasts. As the cold, squashy mess touched my nipples they popped out, actually a lovely sensation, making me want to wiggle my bottom in the mud and holly leaves as I began to get a clearer idea of the pleasures of being a naked piggy-girl.

It was no time for masturbation and I got up. A few smears of mud on my legs, bum and back completed my impromptu camouflage, and I set off, this time direct to the path, where I stood, listening. There was silence, then voices from a good way ahead, male and urgent, female and alarmed, seriously alarmed, then male again, triumphant, and squeals. Someone had been caught.

I moved forward, cautiously, alert to every noise, ducking down again and again to hide myself in the foliage. Voices sounded again, a girlish giggle, a cruel laugh, Morris Rathwell's, then another voice, Marcus. I crossed my fingers as I moved closer, praying it wasn't Kay they'd caught.

It wasn't, it was Jade. She had been tied up, with her knees pulled up to her chin and her hands bound to her calves to lock them in place. She lay on her side, plump pink bottom stuck out towards me, her fanny and anus on open show, and ready for fucking.

It was going to happen, too, lesbian or not. Morris was squatted down by her head, feeding his cock in and out of her mouth. Marcus knelt by her too, fondling one big breast where it squashed out to the side by her raised knees. She was sucking willingly enough, her nipples were hard, and her sex juicy, so I knew she could take it well enough. The sight had my stomach tightening anyway, not because of what was happening to her, but because I knew it could have been me, and still might.

Knowing I could not afford to pass them, I waited, crouched down among thick foliage. They were quick, Rathwell pulling out to briefly stick his cock into her fanny, a gesture of conquest really, then come across her buttocks. By then Marcus had his cock in her mouth, but pulled it out to ejaculate in her face.

Captures were to be marked with bright blue dye. They painted Jade's boobs blue to add to her humiliation, and left her tied on the ground. I counted to a hundred and moved forward, to kiss Jade and check that her bonds weren't too tight, then on.

None of the others had been caught so easily, and the sounds I heard were well ahead. I knew Henry had set up a table well on to his land, with cold beer and sandwiches to tempt them, but I was not at all sure it would work. Certainly when Bulmer got to the end and found I wasn't there, he wasn't going to hang around. So my timing had to be perfect, and I'd lost ground waiting for Morris and Marcus to finish using Jade. I began to go faster, worried that they might turn back before I caught up. I began to jog, peering ahead to watch for Morris and Marcus, towards a large puddle where the two tracks crossed . . .

. . . and I was falling, my legs tangled in something, pitching forward, into the puddle, going down face first into the dirty water, saving my face but not my breasts, dirty water splashing into my eyes and mouth, as my thighs were jerked hard together and the bushes to either side of me erupted. I twisted, frantically, clutching at the noose around my thighs, but too late, as Fat Jeff's body sprawled across mine, crushing me back into the mud and water and knocking the breath from my body. I lashed out, hitting his leg, and kicked as my ankles were grabbed, drawing a cry of pain and a curse from someone else, not Fat Jeff, Bulmer.

'Bitch!' he spat, and my hair had been grabbed and my face forced under the surface of the puddle.

I went crazy, kicking and thrashing and twisting my body, but I could do nothing, with Fat Jeff's weight on my back, one arm trapped under his leg, my head held hard down in the water. They had me and I should have given in, but I didn't care. I couldn't think, I was in a state of utter panic, struggling by pure instinct, unable to breathe, unable to see, terrified and furious at the same time. For an instant I managed to get my face above water, only to have it forced hard down, filling my open mouth with soil and leaves. Hands gripped my ankles. I kicked with all my strength. Bulmer cursed as my shoe caught him. Something was twisted hard around my ankles and pulled – rope – and my legs were together, splashing pathetically in the mud and water, even as Fat Jeff trapped my other arm. Abruptly my head was jerked up, free of the water. I spat out my mouthful of soil, and immediately I was gasping for air, unable to speak, with my eyes shut behind clotted mud, and vile-tasting water dribbling from the holes in my piggy snout down into my mouth. That broke me, being allowed to breathe, and my wrists had been tied before I could recover, and hauled together in the small of my back.

'Got her!' Bulmer declared triumphantly as I went limp in defeat.

'Sweet and easy!' Jeff Jones added as he let go of my hair.

'Here, let me help,' Fat Jeff laughed as he pushed a handkerchief into my face to wipe the mud from my eyes. 'And now you've learnt rule number one, never trust the enemy!'

I didn't need telling.

They hogtied me, lashing my ankles, tying my hands behind my back, and pulling the two together. More rope was wrapped tight around my thighs, closing my knees, and a last twist used to fasten my wrists around my waist. The handkerchief Fat Jeff had used to wipe my face was forced into my mouth and tied off behind my head. Utterly helpless, I was lifted on to a net and wrapped in it, then hoisted high and held up by Bulmer and Fat Jeff as Jeff Jones threw a rope across a branch and tied it off. Fat Jeff took a moment to adjust my breasts, leaving them hanging down through the mesh, a sight all three of them found hilarious, and I was left dangling there.

It had been simple, a noose hidden beneath the surface of a puddle where the tracks intersected, plenty of camouflage, plenty of extra rope, and three against one. So I was caught, and would hang in my bonds until they came back, to be used sexually at their convenience.

I was so exhausted mentally that when the pressure in my bladder grew strong I simply wet myself, watching as my urine dribbled down into the puddle beneath me. I would have soiled myself as easily, with little more feeling.

It must have been an hour before I saw anyone else. First was Vicky, at a run, pausing only to kiss me on the lips and stroke my cheek in sympathy, before dashing on as voices and the thud of boots sounded behind her. She had her apple, and I knew she'd done it, with no men between me and the Razorback ground. That lifted my spirits, but I was in pain, and felt the most pathetic gratitude when Jeff Jones appeared a few moments later.

He stopped and began to play with one of my dangling breasts. I shook my head, trying to make myself understood through my gag, but he just gave me a weasel-like grin went on, now teasing both my nipples. As I felt them start to grow I knew it was going to happen again, and that there was nothing I could do about it.

More people appeared, a little cavalcade of triumphant men and sorry-looking girls. They had caught all six others. The three smallest, Kay, Penny and Sophie, were on halters, with their hands tied behind their backs, fixed together in a coffle with Henry holding them. Each bare bottom bore a splash of blue dye. Annabelle had her ankles and wrists tied, and had been slung over Morris's shoulder, with her trim bottom high and wide and the protruding lips of her fanny painted blue to mark her capture. Harmony had been hobbled as well as having her wrists bound, and Marcus had her on a short lead. Melody had obviously put up the best fight, as they'd had to hogtie her as they had me, and put her in a net, which Fat Jeff and Bulmer had slung from a newly cut hazel pole. Both twins had their snouts painted blue.

'Number seven!' Marcus said as he reached me. 'Oh dearie me, what a sight!'

'And she's pissed herself,' Jeff Jones added. 'Look.'

There were still drops of pee caught where it had dribbled down through my pubic hair. Morris flicked them away with a switch he had cut, something he'd obviously put to use already to judge from the thin red lines decorating Annabelle's bottom.

'Is that a full house then?' Anderson asked as he appeared behind the others.

'No,' Jeff answered, still playing with my tits, 'not the tall one, Vicky. She's covered herself in lard, and when I got her around the waist she bit me!'

'That's pigs for you,' Anderson said casually, 'vicious blighters. My girlfriend, by the way.'

'She got away then?' Henry asked.

'I couldn't catch her,' Jeff admitted. 'Not that I tried too hard. She's not the one that matters.'

He grinned at Bulmer. Bulmer grinned back.

'Eight out of nine then,' Anderson went on, 'including Jade. Seven of us, so that's one each and one over.'

'This one we all fuck,' Bulmer said, and slid a finger up into the crease of my fanny.

I felt my body jerk to the sudden touch on my clitoris, and a spurt of pee shot out, down Bulmer's arm. He made a disgusted sound. Jeff Jones laughed.

'Let's draw lots for the rest,' Fat Jeff said gleefully.

'No, we can fuck who we like,' Bulmer answered as he moved on past me.

They began to argue as they carried on down the path, discussing the best way to get the most out of us, and completely ignoring the wriggling Melody slung in the net between them. Anderson and Jeff Jones stayed back to release me. I had to be helped down and have the circulation massaged back into my legs and arms. My gag was removed but my wrists left tied, and the spare rope used to make a halter, which was tied around my neck. Even Anderson, for all his care and sympathy, was clearly aroused by having me helpless, and took the opportunity to stroke my hard nipples and squeeze my bottom. Jeff Jones fondled me openly, even slipping a finger between my buttocks to tickle my anus.

I let them play, surrendered to my fate and with no wish to hurry whatever Bulmer had in mind for me. Already he had suggested I be made a general plaything, and I was sure that would be the least of it. When they had had their fun, Anderson took my halter and I was led back towards the Razorback Ground. I'd come less than halfway, a pretty comprehensive failure at the Pig Sticking game, and now I was about to pay the price, and get stuck.

At the Razorback Ground the men were standing around drinking beer and comparing notes. The seven captured girls hung in nets from the base of the pylon, like so many chrysalises. Their hands were still tied behind their backs, but they had been rolled up, so that their fannies were poking out through the mesh and could be used without them having to be untied, while each snouted face protruded from the neck of the net, ready for cock-sucking duty. The rude position left their bumholes showing too, six anal stars, pink or pale brown, and no less available, which made my own give an uneasy twinge. The exception was Vicky, sat by the captured pigs, calmly munching her apple and reaching out occasionally to make Penny's tail bounce or stroke the bits of flesh sticking out through the mesh.

Jeff had my net, and he and Anderson were going to string me up with the others, when Bulmer and Fat Jeff walked over, each with a beer in his hand and a gloating expression on his face.

'Not just yet, guys,' Bulmer said. 'We haven't marked her, and we wouldn't want to break the rules, would we?'

'Yeah, right,' Jeff Jones answered, pulling his dye pen from a pocket. 'So, her tits, her cunt?'

'We can do better than that,' Fat Jeff answered. 'Stick your arse out, Amber.'

'Not a clown, please, Jeff,' I managed.

'No, not a clown,' he answered, ducking down to apply his own dye pen to my out-thrust bottom, 'a blue-arsed baboon!'

He gave a crow of laughter, echoed immediately by both Bulmer and Jeff Jones, even Anderson suppressing a snigger behind his hand. I just sighed and held my rude position. They closed in on me, Anderson alone standing back, but watching just the same. My bottom was painted blue, even the hole, my fanny lips too and my face, my snout and cheeks coloured up, to leave me no longer a sweet little piggy-girl, but a baboon-girl, looking as lewd as I did ridiculous.

I was put in the net nonetheless, rolled up like the others, with my fat blue baboon's bottom sticking out of the mesh in fleshy bulges, and hung up beside Kay but lower, with her bottom almost in my face. Her fanny and anus were easily available through the holes, and so were mine. I could smell her sex too, and tell she was aroused, physically, but it was impossible to see her eyes.

'Are you all right?' I managed as the men returned to the others.

'I . . . I don't know,' she managed. 'I . . . I want it, but I'm scared . . . I'm not sure, Amber. You?'

'I can take it,' I sighed. 'Like at the club . . . Don't mind what I do, Kay.'

'I won't,' she promised, and went silent at a sudden peel of laughter from the men.

They began to disperse, Bulmer and Jeff Jones going into the HQ building, Morris and Marcus following them, Fat Jeff to the store. Anderson walked towards us.

'The Razorback boys want to compete for who gets who,' he stated, 'or rather, for who gets to actually have full sex with who. I've also suggested that Ira be allowed to compete, making eight girls for eight men, and meaning you're not put out for general use at the end.'

'Thank you, Anderson.'

'My pleasure.'

He stepped away. Bulmer was already coming back, a paintball gun in his hand. Morris and Marcus appeared, tugging one of the big floor mats used for demonstrations between them. Fat Jeff brought a target out, a board with a picture of a charging soldier on it, with a set of concentric circles in the middle.

All we could do was hang there and watch as our fates were decided. They set up the range and quickly worked out rules, three shots each, and Vicky to judge any disputes. Bulmer went up first, and grouped the scarlet splashes of his paintballs neatly, two in the bull, one an inch outside. It was good, and I felt my fanny tighten at the thought of becoming his plaything, his property really.

He gave the gun to Henry, who did well, but not so well, and my stomach knotted tighter still. Morris followed, and made a complete hash of it. Ira was worse still. Jeff Jones did better than the others, but still less well than Bulmer, as did Marcus, and I was left with two to shoot, and the chances of Bulmer having me rising high. It had always been a chance, but now I was facing it, and I found myself shaking. I was going to melt, I knew it, if he chose me, and do something, really stupid, something really obscene. I was on the edge of panic as Fat Jeff stepped up to the line, brought up the gun, and planted three perfect shots into the bull.

I nearly wet myself with relief, only to be hit by a great wash of shame as I realised that I actually wanted Fat Jeff to take me. Then I did do it, pee spurting out in a little fountain from my fanny, to tinkle on to the ground, then slow, to trickle down into my hole and between my cheeks, wetting my anus and dripping from beneath me. I shut my eyes in pure shame, but quickly opened them as Anderson had taken the gun. He raised, aimed and fired, three quick shots, all in the bull.

He gave a complacent nod and walked forward. I knew he'd pick me if he won, but as he and Vicky and Fat Jeff ducked down, he was shaking his head. It was Fat Jeff who stood up first to walk towards us, rubbing his podgy hands and beaming. I was still hoping he'd pick me, to spare me the ignominy of being fucked by Bulmer, for all the humiliation of being done by him in front of others, but he paused only to slip a finger into the wet cavity of my fanny, and moved on, to Melody. I cursed, wriggling in my bonds, feeling frustrated, impotent and deeply rude, but not enough to call for him and beg, not quite.

Mel's eyes went wide with shock as she realised it was to be her. She was going to speak, but all that came out was an indignant yelp as he reached up to tug loose the slip knot. She landed hard on her bottom in the dirt. Then she did speak, calling him a string of names, which he ignored as he lifted her on to his back as if she had been a sack of potatoes. She was dumped once again, on the training mat, and he set to work, pulling out his cock and stroking it as he began to fondle her. He took his time, stroking her breasts and feet, her bottom and thighs, tickling her bumhole and fingering her fanny, until his cock was a rigid bar on his hand, and she had begun to juice despite herself. Up it went, the thick, pale shaft of his penis pushed in between the smooth, chocolate-brown lips of her fanny, and in, deep up her vagina. He propped his great belly on her hips as he began to fuck her, a truly obscene sight, but she was soon sighing, then moaning, her pleasure rising until she had begun to move her bottom on the intruding penis. That was when he came, pulling out to jerk at his cock and send a long streamer of thick, white sperm out across her buttocks and hip. Done, he rocked back on his heels, panting, his come left, cream on brown across her lovely skin, one piece hanging from a strand of net over her open bottom.

'Make me come, you fat bastard!' she hissed.

Jeff moved forward again, to rub his still hard cock between her buttocks, catching the strand of sperm, to smear it over the richly coloured dimple of her anus, then to her clitoris. He started to rub and she sighed in pleasure, her eyes closing, only to open in abrupt consternation as he stopped.

'For goodness' sake, man, wank her off,' Morris called. 'Can't you see the state she's in?'

'I have a better idea,' Jeff said and leant down, to lift her, stagger a few paces and put her down in the mud.

'We put them all there, yeah?' he said. 'In a pile, and when we're done, they can make each other come. How about it?'

'Nice one, Jeff,' Bulmer called.

Not one man objected, and Anderson's mouth was curved up into a smile as he came over to us. Morris alone went to Melody, but when he reached her he simply squatted down by her head and pulled his cock out for her to suck. Bulmer followed Anderson, speaking as they reached me.

'So who're you going to choose, mate?' Bulmer demanded. 'Amber, or her little tart?'

Anderson lifted an eyebrow in distaste. I let out a sob, knowing that if Anderson chose me, Bulmer would take Kay. It was more than I could bear. Anderson had already reached out, to stroke my hair.

'No, not me,' I managed. 'Take Kay, Anderson, please. That or nothing. Kay, what do you want, tell me?'

Kay didn't answer, but the look which passed between us said everything. She was like me, more than I could ever have suspected. Then her eyes turned to Anderson, full of apprehension, but also lust, and she nodded. He returned a polite smile and lifted her, easily, as his hand reached up for her knot.

Loose, Kay was carried gently to the mat and laid down. He took her head, stroking her hair to soothe her as he pulled out his big, beautiful cock. Her lips came wide without prompting, and she was sucking on him, his cock growing in her mouth as he petted her. It was still hard to watch, to see my new girlfriend sucking cock, even my closest male friend's cock. Not that I could take my eyes away, but only stare, as he grew hard, then urgent, and came, full down her throat. Her eyes popped as her mouth filled with come, but she swallowed bravely, taking it all down, and sucking him until he was satisfied. He thanked her as he pulled free, lifted her, and set her down beside Melody. Bulmer gave a satisfied nod and began to fondle my bottom as he spoke.

'I'll have Amber, as she's made so much effort to get herself into this position, but I want to go last, yeah?'

Nobody protested, and as his fingers moved to the crease of my bottom, I could only manage a resigned groan. Marcus stepped forward, looking thoroughly pleased with himself. He walked to Annabelle, kissed her, and spent a moment to bring her nipples to erection, and moved on. Harmony was beside Annabelle, and he slapped her bottom, then spent a moment examining Jade's huge breasts, as if he were selecting watermelons. I thought he would take her, but he moved to Sophie, slapped her bottom, then to Penny, kissed her as he had Annabelle, and casually pushed a finger up her bumhole. She hadn't been expecting it, and she squeaked, but she must have been ready, because she was moaning in pleasure within moments. Marcus was smiling as he took his finger out and fed it to her, Penny's face setting in bliss as she sucked. She was ready, but he moved back, to plant a resounding slap on Harmony's bottom and reach for the knot.

I knew he would have preferred Melody, to let him take his revenge on the woman who had stolen so much of his girlfriend's affection. So did Harmony, and her face was set in sullen consternation as he untied her. He tried to take her weight but dropped her, and was forced to drag her to the mat in her net, leaving her muddier than ever. Melody it might not have been, but there was still an element of revenge, and he put her face down, kneeling awkwardly with her bottom high, and began to spank her where the bulges of rich brown flesh showed through the mesh of the net. He had freed his cock, and wanked as he punished her, until he was hard and her bottom had taken on a rich, purple tint. He took her like that, from the rear, fucking her as he held on to the net and her bound wrists, pulling out at the last second to come in the deep, moist crease between her buttocks. Finished, he lifted her and dumped her unceremoniously on her sister.

Jeff Jones had already come over to us, and was fondling Jade's breasts. Unlike Marcus, he made a quick choice, unfastening her, and showing surprising strength as he heaved her over his shoulder. Mainly lesbian she might have been, but she was highly aroused, eager for his cock as he fed it into her mouth, and sucking with real relish to get him hard, and inside her. He didn't disappoint, quickly erect, then up her, to pump solidly into her and come in her hole and across the fleshy, pouted lips of her fat little fanny.

He paused a moment, wiped his cock on her leg and lifted her into his arms. The other girls were close, Melody and Harmony already kissing, Kay squirming gently where she lay in the mud. Jeff ignored them, walking past, and to where the row of oil barrels stood beside the fence. Jade squealed as she realised what was to be done to her, but she was ignored, Jeff grinning evilly as he lowered her, wriggling in her net. Her bottom met the surface and the expression on her face turned from panic to utter disgust. Then her fanny was in it, and her whole bottom, oil sloshing out around the drum as the level rose. Still she struggled, futiley, as she was forced into the barrel, to her waist, her fat breasts going under, her neck, and at last her face, set in furious consternation for one last instant before her head was pushed under, and held down, Jeff laughing in manic glee as bubbles rose through the filthy oil. It was seconds only, then he pulled her up, spitting oil, her lovely hair black and filthy, the revolting mess running down her face and down her cleavage as the level settled.

She could do nothing, and Jeff simply walked away, leaving her in the barrel. Vicky and Anderson crossed quickly to her, but it was Vicky who lifted Jade from the barrel as Anderson spoke to Jeff in a sharp whisper. That might have broken it and saved me, but Jade made no complaint, just holding on to Vicky as she was lifted with the oil running down their naked bodies.

Henry had paused, but came over to us as he saw that Jade was all right. His choice was immediate, Annabelle. I wasn't surprised, she was lovely, and an ex-domina, just his style, while it was very seldom that Melody allowed anyone else to play with her, bar Morris and Harmony. For all his age, he carried her easily, his sheer bulk making up for the years. His body wasn't the only thing about him that was large, and Annabelle's face was a picture as he freed his huge cock and offered it to her mouth. She took it, her face set in misery, but sucking eagerly enough. He came hard slowly, his cock growing from her lips as she struggled to keep it in, until he could masturbate into her mouth. I thought he would come, but it was not enough, and he pulled out, gripping the net which held her to turn her around and push his cock into her hole. I could see her tattoo, the message declaring her Melody's slave clear above my godfather's huge cock, a sight as satisfying as being made to lick her had been humiliating. When Henry came, he added a final, dirty touch, and did it over the tattoo, before dumping her with her soiled fanny right in front of Melody's face as Morris rose to take his turn.

Morris had been hard in his wife's mouth for some time, and was nursing his erection as he walked across to the pylon. Penny knew it would be her, and could only wait, hanging in a net, which had been drawn tighter than most, so that bits of her stuck out through the mesh, including her piggy tail. Morris tugged it playfully as he closed with her, then reach for the knot, pulling it casually open to let her fall into the mud with a squashy sound. She squeaked, but as he lifted her, upside down, her mouth was already searching for his cock.

She was put on her side on the mat, fucked briefly, then buggered. He really used her too, dipping his cock in the sopping hole of her fanny again and again, and using the juice he pulled out to lubricate her bumhole, until she was loose enough to get up, first his head, then his whole cock, pushed up bit by bit as she gasped and shivered. Even buggering her wasn't enough for him. He kept it in for a while, holding her cheeks wide so that we could see his cock shaft sliding in and out, until she was slimy and open. Then it came out, and into her mouth. She was made to suck, but only for a moment, then back it went up her sloppy bottom hole, for a few hard pumps, then once more out, and into her mouth. Again and again he did the same, bumhole to mouth, bumhole to mouth, until she was shaking with emotion, reduced to a state of utter wantonness, her mouth agape for more, her bumhole an open red cavity, each leaking fluid as the other was used. He must have done it a dozen times before he chose to come, Penny sucking with desperate need on his dirty penis as he fucked her mouth. At the last second he pulled out, and came in her face, filling one eye and splashing her hair before his cock was popped back in her mouth to be sucked clean and finally wiped on her cheek. As he stood, she began to beg to be made to come, but he merely laughed.

She was dumped with the others, on top of Jade. Ira Edelberg had been waiting shyly all the time, and came over to us as Jade took mercy on Penny and wriggled into licking position. He alone asked for help, Bulmer assisting him in lowering Sophie to the ground. He was also alone in releasing his pig from the netting, and in asking her for her favour. Sophie accepted, I think to his surprise, and she was kind in return, kneeling to suck him hard, and squatting over him to lower herself on to his cock, despite her bound hands. Mounted, she bounced happily away, until he came inside her, then crawled to the others, burying her face in Melody's sex, ever helpful and obedient.

That left me, and as Bulmer took me in his arms and tugged my rope free, my mind was swimming with images of the others' dirty, submissive behaviour. Even Kay had done it, and I knew she was like me at heart, which made it so much easier as I was laid down on the mat and Bulmer's penis pushed into my mouth. I sucked immediately, my resistance gone, as submissive as any of the others, just one more grovelling little slut turned on to dirty, humiliating sex.

'I knew it!' he cried laughing. 'You little tart! You fucking love it, don't you?'

He twisted his hand into my hair, still laughing as he fucked my head, feeding his now solid cock in and out of the ludicrous baboon mouth they had painted on me. I could barely move, but I managed, straining my knees around to crawl up into a doggy position for what I knew was coming next, only of course I wouldn't be fucked like a bitch, not even like the pig I'd made myself, but like a grotesque parody of pig and baboon, my tail waving in the air, my fat blue bottom upended, my wet blue cunt available for cock. He got the message immediately, pulling out of my mouth and moving behind me. A moment later I had been filled, his cock sliding cleanly up into my sopping, ready hole. He took my bound wrists and began to fuck me, hard, short thrusts, his front slapping against my bottom. I was lost, moaning and wriggling to make my nipples rub on my legs, my head still full of the dirty images of my friends, Kay sucking on Anderson's cock, Annabelle's tattoo covered in sperm, Jade in the oil barrel, Penny . . .

'Do it . . .' I gasped, 'treat me like Penny was treated, like . . .'

He laughed. I didn't need to say more. His cock slid from my hole, which closed with a loud fart.

'Yeah, Jeff said you hated it,' he drawled, and the fat, round head of his cock pushed to my bumhole.

It had been so long since I'd been buggered, so very long. Even with Anderson the feelings were so strong I often had to be tied first, maybe spanked too. Now it wasn't Anderson, it was Gavin Bulmer, and as I let my anal ring go slack and felt the dirty little hole start to gape around his cock head, my mouth came open in a long, despairing scream. He just laughed at me, and pushed. My anus gaped wider, stretching to the pressure, lubricated with the juice from my own fanny, sweat and mud, and it was in, suddenly, the mouth of my rectum filling with bloated cock head.

I was being buggered, in public, in front of my friends, in front of my girlfriend, by Gavin Bulmer, a man I thought of myself as so far above, and now he had his cock up my bottom, filling my straining anus, pushing into my already full rectum. He eased back, and pushed again. More cock went up, my bottom now sloppy, as Penny's had been, exactly as Penny's had been. His hands locked in the netting at my hips and he pulled himself in, pushing the breath from my body as another two inches of penis was jammed into my gaping bottom hole. He was nearly all in, but still he pushed, his pubic hair tickling between my open bum cheeks. One more shove and his ball sack met my empty fanny and I knew he was all the way in, right up me, my fat, baboon's bottom stuck full of cock.

He began to move inside me, buggering me, each push making me grunt and puff out air. My bumhole began to make rude squelching noises as he drew himself in and out, faster and faster, only to stop, suddenly. I thought he'd come. I hoped he'd come, somewhere deep in my mind, where a rational spark still lingered. Far more, I was praying that he would really do it, and as he began to ease his cock from my bumhole, I knew he would.

My mouth came open even as his cock came free, in wanton, dirty surrender, not just willing, but eager for the disgusting joke he was about to play on me. He took me by the hair, shuffled round, thrust out his cock, and in it went, full into my mouth, the taste of my own bottom filling my senses as I began to suck. He took moments, just enough to really let what I was doing sink into my befuddled senses. Then he was out, behind me again. His rounded cock head pressed to my sloppy, gaping anus, and up it went, filling my rectum once again, and it was back to the breathlessness and the squelching noises of my buggery.

Three times he repeated his dirty trick, until my head was spinning with reaction and my mouth running dirty saliva as his cock was pushed back up my bottom. He kept it there, deep up, and once more I thought he was going to come, only to feel my body shoved forward on the mat. Someone laughed, and my body moved again. I struggled, trying to look back as I was pushed forward. He was on his knees, shuffling across the mat, with me stuck on his cock.

I realised what he was doing as I saw the other girls right in front of me. Like me, they had given in completely. Penny had come, and was returning the favour, her face filthy as she rubbed her nose into Jade's oil smeared fanny, both still tied. Sophie was loose though, with her face buried between Vicky's thighs, her hands full of bottom, and her own bottom over Annabelle's face for the hole to be licked. Harmony in turn was behind Annabelle, face to fanny, licking as best she could. Melody had also come, and was in the same position, servicing her own sister's sexual needs.

That left Kay, right in front of me, her delectable chubby bottom straining out of the net mesh, her fanny puffy and moist, her pouty, dark brown bumhole winking at me, all of it just dying to be licked. I had no option. I was shoved forward, right into her sex, my snout pressing into the open hole of her vagina. My tongue came out and I was lapping at her bumhole.

My humiliation was complete, absolute, perfect. I'd been captured, tied, done up like a baboon, and buggered in public. I was on my knees, rubbing my face in my submissive little girlfriend's sex as I licked out her anus. I hadn't even been given the courtesy of a tongue or finger to my clitty, but was going to come with Gavin Bulmer's crinkly pubic hair and the rough skin of his scrotum rubbing in my crease.

It was enough, easily enough. I just let myself go. My tongue burrowed up Kay's bumhole, her tiny ring opening to the pressure. Her taste mingled with my own, even as Bulmer began to push harder, bringing himself towards orgasm up my bottom, up my dirty pig's bottom, up my fat dirty baboon's bottom, squelching in my mess as I fed on my darling's own bumhole . . .

I was coming, and Kay let go at the perfect moment, her piddle exploding full in my face, as my orgasm exploded in my head, a blinding, all-consuming climax that tore through and through me as my mouth filled with Kay's pee, as my rectum filled with Bulmer's sperm, as my mouth filled again, and at last my need for submission was truly and fully satisfied.

That wasn't the only thing. As we untangled ourselves my mind slowly cleared. It was done, perhaps taken far beyond the point I had intended it to go, but done all the same. Even as I watched Bulmer take rude advantage of Jade by stuffing his dirty cock in her mouth as she was coming I was starting to smile in satisfaction. All my uncertainty was gone. I knew what I needed, and I had it – success.

Bulmer turned to me, grinning as Jade mouthed eagerly on his penis.

'So, Amber, babe,' he crowed. 'What's it to be next time, you dirty little fuck-slut?'

'Next time?' I said sweetly. 'I think if you look very carefully at the agreement you signed earlier, Gavin, you will find that it's not me who needs to get through unscathed to win. It's Vicky.'

Nexus

NEXUS NEW BOOKS

To be published in March

STRAPPING SUZETTE
Yolanda Celbridge

The fetid heat of French Guyana affords manifold possibilities for the perverted. Suze, a famous English model thinking to get away from it all, finds herself prey to the locals and their arcane, mysterious SM rituals. But the gifted employees of the French space programme have sexual foibles eclipsed in bizarreness only by their own intellects, and make the locals look like rank amateurs in the ways of corporal punishment and kinky sex. Against the forbidding background of the old penal institution that is Devil's Island, Suze realises that if she wanted to find freedom, this is the last place she should have come . . .

£6.99   ISBN 0 352 33783 4

COMPANY OF SLAVES
Christina Shelly

Michael is twenty-one, and a recent graduate looking for a career. Winsome, slightly feminine and sexually unsure, he's recruited by Lovelace Fashion and Design, purveyors of classy women's fashion and lingerie. Armed with a letter of introduction from his stentorian aunt and friend of Emily Lovelace, the imperious MD, he is appointed in no time. Michael does not at first realise the compromises he must make for the sake of his career, however, nor quite how much he will learn to enjoy them. Feminised, sissified and constantly aroused by the application of strict discipline, Michael completes his transformation into the perfect embodiment of LFD's ideals.

£6.99   ISBN 0 352 33784 2

TAKING PAINS TO PLEASE
Arabella Knight

It can be a punishing experience for willing young women striving to please and obey exacting employers. On the job, they quickly come to learn that giving complete satisfaction demands their strict devotion to duty. Maid, nanny or nurse – each must submit to the discipline of the daily grind. In their capable hands, the urgent needs and dark desires of their paymasters are always fulfilled: for these working girls find pleasure in taking pains to please.

£6.99   ISBN 0 352 33785 0

To be published in April

THE PALACE OF PLEASURES
Christobel Coleridge

The city-state of Estra is a thriving port and trading centre, ruled over by a Sultan who finds relief from the pressures of power amidst a selected bevy of intimate Companions. Carria, a mysterious and striking young woman arrives one night aboard a trading ship and rapidly finds herself offered the opportunity of joining the Companions. However, before she can she has to pass the schooling and selection, run by the Sultan's mistress Jnie. The training is, of course, very rigorous, and discipline is maintained with a firm hand. There are many different uniforms and articles to wear, and there are many strange and elaborate punishments for failure, including both humiliation and pain. Carria, however, has her own agenda. When it comes to fruition, nothing in Estra will be quite the same again.

£6.99   ISBN 0 352 33801 6

PEACH
Penny Birch

Penny Birch is currently the filthiest little minx on the Nexus list, with 15 titles already published by Nexus. All are equally full of messy, kinky fun and, frankly, no other erotic writer has ever captured the internal thrills afforded by the perverse shamings and humiliations her characters undergo! In *Peach*, Penny's friend Natasha comes unstuck – stickily. The peach in question is of course Natasha's bottom, as ripe as ever for a spanking, and everyone want a piece. The pert but mischievous Natasha is bound to get her just desserts.

£6.99   ISBN 0 352 33790 1

MISS RATTAN'S LESSON
Yolanda Celbridge

Thomas Peake joins an Oxford set of female devotees of discipline: dominant Edwina Cheshunt; voluptuous mulatto dancer Lucinda Lalage; and Miss Mann, whose disciplinary academy painfully recreates a Lady's schooldays. Thomas's London delights with his group of enthusiastic submissives are interrupted by a summons to claim his Caribbean inheritance. Ransomed after enslavement by the fierce Queen Orchid, he makes his plantation a ladies' holiday resort with a difference – always governed by Miss Rattan's rules.

£6.99   ISBN 0 352 33791 5

If you would like more information about Nexus titles, please visit our website at www.nexus-books.co.uk, or send a stamped addressed envelope to:
  Nexus, Thames Wharf Studios,
  Rainville Road, London W6 9HA

Nexus

NEXUS BACKLIST

This information is correct at time of printing. For up-to-date information, please visit our website at www.nexus-books.co.uk

All books are priced at £5.99 unless another price is given.

Nexus books with a contemporary setting

ACCIDENTS WILL HAPPEN	Lucy Golden ISBN 0 352 33596 3	☐
ANGEL	Lindsay Gordon ISBN 0 352 33590 4	☐
BARE BEHIND £6.99	Penny Birch ISBN 0 352 33721 4	☐
BEAST	Wendy Swanscombe ISBN 0 352 33649 8	☐
THE BLACK FLAME	Lisette Ashton ISBN 0 352 33668 4	☐
BROUGHT TO HEEL	Arabella Knight ISBN 0 352 33508 4	☐
CAGED!	Yolanda Celbridge ISBN 0 352 33650 1	☐
CANDY IN CAPTIVITY	Arabella Knight ISBN 0 352 33495 9	☐
CAPTIVES OF THE PRIVATE HOUSE	Esme Ombreux ISBN 0 352 33619 6	☐
CHERI CHASTISED £6.99	Yolanda Celbridge ISBN 0 352 33707 9	☐
DANCE OF SUBMISSION	Lisette Ashton ISBN 0 352 33450 9	☐
DIRTY LAUNDRY £6.99	Penny Birch ISBN 0 352 33680 3	☐
DISCIPLINED SKIN	Wendy Swanscombe ISBN 0 352 33541 6	☐

DISPLAYS OF EXPERIENCE	Lucy Golden ☐
	ISBN 0 352 33505 X
DISPLAYS OF PENITENTS	Lucy Golden ☐
£6.99	ISBN 0 352 33646 3
DRAWN TO DISCIPLINE	Tara Black ☐
	ISBN 0 352 33626 9
EDEN UNVEILED	Maria del Rey ☐
	ISBN 0 352 32542 4
AN EDUCATION IN THE	Esme Ombreux ☐
PRIVATE HOUSE	ISBN 0 352 33525 4
EMMA'S SECRET DOMINATION	Hilary James ☐
	ISBN 0 352 33226 3
GISELLE	Jean Aveline ☐
	ISBN 0 352 33440 1
GROOMING LUCY	Yvonne Marshall ☐
	ISBN 0 352 33529 7
HEART OF DESIRE	Maria del Rey ☐
	ISBN 0 352 32900 9
HIS MISTRESS'S VOICE	G. C. Scott ☐
	ISBN 0 352 33425 8
IN FOR A PENNY	Penny Birch ☐
	ISBN 0 352 33449 5
INTIMATE INSTRUCTION	Arabella Knight ☐
	ISBN 0 352 33618 8
THE LAST STRAW	Christina Shelly ☐
	ISBN 0 352 33643 9
NURSES ENSLAVED	Yolanda Celbridge ☐
	ISBN 0 352 33601 3
THE ORDER	Nadine Somers ☐
	ISBN 0 352 33460 6
THE PALACE OF EROS	Delver Maddingley ☐
£4.99	ISBN 0 352 32921 1
PALE PLEASURES	Wendy Swanscombe ☐
£6.99	ISBN 0 352 33702 8
PEACHES AND CREAM	Aishling Morgan ☐
£6.99	ISBN 0 352 33672 2

PEEPING AT PAMELA	Yolanda Celbridge ISBN 0 352 33538 6	☐
PENNY PIECES	Penny Birch ISBN 0 352 33631 5	☐
PET TRAINING IN THE PRIVATE HOUSE	Esme Ombreux ISBN 0 352 33655 2	☐
REGIME £6.99	Penny Birch ISBN 0 352 33666 8	☐
RITUAL STRIPES £6.99	Tara Black ISBN 0 352 33701 X	☐
SEE-THROUGH	Lindsay Gordon ISBN 0 352 33656 0	☐
SILKEN SLAVERY	Christina Shelly ISBN 0 352 33708 7	☐
SKIN SLAVE	Yolanda Celbridge ISBN 0 352 33507 6	☐
SLAVE ACTS £6.99	Jennifer Jane Pope ISBN 0 352 33665 X	☐
THE SLAVE AUCTION	Lisette Ashton ISBN 0 352 33481 9	☐
SLAVE GENESIS	Jennifer Jane Pope ISBN 0 352 33503 3	☐
SLAVE REVELATIONS	Jennifer Jane Pope ISBN 0 352 33627 7	☐
SLAVE SENTENCE	Lisette Ashton ISBN 0 352 33494 0	☐
SOLDIER GIRLS	Yolanda Celbridge ISBN 0 352 33586 6	☐
THE SUBMISSION GALLERY	Lindsay Gordon ISBN 0 352 33370 7	☐
SURRENDER	Laura Bowen ISBN 0 352 33524 6	☐
THE TAMING OF TRUDI £6.99	Yolanda Celbridge ISBN 0 352 33673 0	☐
TEASING CHARLOTTE £6.99	Yvonne Marshall ISBN 0 352 33681 1	☐
TEMPER TANTRUMS	Penny Birch ISBN 0 352 33647 1	☐

THE TORTURE CHAMBER	Lisette Ashton	☐
	ISBN 0 352 33530 0	
UNIFORM DOLL	Penny Birch	☐
£6.99	ISBN 0 352 33698 6	
WHIP HAND	G. C. Scott	☐
£6.99	ISBN 0 352 33694 3	
THE YOUNG WIFE	Stephanie Calvin	☐
	ISBN 0 352 33502 5	

Nexus books with Ancient and Fantasy settings

CAPTIVE	Aishling Morgan	☐
	ISBN 0 352 33585 8	
DEEP BLUE	Aishling Morgan	☐
	ISBN 0 352 33600 5	
DUNGEONS OF LIDIR	Aran Ashe	☐
	ISBN 0 352 33506 8	
INNOCENT	Aishling Morgan	☐
£6.99	ISBN 0 352 33699 4	
MAIDEN	Aishling Morgan	☐
	ISBN 0 352 33466 5	
NYMPHS OF DIONYSUS	Susan Tinoff	☐
£4.99	ISBN 0 352 33150 X	
PLEASURE TOY	Aishling Morgan	☐
	ISBN 0 352 33634 X	
SLAVE MINES OF TORMUNIL	Aran Ashe	☐
£6.99	ISBN 0 352 33695 1	
THE SLAVE OF LIDIR	Aran Ashe	☐
	ISBN 0 352 33504 1	
TIGER, TIGER	Aishling Morgan	☐
	ISBN 0 352 33455 X	

Period

CONFESSION OF AN ENGLISH SLAVE	Yolanda Celbridge	☐
	ISBN 0 352 33433 9	
THE MASTER OF CASTLELEIGH	Jacqueline Bellevois	☐
	ISBN 0 352 32644 7	
PURITY	Aishling Morgan	☐
	ISBN 0 352 33510 6	
VELVET SKIN	Aishling Morgan	☐
	ISBN 0 352 33660 9	

Samplers and collections

NEW EROTICA 5	Various ISBN 0 352 33540 8	☐
EROTICON 1	Various ISBN 0 352 33593 9	☐
EROTICON 2	Various ISBN 0 352 33594 7	☐
EROTICON 3	Various ISBN 0 352 33597 1	☐
EROTICON 4	Various ISBN 0 352 33602 1	☐
THE NEXUS LETTERS	Various ISBN 0 352 33621 8	☐
SATURNALIA £7.99	ed. Paul Scott ISBN 0 352 33717 6	☐
MY SECRET GARDEN SHED £7.99	ed. Paul Scott ISBN 0 352 33725 7	☐

Nexus Classics

A new imprint dedicated to putting the finest works of erotic fiction back in print.

AMANDA IN THE PRIVATE HOUSE £6.99	Esme Ombreux ISBN 0 352 33705 2	☐
BAD PENNY	Penny Birch ISBN 0 352 33661 7	☐
BRAT £6.99	Penny Birch ISBN 0 352 33674 9	☐
DARK DELIGHTS £6.99	Maria del Rey ISBN 0 352 33667 6	☐
DARK DESIRES	Maria del Rey ISBN 0 352 33648 X	☐
DISPLAYS OF INNOCENTS £6.99	Lucy Golden ISBN 0 352 33679 X	☐
DISCIPLINE OF THE PRIVATE HOUSE £6.99	Esme Ombreux ISBN 0 352 33459 2	☐
EDEN UNVEILED	Maria del Rey ISBN 0 352 33542 4	☐

HIS MISTRESS'S VOICE	G. C. Scott ISBN 0 352 33425 8	☐
THE INDIGNITIES OF ISABELLE £6.99	Penny Birch writing as Cruella ISBN 0 352 33696 X	☐
LETTERS TO CHLOE	Stefan Gerrard ISBN 0 352 33632 3	☐
MEMOIRS OF A CORNISH GOVERNESS £6.99	Yolanda Celbridge ISBN 0 352 33722 2	☐
ONE WEEK IN THE PRIVATE HOUSE £6.99	Esme Ombreux ISBN 0 352 33706 0	☐
PARADISE BAY	Maria del Rey ISBN 0 352 33645 5	☐
PENNY IN HARNESS	Penny Birch ISBN 0 352 33651 X	☐
THE PLEASURE PRINCIPLE	Maria del Rey ISBN 0 352 33482 7	☐
PLEASURE ISLAND	Aran Ashe ISBN 0 352 33628 5	☐
SISTERS OF SEVERCY	Jean Aveline ISBN 0 352 33620 X	☐
A TASTE OF AMBER	Penny Birch ISBN 0 352 33654 4	☐

------ ✂ ------------------------

Please send me the books I have ticked above.

Name ....

Address ....

....

....

.... Post code....................

Send to: **Cash Sales, Nexus Books, Thames Wharf Studios, Rainville Road, London W6 9HA**

US customers: for prices and details of how to order books for delivery by mail, call 1-800-343-4499.

Please enclose a cheque or postal order, made payable to **Nexus Books Ltd**, to the value of the books you have ordered plus postage and packing costs as follows:
 UK and BFPO – £1.00 for the first book, 50p for each subsequent book.
 Overseas (including Republic of Ireland) – £2.00 for the first book, £1.00 for each subsequent book.

If you would prefer to pay by VISA, ACCESS/MASTERCARD, AMEX, DINERS CLUB or SWITCH, please write your card number and expiry date here:

....

Please allow up to 28 days for delivery.

Signature ....

Our privacy policy.

We will not disclose information you supply us to any other parties. We will not disclose any information which identifies you personally to any person without your express consent.

From time to time we may send out information about Nexus books and special offers. Please tick here if you do *not* wish to receive Nexus information. ☐

------ ✂ ------------------------